THE VISION
SPLENDID

WILLIAM MACLEOD RAINE

The Vision Splendid

William MacLeod Raine

© 1st World Library, 2009
PO Box 2211
Fairfield, IA 52556
www.1stworldlibrary.com
First Edition

LCCN: 2009923514

Softcover ISBN: 978-1-4218-8897-2
Hardcover ISBN: 978-1-4218-8996-2
eBook ISBN: 978-1-4218-8798-2

Purchase *"The Vision Splendid"*
as a traditional bound book at:
www.1stWorldLibrary.com/purchase.asp?ISBN=978-1-4218-8897-2

1st World Library is a literary, educational organization
dedicated to:

- Creating a free internet library of downloadable ebooks

- Hosting writing competitions and offering book publishing
scholarships.

Interested in more 1st World Library books? contact:
literacy@1stworldlibrary.com
Check us out at: www.1stworldlibrary.com

1ˢᵗ World Library Literary Society

Giving Back to the World

"If you want to work on the core problem, it's early school literacy."

- James Barksdale, former CEO of Netscape

"No skill is more crucial to the future of a child, or to a democratic and prosperous society, than literacy."

- Los Angeles Times

"Literacy... means far more than learning how to read and write... The aim is to transmit... knowledge and promote social participation."

- UNESCO

"Literacy is not a luxury, it is a right and a responsibility. If our world is to meet the challenges of the twenty-first century we must harness the energy and creativity of all our citizens."

- President Bill Clinton

"Parents should be encouraged to read to their children, and teachers should be equipped with all available techniques for teaching literacy, so the varying needs and capacities of individual kids can be taken into account."

- Hugh Mackay

CHAPTER 1

Of all the remote streams of influence that pour both before and after birth into the channel of our being, what an insignificant few—and these only the more obvious—are traceable at all. We swim in a sea of environment and heredity, are tossed hither and thither by we know not what cross currents of Fate, are tugged at by a thousand eddies of which we never dream. The sum of it all makes Life, of which we know so little and guess so much, into which we dive so surely in those buoyant days before time and tide have shaken confidence in our power to snatch success and happiness from its mysterious depths.

—From the Note Book of a Dreamer

A REBEL IN THE MAKING

Part 1

The air was mellow with the warmth of the young spring sun. Locusts whirred in rhapsody. Bluebirds throbbed their love songs joyously. The drone of insects, the shimmer of hear, were in the atmosphere. One could almost see green things grow. To confine youth within four walls on such a day was an outrage against human nature.

A lean, wiry boy, hatchet-faced, stared with dreamy eyes out of the window of his prison. By raising himself in his seat while the teacher was not looking he could catch a silvery gleam of the river through the great firs. His thoughts were far afield. They were not concerned with the capitals of the States he was supposed to be learning, but had fared forth to the reborn earth, to the stir and movement of creeping things. The call of nature awakening from its long winter sleep drummed in his heart. He could sympathize with the bluebottle buzzing against the sunny windowpane in its efforts to reach the free world outside.

Recess! With the sound of the gong his heart leaped, but he kept his place in the line with perfect decorum. It would never do to be called back now for a momentary indiscretion. From the school yard he slipped the back way and dived into a bank of great ferns. In the heart of this he lay until the bell had called his classmates back to work. Cautiously he crept from his hiding place and ran down to the river.

Flinging himself on Big Rock, with his chin over the edge, he looked into the deep holes under the bank where the trout lay close to the strings of shiny moss, their noses to the current, motionless save for the fanning tails.

Idly he enjoyed himself for a happy hour, letting thoughts happen as they would. Not till the school bell rang for dismissal did he drag himself back with a sigh to the workaday world that called. He had a lawn to mow and a back yard to clean up for Mr. Rawson.

With his cap stuck on the back of his head and his hands in the pockets of his patched trousers, the boy went whistling townward on his barefoot way. At Adams Street he met the schoolchildren bound for home. A dozen boys from his own room closed in on him with shouts of joyous malice.

William MacLeod Raine

"Played hookey! Played hookey! Jeff Farnum played hookey!" they shrilled at him.

Ned Merrill assumed leadership of the young Apaches. "You're goin' to catch it. Old Webber was down askin' for you. Wasn't he, Tom? Wasn't he, Dick?"

Tom and Dick lied cheerfully to increase Jeff's dread. They added graphic details to help the story.

The victim looked around with stoicism. He remembered the philosophy of the optimist that a licking does not last long.

"Don't care if he was down," the boy bluffed.

"Huh! Mr. Don't Care! Mr. Don't Care!" shrieked Merrill gleefully.

They made a circle around Jeff and mocked him. Once or twice a bolder tormentor snatched at his cap or pushed a neighbor against him. Then, with the inconstancy of youth, they suddenly deserted him for more diverting game.

A forlorn little Italian girl was trying to slip past on the other side of the street. Someone caught sight of her and with a whoop the Apaches were upon her pell-mell. She began to run, but they hemmed her in. One tugged at her braided hair. Another flipped mud at her dress from the end of a stick. Merrill snatched her slate and made off with it.

Jeff cut swiftly across the street. Merrill was coming directly toward him, his head turned to the girl. Triumphant whoops broke from his throat. He bumped into Jeff, stumbled, and went down in the mud.

Young Merrill was up in an instant, clamorous for battle. His hands and clothes were plastered with filth.

"I'm goin' to lick the stuffin' out of you," he bellowed.

Jeff said nothing. He was very white. His fingers worked nervously.

"Yah! Yah! He's scared," the mob jeered.

Jeff was. In that circle of hostile faces he found no sympathy. He had to stand up to the bully of the class, a boy who could have given him fifteen pounds. Looking around for help, he saw that none was at hand. The thin legs of the rescued Italian girl were flashing down the street. On the steps of the big house of P. C. Frome a six-year-old little one was standing with her nurse. Nobody else was in sight except his cousin, James, and the Apaches.

"You're goin' to get the maulin' of your life," Ned Merrill promised as he slipped out of his coat. "Webber'll lick you if he finds out you been fightin'," James Farnum prophesied cheerfully to his cousin. He intended to do his duty in the way of protest and then watch the fight.

Ned worked his wiry little foe to the fence and pummeled him. Jeff ducked and backed out of danger. Keeping to the defensive, he was being badly punished. Once he slipped in the mud and went down, but he was up again before his slower antagonist could close with him. Blood streamed from his nose. His lip was gashed. Under the buffeting he was getting his head began to sing.

"Punch him good, Ned," one of the champion's friends advised.

"You bet he is," another chortled.

Their jeers had an unexpected effect. Jeff's fears were blotted out by his desperate need. Some spark of the fighting edge, inherited from his father, was fanned to a flame in the heart of the bruised little warrior. Like a tiger cat he leaped for Ned's throat, twisted his slim legs round the sturdy ones of his enemy, and went down with him in a heap.

Jeff landed on the bottom, but like an eel he squirmed to the top before the other had time to get set. The champion's patrician head was thumped down into the mud and a knobby little fist played a painful tattoo on his mouth and cheek.

"Take him off! Take him off!" Merrill shrieked after he had tried in vain to roll away the incubus clamped like a vise to his body.

His henchmen ran forward to obey. An unexpected intervention stopped them. A one-armed little man who had drifted down the street in time to see part of the fracas pushed forward.

"I reckon not just yet. Goliath's had a turn. Now David gets his."

"Lemme up," sobbed Goliath furiously.

"Say you're whopped." Jeff's fist emphasized the suggestion.

"Doggone you!"

This kind of one-sided warfare did not suit Jeff. He made as if to get up, but his backer stopped him.

"Hold on, son. You're not through yet. When you do a job do it thorough." To the former champion he spoke. "Had plenty yet?"

"I—I'll have him skinned," came from the tearful champion with a burst of profanity.

"That ain't the point. Have you had enough so you'll be good? Or do you need some more?"

"I'm goin' to tell Webber."

"Needs just a leetle more, son," the one-armed man told Jeff, dragging at his goatee.

But young Farnum had made up his mind. With a little twist of his body he got to his feet.

Merrill rose, tearful and sullen. "I—I'll fix you for this," he gulped, and went sobbing toward the schoolhouse.

"Better duck," James whispered to his cousin.

Jeff shook his head.

The little man looked at the boy sharply. The eyes under his shaggy brows were like gimlets.

"Come up to the school with me. I'll see your teacher, son."

Jeff walked beside him. He knew by the sound of the voice that his rescuer was a Southerner and his heart warmed to him. He wanted greatly to ask a question. Presently it plumped out.

"Was it in the war, sir?"

"I reckon I don't catch your meaning."

William MacLeod Raine

"That you lost your arm?" The boy added quickly, "My father was a soldier under General Early."

The steel-gray eyes shot at him again. "I was under Early myself."

"My father was a captain—Captain Farnum," the young warrior announced proudly.

"Not Phil Farnum!"

"Yes, sir. Did you know him?" Jeff trembled with eagerness. His dead soldier-father was the idol of his heart.

"Did I?" He swung Jeff round and looked at him. "You're like him, in a way, and, by Gad! you fight like him. What's your name?"

"Jefferson Davis Farnum."

"Shake hands, Jefferson Davis Farnum, you dashed little rebel. My name is Lucius Chunn. I was a lieutenant in your father's company before I was promoted to one of my own."

Jeff forgot his troubles instantly. "I wish I'd been alive to go with father to the war," he cried.

Captain Chunn was delighted. "You doggoned little rebel!"

"I didn't know we used that word in the South' sir."

Chunn tugged at his goatee and laughed. "We're not in the South, David."

The former Confederate asked questions to piece out his patchwork information. He knew that Philip Farnum had come out of the war with a constitution weakened by the hardships of the service. Rumors had drifted to him that the taste for liquor acquired in camp as an antidote for sickness had grown upon his comrade and finally overcome him. From Jeff he learned that after his father's death the widow had sold her mortgaged place and moved to the Pacific Coast. She had invested the few hundreds left her in some river-bottom lots at Verden and had later discovered that an unscrupulous real estate dealer had unloaded upon her worthless property. The patched and threadbare clothes of the boy told him that from a worldly point of view the affairs of the Farnums were at ebb tide.

"Did... did you know father very well?" Jeff asked tremulously.

Chunn looked down at the thin dark face of the boy walking beside him and was moved to lay a hand on his shoulder. He understood the ache in that little heart to hear about the father who was a hero to him. Jeff was of no importance in the alien world about him. The Captain guessed from the little scene he had witnessed that the lad trod a friendless, stormy path. He divined, too, that the hungry soul was fed from within by dreams and memories.

So Lucius Chunn talked. He told about the slender, soldierly officer in gray who had given himself so freely to serve his men, of the time he had caught pneumonia by lending his blanket to a sick boy, of the day he had led the charge at Battle Creek and received the wound which pained him so greatly to the hour of his death. And Jeff drank his words in like a charmed thing. He visualized it all, the bitter nights in camp, the long wet marches, the trumpet call to battle. It was this last that his imagination seized upon most eagerly. He saw the silent massing of troops, the stealthy advance through the woods; and he heard the blood-curdling rebel yell as the line swept forward from cover like a tidal wave, with his father at its head.

Captain Chunn was puzzled at the coldness with which Mr. Webber listened to his explanation of what had taken place. The school principal fell back doggedly upon one fact. It would not have happened if Jeff had not been playing truant. Therefore he was to blame for what had occurred.

Nothing would be done, of course, without a thorough investigation.

The Captain was not satisfied, but he did not quite see what more he could do.

"The boy is a son of an old comrade of mine. We were in the war together. So of course I have to stand by Jeff," he pleaded with a smile.

"You were in the rebel army?" The words slipped out before the schoolmaster could stop them.

"In the Confederate army," Chunn corrected quietly.

Webber flushed at the rebuke. "That is what I meant to say."

"I leave to-morrow for Alaska. It would be pleasant to know before I go that Jeff is out of his trouble."

"I'm afraid Jeff always will be in trouble. He is a most insubordinate boy," the principal answered coldly.

"Are you sure you quite understand him?"

"He is not difficult to understand." Webber, resenting the interference of the Southerner as an intrusion, disposed of the matter in a sentence. "I'll look into this matter carefully, Mr. Chunn."

Webber called immediately at the office of Edward B. Merrill, president of the tramway company and of the First National Bank. It happened that the vice-president of the bank was a school director; also that the funds of the district were kept in the First National. The schoolteacher did not admit that he had come to ingratiate himself with the powers that ruled his future, but he was naturally pleased to come in direct touch with such a man as Merrill.

The financier was urbane and spent nearly half an hour of his valuable time with the principal. When the latter rose to go they shook hands. The two understood each other thoroughly.

"You may depend upon me to do my duty, Mr. Merrill, painful though such a course may be to me."

"I am very glad to have met you, Mr. Webber. It is a source of satisfaction to me that our educational system is in the care of men of your stamp. I leave this matter with confidence entirely in your hands. Do what you think best."

His confidence was justified. After school opened next morning Jeff was called up and publicly thrashed for playing truant. As a prelude to the corporal punishment the principal delivered a lecture. He alluded to the details of the fight gravely, with selective discrimination, giving young Farnum to understand that he had reached the end of his rope. If any more such brutal affairs were reported to him he would be punished severely.

The boy took the flogging in silence. He had learned to set his teeth and take punishment without whimpering. From the

William MacLeod Raine

hardest whipping Webber had ever given he went to his seat with a white, set face that stared straight in front of him. Young as he was, he knew it had not been fair and his outraged soul cried out at the injustice of it. The principal had seized upon the truancy as an excuse to let him escape from an investigation of the cause of the fight. Ned Merrill got off because his father was a rich man and powerful in the city. He, Jeff, was whipped because he was an outcast and had dared lift his hand against one of his betters.

And there was no redress. It was simply the way of the world.

Jeff and his mother were down that afternoon to see their new friend off in the *City of Skook*. Captain Chunn found a chance to draw the boy aside for a question.

"Is it all right with Mr. Webber? What did he do?"

"Oh, he gave me a jawing," the boy answered.

The little man nodded. "I reckoned that was what he would do. Be a good boy, Jeff. I never knew a man more honorable than your father. Run straight, son."

"Yes, sir," the lad promised, a lump in his throat.

It was more than ten years before he saw Captain Chunn again.

Part 2

As an urchin Jeff had taken things as they came without understanding causes. Thoughts had come to him in flashes, without any orderly sequence, often illogically. As a gangling boy he still took for granted the hard knocks of a world he did not attempt to synthesize.

Even his mother looked upon him as "queer." She worried plaintively because he was so careless about his clothes and because his fondness for the outdoors sometimes led him to play truant. Constantly she set before him as a model his cousin, James, who was a good-looking boy, polite, always well dressed, with a shrewd idea of how to get along easily.

"Why can't you be like Cousin James? He isn't always in trouble," she would urge in her tired way.

It was quite true that the younger cousin was more of a general favorite than harum-scarum Jeff, but the mother might as well have asked her boy to be like Socrates. It was not that he could not learn or that he did not want to study. He simply did not fit into the school groove. Its routine of work and discipline, its tendency to stifle individuality, to run all children through the same hopper like grist through a mill, put a clamp upon his spirits and his imagination. Even thus early he was a rebel.

Jeff scrambled up through the grades in haphazard fashion until he reached the seventh. Here his teacher made a discovery. She was a faded little woman of fifty, but she had that loving insight to which all children respond. Under her guidance for one year the boy blossomed. His odd literary fancy for Don Quixote, for Scott's poems and romances she encouraged, quietly eliminating the dime novels he had read indiscriminately with these. She broke through the shell of

William MacLeod Raine

his shyness to find out that his diffidence was not sulkiness nor his independence impudence.

The boy was a dreamer. He lived largely in a world of his own, where Quentin Durward and Philip Farnum and Robert E. Lee were enshrined as heroes. From it he would emerge all hot for action, for adventure. Into his games then he would throw a poetic imagination that transfigured them. Outwardly he lived merely in that boys' world made to his hand. He adopted its shibboleths, fought when he must, went through the annual routine of marbles, tops, kites, hop scotch, and baseball. From his fellows he guarded jealously the knowledge of even the existence of his secret world of fancy.

His progress through the grades and the high school was intermittent. Often he had to stop for months at a time to earn money for their living. In turn he was newsboy, bootblack, and messenger boy. He drove a delivery wagon for a grocer, ushered at a theater, was even a copyholder in the proofroom of a newspaper. Hard work kept him thin, but he was like a lath for toughness.

Seven weeks after he was graduated from the high school his mother died. The day of the funeral a real estate dealer called to offer three, hundred dollars for the lots in the river bottom bought some years earlier by Mrs. Farnum.

Jeff put the man off. It was too late now to do his mother any good. She had had to struggle to the last for the bread she ate. He wondered why the good things in life were so unevenly distributed.

Twice during the next week Jeff was approached with offers for his lots. The boy was no fool.

He found out that the land was wanted by a new railroad pushing into Verden. Within three days he had sold direct to the agent of the company for nine hundred dollars. With what he could earn on the side and in his summers he thought that sum would take him through college.

William MacLeod Raine

CHAPTER 2

I wonder if Morgan, the Pirate,
When plunder had glutted his heart,
Gave part of the junk from the ships he had sunk
To help some Museum of Art;
If he gave up the role of "collector of toll"
And became a Collector of Art?

I wonder if Genghis, the Butcher,
When he'd trampled down nations like grass,
Retired with his share when he'd lost all his hair
And started a Sunday-school class;
If he turned his past under and used half his plunder
In running a Sunday-school class?

I wonder if Roger, the Rover,
When millions in looting he'd made,
Built libraries grand on the jolly mainland
To honor success and "free trade";
If he founded a college of nautical knowledge
Where Pirates could study their trade?

I wonder, I wonder, I wonder,
If Pirates were ever the same,
Ever trying to lend a respectable trend
To the jaunty old buccaneer game

Or is it because of our Piracy Laws
That philanthropists enter the game?

—Wallace Irwin, in Life

THE REBEL IS INSTRUCTED IN THE WORSHIP OF THE GOD-OF-THINGS-AS-THEY-ARE

Part 1

Jeff was digging out a passage in the "Apology" when there came a knock at the door of his room. The visitor was his cousin, James, and he radiated such an air of prosperity that the plain little bedroom shrank to shabbiness.

James nodded in offhand fashion as he took off his overcoat. "Hello, Jeff! Thought I'd look you up. Got settled in your diggings, eh?" Before his host could answer he rattled on: "Just ran in for a moment. Had the devil of a time to find you. What's the object in getting clear off the earth?"

"Cheaper," Jeff explained.

"Should think it would be," James agreed after he had let his eyes wander critically around the room. "But you can't afford to save that way. Get a good suite. And for heaven's sake see a tailor, my boy. In college a man is judged by the company he keeps."

"What have my room and my clothes to do with that?" Jeff wanted to know, with a smile.

"Everything. You've got to put up a good front. The best fellows won't go around with a longhaired guy who doesn't know how to dress. No offense, Jeff."

William MacLeod Raine

His cousin laughed. "I'll see a barber to-morrow."

"And you must have a room where the fellows can come to see you."

"What's the matter with this one?"

A hint of friendly patronage crept into the manner of the junior. "My dear chap, college isn't worth doing at all unless you do it right. You're here to get in with the best fellows and to make connections that will help you later. That sort of thing, you know."

Into Jeff's face came the light that always transfigured its plainness when he was in the grip of an idea. "Hold on, J. K. Let's get at this right. Is that what I'm here for? I didn't know it. There's a hazy notion in my noodle that I'm here to develop myself."

"That's what I'm telling you. Go in for the things that count. Make a good frat. Win out at football or debating. I don't give a hang what you go after, but follow the ball and keep on the jump. I'm strong with the crowd that runs things and I'll see they take you in and make you a cog of the machine. But you'll have to measure up to specifications."

"But, hang it, I don't want to be a cog in any machine. I'm here to give myself a chance to grow—sit out in the sun and hatch an individuality—give myself lots of free play."

"Then you've come to the wrong shop," James informed him dryly. "If you want to succeed at college you've got to do the things the other fellows do and you've got to do them the same way."

"You mean I've got to travel in a rut?"

"Oh, well! That's a way of putting it. I mean that you have to accept customs and traditions. You have to work like the devil doing things that count. If you make the team you've got to think football, talk it, eat it, dream it."

"But is it worth while?"

James waved his protest aside. "Of course it's worth while. Success always is. Get this in your head. Four-fifths of the fellows at college don't count. They're also-rans. To get in with the right bunch you've got to make a good showing. Look at me. I'm no John D. Rockefeller, Jr. Athletics bore me. I can't sing. I don't grind. But I'm in everything. Best frat. Won the oratorical contest. Manager of the football team next season. President of the Dramatic Club. Why?"

He did not wait for Jeff to guess the reason. "Because our set runs things and I go after the honors."

"But a college ought to be a democracy," Jeff protested.

"Tommyrot! It's an aristocracy, that's what it is, just like the little old world outside, an aristocracy of the survival of the fittest. You get there if you're strong. You go to the wall if you're weak. That's the law of life."

The freshman came to this squint of pragmatism with surprise. He had thought of Verden University as a splendid democracy of intellectual brotherhood that was to leaven the world with which it came in touch.

"Do you mean that a fellow has to have money enough to make a good showing before he can win any of the prizes?"

James K. nodded with the sage wisdom of a man of the world. "The long green is a big help, but you've got to have the stuff in you. Success comes to the fellow who goes after it in the right way."

"And suppose a fellow doesn't care to go after it?"

"He stays a nobody."

James was in evening dress, immaculate from clean-shaven cheek to patent leather shoes. He had a well-filled figure and a handsome face with a square, clean-cut jaw. His cousin admired the young fellow's virile competency. It was his opinion that James K. Farnum was the last person he knew likely to remain a nobody. He knew how to conform, to take the color of his thinking from the dominant note of his environment, but he had, too, a capacity for leadership.

"I'm not going to believe you if I can help it," Jeff answered with a smile.

The upper classman shrugged. "You'd better take my advice, just the same. At college you don't get a chance to make two starts. You're sized up from the crack of the pistol."

"I haven't the money to make a splurge even if I wanted to."

"Borrow."

"Who from?" asked Jeff ungrammatically.

"You can rustle it somewhere. I'm borrowing right now."

"It's different with you. I'm used to doing without things. Don't worry about me. I'll get along."

James came with a touch of embarrassment to the real object of his visit. "I say, Jeff. I've had a tough time to win out. You won't—you'll not say anything—let anything slip, you know —something that might set the fellows guessing."

His cousin was puzzled. "About what?"

"About the reason why Mother and I left Shelby and came out to the coast."

"What do you take me for?"

"I knew you wouldn't. Thought I'd mention it for fear you might make a slip."

"I don't chatter about the private affairs of my people."

"Course not. I knew you didn't." The junior's hand rested caressingly on the shoulder of the other. "Don't get sore, Jeff. I didn't doubt you. But that thing haunts me. Some day it will come out and ruin me when I'm near the top of the ladder."

The freshman shook his head. "Don't worry about it, James. Just tell the plain truth if it comes out. A thing like that can't hurt you permanently. Nothing can really injure you that does not come from your own weakness."

"That's all poppycock," James interrupted fretfully. "Just that sort of thing has put many a man on the skids. I tell you a young fellow needs to start unhampered. If the fellows got onto it that my father had been in the pen because he was a defaulting bank cashier they would drop me like a hot potato."

"None but the snobs would. Your friends would stick the closer."

"Oh' friends!" The young man's voice had a note of angry derision.

William MacLeod Raine

Jeff's affectionate grin comforted him. "Don't let it get on your nerves, J. K. Things never are as bad as we expect at their worst."

The junior set his teeth savagely. "I tell you, sometimes I hate him for it. That's a fine heritage for a father to give his son, isn't it? Nothing but trouble and disgrace."

His cousin spoke softly. "He's paid a hundred times for it, old man."

"He ought to pay. Why shouldn't he? I've got to pay. Mother had to as long as she lived." His voice was hard and bitter.

"Better not judge him. You're his only son, you know."

"I'm the one he's injured most. Why shouldn't I judge him? I've been a pauper all these years, living off money given us by my mother's people. I had to leave our home because of what he did. I'd like to know why I shouldn't judge him."

Jeff was silent.

Presently James rose. "But there's no use talking about it. I've got to be going. We have an eat to-night at Tucker's."

Part 2

Jeff came to his new life on the full tide of an enthusiasm that did not begin to ebb till near the close of his first semester. He lived in a new world, one removed a million miles from the sordid one through which he had fought his way so many years. All the idealism of his nature went out in awe and veneration for his college. It stood for something he could not phrase, something spiritually fine and intellectually strong. When he thought of the noble motto of the university, "To Serve," it was always with a lifted emotion that was half a prayer. His professors went clothed in majesty. The chancellor was of godlike dimensions. Even the seniors carried with them an impalpable aura of learning.

The illusion was helped by reason of the very contrast between the jostling competition of the street and the academic air of harmony in which he now found himself. For the first time was lifted the sense of struggle that had always been with him.

The outstanding notes of his boyhood had been poverty and meagerness. It was as if he and his neighbors had been flung into a lake where they must keep swimming to escape drowning. There had been no rest from labor. Sometimes the tragedy of disaster had swept over a family. But on the campus of the university he found the sheltered life. The echo of that battling world came to him only faintly.

He began to make tentative friendships, but in spite of the advice of his cousin they were with the men who did not count. Samuel Miller was an example. He was a big, stodgy fellow with a slow mind which arrived at its convictions deliberately. But when he had made sure of them he hung to his beliefs like a bulldog to a bone.

It was this quality that one day brought them together in the classroom. An instructor tried to drive Miller into admitting he was wrong in an opinion. The boy refused to budge, and the teacher became nettled.

"Mr. Miller will know more when he doesn't know so much," the instructor snapped out.

Jeff's instinct for fair play was roused at once, all the more because of the ripple of laughter that came from the class. He spoke up quietly.

"I can't see yet but that Mr. Miller is right, sir."

"The discussion is closed," was the tart retort.

After class the dissenters walked across to chapel together.

"Poke the animal up with a stick and hear him growl," Jeff laughed airily.

"Page always thinks a fellow ought to take his say-so as gospel," Miller commented.

Most of the students saw in Jeff Farnum only a tallish young man, thin as a rail, not particularly well dressed, negligent as to collar and tie. But Miller observed in the tanned face a tender, humorous mouth and eager, friendly eyes that looked out upon the world with a suggestion of inner mirth. In course of time he found out that his friend was an unconquerable idealist.

Jeff made discoveries. One of them was a quality of brutal indifference in some of his classmates to those less fortunate. These classy young gentlemen could ignore him as easily as a hurrying business man can a newsboy trying to sell him a paper. If he was forced upon their notice they were perfectly courteous; otherwise he was not on the map for them.

Another point that did not escape his attention was the way in which the institution catered to Merrill and Frome, because they were large donors to the university. He had once heard Peter C. Frome say in a speech to the students that he contributed to the support of Verden University because it was a "safe and conservative citadel which never had yielded to demagogic assaults." At the time he had wondered just what the president of the Verden Union Water Company had meant. He was slowly puzzling his way to an answer.

Chancellor Bland referred often to the "largehearted Christian gentlemen who gave of their substance to promote the moral and educational life of the state." But Jeff knew that many believed Frome and Merrill to be no better than robbers on a large scale. He knew the methods by which they had gained their franchises and that they ruled the politics of the city by graft and corruption. Yet the chancellor was always ready to speak or write against municipal ownership. It was common talk on the streets that Professor Perkins, of the chair of political science, had had his expenses paid to England by Merrill to study the street railway system of Great Britain, and that Perkins had duly written several bread-and-butter articles to show that public ownership was unsuccessful there.

The college was a denominational one and the atmosphere wholly orthodox. Doubt and skepticism were spoken of only with horror. At first it was of himself that Jeff was critical. The spirit of the place was opposed to all his convictions, but he felt that perhaps his reaction upon life had been affected too much by his experiences.

He asked questions, and was suppressed with severity or

kindly paternal advice. It came to him one night while he was walking bareheaded under the stars that there was in the place no intellectual stimulus, though there was an elaborate presence of it. The classrooms were arid. Everywhere fences were up beyond which the mind was not expected to travel. A thing was right, because it had come to be accepted. That was the gospel of his fellows, of his teachers. Later he learned that it is also the creed of the world.

What Jeff could not understand was a mind which refused to accept the inevitable conclusions to which its own processes pushed it. Verden University lacked the courage which comes from intellectual honesty. Wherefore its economics were devitalized and its theology an anachronism.

But Jeff had been given a mind unable to lie to itself. He was in very essence a non-conformist. To him age alone did not lend sanctity to the ghosts of dead yesterdays that rule to-day.

CHAPTER 3

"Whoso would be a man must be a non-conformist. He who would gather immortal palms must not be hindered by the name of goodness, but must explore if it be goodness. Nothing is at last sacred but the integrity of your own mind,"

—Emerson

CONVERSING ON RELIGION AND PHILOSOPHY, THE REBEL LEARNS THAT IT IS SOMETIMES WISE TO SOFT PEDAL IDEAS UNLESS THEY ARE ACCEPTED ONES

During his freshman year Jeff saw little of his cousin beyond the usual campus greetings, except for a period of six weeks when the junior happened to need him. But the career of James K. tickled immensely the under classman's sense of humor. He was becoming the most dazzling success ever developed by the college. Even with the faculty he stood high, for if he lacked scholarship he had the more showy gifts that went farther. He knew when to defer and when to ride roughshod to his end. It was felt that his brilliancy had a solidity back of it, a quality of flintiness that would endure.

William MacLeod Raine

James was inordinately ambitious and loved the spotlight like an actor. The flamboyant oratory at which he excelled had won for him the interstate contest. He was editor-in-chief of the "Verdenian," manager of the varsity football team, and president of the college senate.

With the beginning of his senior year James entered another phase of his development. He offered to the college a new, or at least an enlarged, interpretation of himself. Some of his smiling good-fellowship had been sloughed to make way for the benignity of a budding statesman. He still held a tolerant attitude to the antics of his friends, but it was easy to see that he had put away childish things. To his many young women admirers he talked confidentially of his aims and aspirations. The future of James K. Farnum was a topic he never exhausted.

It was, too, a subject which greatly interested Jeff and Sam Miller. His cousin might smile at his poses, and often did, but he never denied James qualities likely to carry him far.

"His one best bet is his belief in himself," Sam announced one night.

"It's a great thing to believe in yourself."

"He's so dead sure he's cast for a big part. The egoism just oozes out of him. He doesn't know himself that he's a faker."

"He is a long way from that," Jeff protested warmly.

"Take his oratory," Miller went on irritably. "It's all bunk. He throws a chest and makes you feel he's a big man, but what he says won't stand analysis—just a lot of platitudes."

"Don't forget he's young yet. James K. hasn't found himself."

"Sure there's anything to find?"

"There's a lot in him. He's the biggest man in the university to-day."

"You practically wrote the oration that won the interstate contest. Think I don't know that?" Miller snorted.

Jeff's mouth took on a humorous twist. "I gave him some suggestions. How did you know?"

"Knew he wasn't hanging around last term for nothing. He's selfish as the devil."

"You're all wrong about him, Sam. He isn't selfish at all at bottom."

"Shoot the brains out of that oration and what's left would be the part he supplied. The fellow's got a gift of absorbing new ideas superficially and dressing them up smartly."

"Then he's got us beat there," Jeff laughed goodnaturedly. He had not in his make-up a grain of envy. Even his laughter was generally genial, though often irreverent to the God-of-things-as-they-are.

"When he won the interstate he lapped up flattery like a thirsty pup, but his bluff was that it was only for the college he cared to win."

"Most of us have mixed motives."

"Not J. K. Reminds me of old Johnson's 'Patriotism is the last refuge of a scoundrel.'"

Jeff straightened. "That won't do, Sam. I believe in J. K. You've got nothing against him except that you don't like him."

"Forgot you were his cousin, Jeff," Miller grumbled. "But it's a fact that he works everybody to shove him along."

"He's only a kid. Give him time. He'll be a big help to any community."

"James K.'s biggest achievement will always be James K."

Jeff chuckled at the apothegm even while he protested. Sam capped it with another.

"He's always sitting to himself for his own portrait."

"He'll get over that when he brushes up against the world." Jeff added his own criticism thoughtfully. "The weak spot in him is a sort of flatness of mind. This makes him afraid of new ideas. He wants to be respectable, and respectability is the most damning thing on earth."

After Miller had left Jeff buckled down to Ely's "Political Economy." He had not been at it long when James surprised him by dropping in. His host offered the easiest chair and shoved tobacco toward him.

"Been pretty busy with the team, I suppose?" Jeff suggested.

"It's taken a lot of my time, but I think I've put the athletic association on a paying basis at last."

"I see by your report in the 'Verdenian' that you made good."

"A fellow ought to do well whatever he undertakes to do."

Jeff grinned across at him from where he lay on the bed with his fingers laced beneath his head. "That's what the copy-books used to say."

"I want to have a serious talk with you, Jeff."

"Aren't you having it? What can be more important than the successes of James K. Farnum?"

The senior looked at him suspiciously. He was not strongly fortified with a sense of humor. "Just now I want to talk about the failures of Jefferson D. Farnum," he answered gravely.

Jeff's eyes twinkled. "Is it worth while? I am unworthy of this boon, O great Cesar."

"Now that's the sort of thing that stands in your way," James told him impatiently. "People never know when you're laughing at them. There is no reason why you shouldn't succeed. Your abilities are up to the average, but you fritter them away."

"Thank you." Jeff wore an air of being immensely pleased.

"The truth is that you're your own worst enemy. Now that you have taken to dressing better you are not bad looking. I find a good many of the fellows like you—or they would if you'd let them."

"Because I'm so well connected," Jeff laughed.

"I suppose it does help, your being my cousin. But the thing depends on you. Unless you make a decided change you'll never get on."

"What change do you suggest? Item one, please?"

William MacLeod Raine

James looked straight at him. "You lack bedrock principles, Jeff."

"Do I?"

"Take your habits. Two or three times you've been seen coming out of saloons."

"Expect I went in to get a drink."

"It's not generally known, of course, but if it reached Prexy he'd fire you so quick your head would swim."

"I dare say."

The senior looked at him significantly. "You're the last man that ought to go to such places. There's such a thing as an inherited tendency."

The jaw muscles stood out like ropes under the flesh of Jeff's lean face. "We'll not discuss that."

"Very well. Cut it out. A drinking man is handicapped too heavily to win."

"Much obliged. Second count in the indictment, please."

"You've got strange, unsettling notions. The profs don't like them."

"Don't they?"

"You know what I mean. We didn't make this world. We've got to take it as it is. You can't make it over. There are always going to be rich people and poor ones. Just because you've fed indigestibly on Ibsen and Shaw you can't change facts."

"So you advise?"

"Soft pedal your ideas if you must have them."

"Hasn't a man got to see things as straight as he can?"

"That's no reason for calling in the neighbors to rejoice with him because he has astigmatism."

Jeff came back with a tag of Emerson, whose phrases James was fond of quoting in his speeches. "Whoso would be a man must be a non-conformist. Nothing is at last sacred but the integrity of your own mind."

"You can push that too far. It isn't practical. We've got to make compromises, especially with established things."

Jeff sat up on the bed. Points of light were dancing in his big eyes. "That's what the Pharisees said to Jesus when he wouldn't stand for lies because they were deep rooted and for injustice because it had become respectable."

"Oh, if you're going to compare yourself to Christ—"

"Verden University is supposed to stand for Christianity, isn't it? It was because Jesus whanged away at social and industrial freedom, at fraternity, at love on earth, that he had to endure the Cross. He got under the upper class skin when he attacked the traditional lies of vested interests. Now why doesn't Bland preach the things that Jesus taught?"

"He does."

"Yes, he does," Jeff scoffed. "He preaches good form, respectability, a narrow personal righteousness, a salvation canned and petrified three hundred years ago."

"Do you want him to preach socialism?"

"I want him to preach the square deal in our social life, intellectual honesty, and a vital spiritual life. Think of what this college might mean, how it might stand for democracy It ought to pour out into the state hundreds of specialists on the problems of the country. Instead, it is only a reflection of the caste system that is growing up in America."

James shrugged his broad shoulders. "I've been through all that. It's a phase we pass. You'll get over it. You've got to if you are going to succeed."

A quizzical grin wrinkled Jeff's lean face. "What is success?"

"It's setting a high goal and reaching it. It's taking the world by the throat and shaking from it whatever you want." James leaned across the table, his eyes shining. "It's the journey's end for the strong, that's what it is. I don't care whether a man is gathering gilt or fame, he's got to pound away with his eye right on it. And he's got to trample down the things that get in his way."

Jeff's eye fell upon a book on the table. "Ever hear of a chap called Goldsmith?"

"Of course. He wrote 'The School for Scandal.' What's he got to do with it?"

Jeff smiled, without correcting his cousin. "I've been reading about him. Seems to have been a poor hack writer 'who threw away his life in handfuls.' He wrote the finest poem, the best novel, the most charming comedy of his day. He knew how to give, but he didn't know how to take. So he died alone in a garret. He was a failure."

"Probably his own fault."

"And on the day of his funeral the stairway was crowded with poor people he had helped. All of them were in tears."

"What good did that do him? He was inefficient. He might have saved his money and helped them then."

"Perhaps. I don't know. It might have been too late then. He chose to give his life as he was living it."

"Another reason for his poverty, wasn't there?"

Jeff flushed. "He drank."

"Thought so." James rose triumphantly and put on his overcoat. "Well, think over what I've said."

"I will. And tell the chancellor I'm much obliged to him for sending you."

For once the Senior was taken aback. "Eh, what—what?"

"You may tell him it won't be your fault that I'll never be a credit to Verden University."

As he walked across the campus to his fraternity house James did not feel that his call had been wholly successful. With him he carried a picture of his cousin's thin satiric face in which big expressive eyes mocked his arguments. But he let none of this sense of futility get into the report given next day to the Chancellor.

"Jeff's rather light-minded, I'm afraid, sir. He wanted to branch off to side lines. But I insisted on a serious talk. Before I left him he promised to think over what I had said."

"Let us hope he may."

"He said it wouldn't be my fault if he wasn't a credit to the University."

"We can all agree with him there, Farnum."

"Thank you, sir. I'm not very hopeful about him. He has other things to contend with."

"I'm not sure I quite know what you mean."

"I can't explain more fully without violating a confidence."

"Well, we'll hope for the best, and remember him in our prayers."

"Yes, sir," James agreed.

CHAPTER 4

"I met a hundred men on the road to Delhi, and they were all my brothers."

—Old Proverb

THE REBEL FLUNKS IN A COURSE ON HOW TO GET ON IN LIFE

Part 1

It would be easy to overemphasize Jeff's intellectual difficulties at the expense of the deep delight he found in many phases of his student life. The daily routine of the library, the tennis courts, and the jolly table talk brought out the boy in him that had been submerged.

There developed in him a vagabond streak that took him into the woods and the hills for days at a time. About the middle of his Sophomore year he discovered Whitman. While camping alone at night under the stars he used to shout out,

"Strong and content, I travel the open road," or

"Allons! The road is before us!

"It is safe—I have tried it—my own feet have tried it well."

Through Stevenson's essay on Whitman Jeff came to know the Scotch writer, and from the first paragraph of him was a sealed follower of R. L. S. In different ways both of these poets ministered to a certain love of freedom, of beauty, of outdoor spaces that was ineradicably a part of his nature. The essence of vagabondage is the spirit of romance. One may tour every corner of the earth and still be a respectable Pharisee. One may never move a dozen miles from the village of his birth and yet be of the happy company of romantics. Jeff could find in a sunset, in a stretch of windswept plain, in the sight of water through leafless trees, something that filled his heart with emotion.

Perhaps the very freedom of these vacation excursions helped to feed his growing discontent. The yeast of rebellion was forever stirring in him. He wanted to come to life with open mind. He was possessed of an insatiable curiosity about it. This took him to the slums of Verden, to the redlight district, to Socialist meetings, to a striking coal camp near the city where he narrowly escaped being killed as a scab. He knew that something was wrong with our social life. Inextricably blended with success and happiness he saw everywhere pain, defeat, and confusion. Why must such things be? Why poverty at all?

But when he flung his questions at Pearson, who had charge of the work in sociology, the explanations of the professor seemed to him pitifully weak.

In the ethics class he met the same experience. A chance reference to Drummond's "Natural Law in the Spiritual world" introduced him to that stimulating book. All one night he sat up and read it—drank it in with every fiber of his thirsty being.

The fire in his stove went out. He slipped into his overcoat. Gray morning found him still reading. He walked out with dazed eyes into a world that had been baptized anew during the night to a miraculous rebirth.

But when he took his discovery to the lecture room Dawson was not only cold but hostile. Drummond was not sound. There was about him a specious charm very likely to attract young minds. Better let such books alone for the present. In the meantime the class would take up with him the discussion of predeterminism as outlined in Tuesday's work.

There were members of the faculty big enough to have understood the boy and tolerant enough to have sympathized with his crude revolt, but Jeff was diffident and never came in touch with them.

His connection with the college ended abruptly during the Spring term of his Sophomore year.

A celebrated revivalist was imported to quicken the spiritual life of the University. Under his exhortations the institution underwent a religious ferment. An extraordinary excitement was astir on the campus. Class prayer meetings were held every afternoon, and at midday smaller groups met for devotional exercises. At these latter those who had made no profession of religion were petitioned for by name. James Farnum was swept into the movement and distinguished himself by his zeal. It was understood that he desired the prayers of friends for that relative who had not yet cast away the burden of his sins.

It became a point of honor with his cousin's circle to win Jeff for the cause. There was no difficulty in getting him to attend the meetings of the revivalist. But he sat motionless through the emotional climax that brought to an end each meeting.

To him it seemed that this was not in any vital sense religion, but he was careful not to suggest his feeling by so much as a word.

One or two of his companions invited him to come to Jesus. He disconcerted them by showing an unexpected familiarity with the Scriptures as a weapon of offense against them.

James invited him to his rooms and labored with him. Jeff resorted to the Socratic method. From what sins was he to be saved? And when would he know he had found salvation?

His cousin uneasily explained the formula. "You must believe in Christ and Him crucified. You must surrender your will to His. Shall we pray together?"

"I'd rather not, J. K. First, I want to get some points clear. Do you mean that I'm to believe in what Jesus said and to try to live as he suggested?"

"Yes."

Jeff picked up his cousin's Bible and read a passage. "'We know that we have passed from death unto life, BECAUSE WE LOVE THE BRETHREN. He that loveth not his brother abideth in death.' That's the test, isn't it?"

"Well, you have to be converted," James said dubiously.

"Isn't that conversion—loving your brother? And if a man is willing to live in plenty while his brother is in poverty, if he exploits those weaker than himself to help him get along, then he can't be really converted, can he?"

"Now see here, Jeff, you've got the wrong idea. Christ didn't come into the world to reform it, but to save it from its sins.

He wasn't merely a man, but the Divine Son of God."

"I don't understand the dual nature of Jesus. But when one reads His life it is easy to believe in His divinity." After a moment the young man added: "In one way we're all divine sons of God, aren't we?"

James was shocked. "Where do you get such notions? None of our people were infidels."

"Am I one?"

"You ought to take advantage of this chance. It's not right to set your opinion up against those that know better."

"And that's what I'm doing, isn't it?" Jeff smiled. "Can't help it. I reckon I can't be saved by my emotions. It's going to be a life job."

James gave him up, but he sent another Senior to make a last attempt. The young man was Thurston Thomas and he had never exchanged six sentences with Jeff in his life. The unrepentant sinner sent him to the right about sharply.

"What the devil do you mean by running about officiously and bothering about other people's souls? Better look out for your own."

Thomas, a scion of one of the best families in Verden, looked as if he had been slapped in the face.

"Why Farnum, I—I spoke for your good."

"No, you didn't," contradicted Jeff flatly. "You don't care a hang about me. You've never noticed me before. We're not friends. You've always disliked me. But you want the credit of bringing me into the fold. It's damned impertinent of you."

The Senior retired with a white face. He was furious, but he thought it due himself to turn the other cheek by saying nothing. He reported his version to a circle of friends, and from them it spread like grass seed in the wind. Soon it was generally known that Jeff Farnum had grossly insulted with blasphemy a man who had tried to save his soul.

Two days later Miller met Jeff at the door of Frome 15.

"You're in bad! Jeff. What the deuce did you do to Sissy Thomas?"

"Gave him some good advice."

Miller grinned. "I'll bet you did. The little cad has been poisoning the wells against you. Look there."

A young woman of their class had passed into the room. Her glance had fallen upon Farnum and been quickly averted.

"That's the first time Bessie Vroom ever cut you," Sam continued angrily. "Thomas is responsible. I've heard the story a dozen times already."

"I only told him to mind his own business."

"He can't. He's a born meddler. Now he's queered you with the whole place."

"Can't help it. I wasn't going to let him get away with his impudence. Why should I?"

Miller shrugged. "Policy, my boy. Better take the advice of Cousin James and crawl into your shell till the storm has pelted past."

Half an hour later Jeff met his cousin near the chapel and was taken to task.

"What's this I hear about your insulting Thomas?"

"You have it wrong. He insulted me," Jeff corrected with a smile.

"Tommyrot! Why couldn't you treat him right?"

"Didn't like to throw him through the window on account of littering up the lawn with broken glass. "

James K.'s handsome square-cut face did not relax to a smile. "You may think this a joke, but I don't. I've heard the Chancellor is going to call you on the carpet."

"If he does he'll learn what I think."

The upper classman's anger boiled over. "You might think of me a little."

"Didn't know you were in this, J. K."

"They know I'm your cousin. It's hurting my reputation."

A faint ironic smile touched Jeff's face. "No, James, I'm helping it. Ever notice how blondes and brunettes chum together. Value of contrasts, you see. I'm a moral brunette. You're a shining example of all a man should be. I simply emphasize your greatness."

"That's not the way it works," his cousin grumbled.

William MacLeod Raine

"That's just how it works. Best thing that could happen to you would be for me to get expelled. Shall I?"

Jeff offered his suggestion debonairly.

"Of course not."

"It would give you just the touch of halo you need to finish the picture. Think of it: your noble head bowed in grief because of the unworthy relative you had labored so hard to save; the sympathy of the faculty, the respect of the fellows, the shy adoration of the co-eds. Great Brutus bowed by the sorrow of a strong man's unrepining emotion. By Jove, I ought to give you the chance. You'd look the part to admiration."

For a moment James saw himself in the role and coveted it. Jeff read his thought, and his laughter brought his cousin back to earth. He had the irritated sense of having been caught.

"It's not an occasion for talking nonsense," he said coldly.

Jeff sensed his disgrace in the stiff politeness of the professors and in the embarrassed aloofness of his classmates. Some of the men frankly gave him a wide berth as if he had been a moral pervert.

His temperament was sensitive to slights and he fell into one of his rare depressions. One afternoon he took the car for the city. He wanted to get away from himself and from his environment.

A chill mist was in the air. Drawn by the bright lights, Jeff entered a saloon and sat down in an alcove with his arms on the table. Why did they hammer him so because he told the truth as he saw it? Why must he toady to the ideas of Bland as everybody else at the University seemed to do? He was not respectable enough for them. That was the trouble. They were pushing him back into the gutter whence he had emerged. Wild fragmentary thoughts chased themselves across the record of his brain.

Almost before he knew it he had ordered and drunk a high-ball. Immediately his horizon lightened. With the second glass his depression vanished. He felt equal to anything.

It was past nine o'clock when he took the University car. As chance had it Professor Perkins and he were the only passengers. The teacher of Economics bowed to the flushed youth and buried himself in a book. It was not till they both rose to leave at the University station that he noticed the condition of Farnum. Even then he stood in momentary doubt.

With a maudlin laugh Jeff quieted any possible explanation of sickness.

"Been havin' little spree down town, Profeshor. Good deal like one ev'body been havin' out here. Yours shpiritual; mine shpirituous. Joke, see! Play on wor'd. Shpiritual—shpirituous."

"You're intoxicated, sir," Perkin,s told him sternly.

"Betcherlife I am, old cock! Ever get shp—shp—shpiflicated yourself?"

"Go home and go to bed, sir!"

"Whaffor? 'S early yet. 'S reasonable man I ask whaffor?"

The professor turned away, but Jeff caught at his sleeve.

"Lesh not go to bed. Lesh talk economicsh."

"Release me at once, sir."

"Jush's you shay. Shancellor wants see me. I'll go now."

He did. What occurred at that interview had better be omitted. Jeff was very cordial and friendly, ready to make up any differences there might be between them. An ice statue would have been warm compared to the Chancellor.

Next day Jeff was publicly expelled. At the time it did not trouble him in the least. He had brought a bottle home with him from town, and when the notice was posted he lay among the bushes in a sodden sleep half a mile from the campus.

Part 2

From a great distance there seemed to come to Jeff vaguely the sound of young rippling laughter and eager girlish voices. Drawn from heavy sleep, he was not yet fully awake. This merriment might be the music of fairy bells, such stuff as dreams are made of. He lay incurious, drowsiness still heavy on his eyelids.

"Oh, Virgie, here's another bunch! Oh, girls, fields of them!"

There was a little rush to the place, and with it a rustle of skirts that sounded authentic. Jeff began to believe that his nymphs were not born of fancy. He opened his eyes languidly to examine a strange world upon which he had not yet focused his mind.

Out of the ferns a dryad was coming toward him, lance straight, slender, buoyantly youthful in the light tread and in the poise of the golden head.

At sight of him she paused, held in her tracks, eyes grown big with solicitude.

"You are ill."

Before he could answer she had dropped the anemones she carried, was on her knees beside him, and had his head cushioned against her arm.

"Tell me! What can I do for you? What is the matter?"

Jeff groaned. His head was aching as if it would blow up, but that was not the cause of the wave of pain which had swept over him. A realization had come to him of what was the matter with him. His eyes fell from hers. He made as if to get

William MacLeod Raine

up, but her hand restrained him with a gentle firmness.

"Don't! You mustn't." Then aloud, she cried: "Girls—girls—there's a sick man here. Run and get help. Quick."

"No—no! I—I'm not sick."

A flood of shame and embarrassment drenched him. He could not escape her tender hands without actual force and his poignant shyness made that impossible. She was like a fairy tale, a creature of dreams. He dared not meet her frank pitiful eyes, though he was intensely aware of them. The odor of violets brings to him even to this day a vision of girlish charm and daintiness, together with a memory of the abased reverence that filled him.

They came running, her companions, eager with question and suggestion. And hard upon their heels a teamster from the road broke through the thicket, summoned by their calls for help. He stooped to pick up something that his foot had struck. It was a bottle. He looked at it and then at Jeff.

"Nothing the matter with him, Miss, but just plain drunk," the man said with a grin. "He's been sleeping it off."

Jeff felt the quiver run through her. She rose, trembling, and with one frightened sidelong look at him walked quickly away. He had seen a wound in her eyes he would not soon forget. It was as if he had struck her down while she was holding out hands to help him.

CHAPTER 5

Lies need only age to make them respectable. Given that, they become traditions and are put upon a pedestal. Then the gentlest word for him who attacks them is traitor.

—From the Note Book of a Dreamer

THE REBEL FOLLOWS THE RAMIFICATIONS OF BIG BUSINESS AND FINDS THAT THE PILLARS OF SOCIETY ARE NOT IN POLITICS FOR THEIR HEALTH

Part 1

"Hmp! Want to be a reporter, do you?"

Warren, city editor on the Advocate, leaned back in his chair and looked Jeff over sharply.

"Yes."

"It's a hell of a life. Better keep out."

"I'd like to try it."

"Any experience?"

"Only correspondence. I've had two years at college."

The city editor snorted. He had the unreasoning contempt for college men so often found in the old-time newspaper hack.

"Then you don't want to be a reporter. You want to be a journalist," he jeered.

"They kicked me out," Jeff went on quietly.

"Sounds better. Why?"

Jeff hesitated. "I got drunk."

"Can't use you," Warren cut in hastily.

"I've quit—sworn off."

The city editor was back on the job, his eyes devouring copy. "Heard that before. Nothing to it," he grunted.

"Give me a trial. I'll show you."

"Don't want a man that drinks. Office crowded with 'em already."

Jeff held his ground. For five minutes the attention of Warren was focused on his work.

Suddenly he snapped out, "Well?"

He met Farnum's ingratiating smile. "You haven't told me yet what to start doing."

"I told you I didn't want you."

"But you do. I'm on the wagon."

"For how long?" jeered the city editor.

"For good."

Warren sized him up again. He saw a cleareyed young fellow without a superfluous ounce of flesh on him, not rugged but with a look of strength in the slender figure and the thin face. This young man somehow inspired confidence.

"Sent in that Colby story to us, didn't you?"

"Yes."

"Rotten story. Not half played up. Report to Jenkins at the City Hall."

"Now?"

"Now. Think I meant next year?"

The city editor was already lost in the reading of more copy.

Inside of half an hour Jeff was at work on his first assignment. Some derelict had committed suicide under the very shadow of the City Hall. Upon the body was a note scrawled on the bask of a dirty envelope.

Sick and out of work. Notify Henry Simmons, 237 River Street, San Francisco.

Jenkins, his hands in his pockets, looked at the body indifferently and turned the story over to the cub with a nod of his head.

"Go to it. Half a stick," he said.

From another reporter Jeff learned how much half a stick is. He wrote the account. When he had read it Jenkins glanced sharply at him. Though only the barest facts were told there was a sob in the story.

"That ain't just how we handle vag suicides, but we'll let 'er go this time," he commented.

It did not take Jeff long to learn how to cover a story to the satisfaction of the city editor. He had only to be conventional, sensational, and in general accurate as to his facts. He fraternized with his fellow reporters at the City Hall, shared stories with them, listened to the cheerful lies they told of their exploits, and lent them money they generally forgot to return. They were a happy-go-lucky lot, full of careless generosities and Bohemian tendencies. Often a week's salary went at a single poker sitting. Most of them drank a good deal.

After a few months' experience Jeff discovered that while the gathering of news tends to sharpen the wits it makes also for the superficial. Alertness, cleverness, persistence, a nose for news, and a surface accuracy were the chief qualities demanded of him by the office. He had only to look around him to see that the profession was full of keen-eyed, nimble-witted old-young men who had never attempted to synthesize the life they were supposed to be recording and interpreting. While at work they were always in a hurry, for to-day's news is dead to-morrow. They wrote on the run, without time for thought or reflection. Knowing beyond their years, the fruit of their wisdom was cynicism. Their knowledge withered for lack of roots.

The tendency of the city desk and of copy readers is to

reduce all reporters to a dead level, but in spite of this Jeff managed to get himself into his work. He brought to many stories a freshness, a point of view, an optimism that began to be noticed. From the police run Jeff drifted to other departments. He covered hotels, the court house, the state house and general assignments.

At the end of a couple of years he was promoted to a desk position. This did not suit him, and he went back to the more active work of the street. In time he became known as a star man. From dramatics he went to politics, special stories and feature work. The big assignments were given him.

It was his duty to meet famous people and interview them. The chance to get behind the scenes at the real inside story was given him. Because of this many reputations were pricked like bubbles so far as he was concerned. The mask of greatness was like the false faces children wear to conceal their own. In the one or two really big men he met Jeff discovered a humility and simplicity that came from self-forgetfulness. They were too busy with their vision of truth to pose for the public admiration.

Part 2

It was while Jeff was doing the City Hall run that there came to him one night at his rooms a man he had known in the old days when he had lived in the river bottom district. If he was surprised to see him the reporter did not show it.

"Hello, Burke! Come in. Glad to see you."

Farnum took the hat of his guest and relieved his awkwardness by guiding him to a chair and helping him get his pipe alight.

"How's everything? Little Mike must be growing into a big boy these days. Let's see. It's three years since I've seen him."
A momentary flicker lit the gloomy eyes of the Irishman. "He's a great boy, Mike is. He often speaks of you, Mr. Farnum.

"Glad to know it. And Mrs. Burke?"

"Fine."

"That leaves only Patrick Burke. I suppose he hasn't fallen off the water wagon yet."

The occupation of Burke had been a threadbare joke between them in the old days. He drove a street sprinkler for the city.

"That's what he has. McGuire threw the hooks into me this morning. I've drove me last day."

"What's the matter?"

"I'm too damned honest.... or too big a coward. Take your choice."

"All right. I've taken it," smiled the reporter.

Pat brought his big fist down on the table so forcefully that the books shook. "I'll not go to the penitentiary for an-ny man.... He wanted me to let him put two other teams on the rolls in my name. I wouldn't stand for it. That was six weeks ago. To-day he lets me out."

Jeff began to see dimly the trail of the serpent graft. He lit his pipe before he spoke.

"Don't quite get the idea, Pat. Why wouldn't you?"

"Because I'm on the level. I'll have no wan tellin' little Mike his father is a dirty thief.... It's this way. The rolls were to be padded, understand."

"I see. You were to draw pay for three teams when you've got only one."

"McGuire was to draw it, all but a few dollars a month." The Irishman leaned forward, his eyes blazing. "And because I wouldn't stand for it I'm fired for neglecting my duty. I missed a street yesterday. If he'd been frientlly to me I might have missed forty.... But he can't throw me down like that. I've got the goods to show he's a dirty grafter. Right now he's drawing pay for seven teams that don't exist."

"And he doesn't know you know it?"

"You bet he don't. I've guessed it for a month. To-day I went round and made sure."

Jeff asked questions, learned all that Burke had to tell him. In the days that followed he ran down the whole story of the graft so secretly that not even the city editor knew what he was about. Then he had a talk with the "old man" and wrote his story.

It was a red-hot exposure of one of the most flagrant of the City Hall gang. There was no question of the proof. He had it in black and white. Moreover, there was always the chance that in the row which must follow McGuire might peach on Big Tim himself, the boss of all the little bosses.

Within twenty-four hours Jeff was summoned to a conference at which were present the city editor and Warren, now managing editor.

"We've killed your story, Farnum," announced the latter as soon as the door was closed.

"Why? I can prove every word of it."

"That was what we were afraid of."

"It's a peach of a story. With the spring elections coming on we need some dynamite to blow up Big Tim. I tell you McGuire would tell all he knows to save his own skin."

"My opinion, too," agreed Warren dryly. "My boy, it's too big a story. That's the whole trouble. If we were sure it would stop at McGuire we'd run it. But it won't. The corporations are backing Big Tim to win this spring. It won't do to get him tied up in a graft scandal."

"But the *Advocate* has been out after his scalp for years."

"Well, we're not after it any more. Of course, we're against him on the surface still."

Jeff did some rapid thinking. "Then the program will be for

us to nominate a weak ticket and elect Big Tim's by default. Is that it?"

"That's about it. The big fellows have to make sure of a Mayor who will be all right about the Gas and Electric franchise. So we're going to have four more years of Big Tim."

"Will Brownell stand for it?"

Brownell was the principal owner of the *Advocate.*

"Will he?" Warren let his eyelash rest for a second upon the cheek nearest Jeff. "He's been seen. My orders come direct from the old man."

The story was suppressed. No more was heard about the McGuire graft scandal exposure. It had run counter to the projects of big business.

Burke had to be satisfied without his revenge.

He got a job with a brewery and charged the McGuire matter to profit and loss.

As for Jeff the incident only served to make clearer what he already knew. More and more he began to understand the forces that dominate our cities, the alliance between large vested interests and the powers that prey. These great corporations were seekers of special privileges. To secure this they financed the machines and permitted vice and corruption. He saw that ultimately most of the shame for the bad government of American cities rests upon the Fromes and the Merrills.

As for the newspapers, he was learning that between the people and an independent press stand the big advertisers.

These make for conservatism, for an unfair point of view, for a slant in both news recording and news interpretation. Yet he saw that the press is in spite of this a power for good. The evil that it does is local and temporary, the good general and permanent.

Part 3

The spirit of commercialism that dominated America during the nineties and the first years of the new century never got hold of Jeff. The air and the light of his land were often the creation of a poet's dream. The delight of life stabbed him, so, too, did its tragedy. Not anchored to conventions, his mind was forever asking questions, seeking answers.

He would come out from a theater into a night that was a flood of illumination. Electric signs poured a glare of light over the streets. Motor cars and electrics whirled up to take away beautifully gowned women and correctly dressed men. The windows of the department stores were filled with imported luxuries. And he would sometimes wonder how much of misery and trouble was being driven back by that gay blare of wealth, how many men and women and children were giving their lives to maintain a civilization that existed by trampling over their broken hearts and bodies.

Preventable poverty stared at him from all sides. He saw that our social fabric is thrown together in the most haphazard fashion, without scientific organization, with the greatest waste, in such a way that non-producers win all the prizes while the toilers do without. Yet out of this system that sows hate and discontent, that is a practical denial of brotherhood, of God, springs here and there love like a flower in a dunghill.

He felt that art and learning, as well as beauty and truth, ought to walk hand in hand with our daily lives. But this is impossible so long as disorder and cruelty and disease are in the world unnecessarily. He heard good people, busy with effects instead of causes, talk about the way out, as if there could be any way out which did not offer an equality of opportunity refused by the whole cruel system of to-day.

But Jeff could be in revolt without losing his temper. The men who profited by present conditions were not monsters. They were as kind of heart as he was, effects of the system just as much as the little bootblack on the corner. No possible good could come of a blind hatred of individuals.

His Bohemian instinct sent Jeff ranging far in those days. He made friends out of the most unlikely material. Some of the most radical of these were in the habit of gathering informally in his rooms about once a week. Sometimes the talk was good and pungent. Much of it was merely wild.

His college friend, Sam Miller, now assistant city librarian, was one of this little circle. Another was Oscar Marchant, a fragile little Socialist poet upon whom consumption had laid its grip. He was not much of a poet, but there burnt in him a passion for humanity that disease and poverty could not extinguish.

One night James Farnum dropped in to borrow some money from his cousin and for ten minutes listened to such talk as he had never heard before. His mind moved among a group of orthodox and accepted ideas. A new one he always viewed as if it were a dynamite bomb timed to go off shortly. He was not only suspicious of it; he was afraid of it.

James was, it happened, in evening dress. He took gingerly the chair his cousin offered him between the hectic Marchant and a little Polish Jew.

The air was blue with the smoke from cheap tobacco. More than one of those present carried the marks of poverty. But the note of the assembly was a cheerful at-homeness. James wondered what the devil his cousin meant by giving this heterogeneous gathering the freedom of his rooms.

Dickinson, the single-taxer, was talking bitterly. He was a big man with a voice like a foghorn. His idea of emphasis appeared to be pounding the table with his blacksmith fist.

"I tell you society doesn't want to hear about such things,"he was declaiming. "It wants to go along comfortably without being disturbed. Ignore everything that's not pleasant, that's liable to harrow the feelings. The sins of our neighbors make spicy reading. Fill the papers with 'em. But their distresses and their poverty! That's different. Let's hear as little about them as possible. Let's keep it a well-regulated world."

Nearly everybody began to talk at once. James caught phrases here and there out of the melee.

"... Democratic institutions must either decay or become revitalized.... To hell with such courts. They're no better than anarchy.... In Verden there are only two classes: those who don't get as much as they earn and those who get more.... Tell you we've got to get back to the land, got to make it free as air. You can't be saved from economic slavery till you have socialism...."

Suddenly the hubbub subsided and Marchant had the floor. "All of life's a compromise, a horrible unholy giving up as unpractical all the best things. It's a denial of love, of Christ, of God."

A young preacher who was conducting a mission for sailors on the water front cut in. "Exactly. The church is radically wrong because—"

"Because it hasn't been converted to Christianity yet. Mr. Moneybags in the front pew has got a strangle hold on the parson. Begging your pardon, Mifflin. We know you're not that kind."

Marchant won the floor again. "Here's the nub of it. A man's a slave so long as his means of livelihood is dependent on some other man. I don't care whether it's lands or railroads or mines. Abolish private property and you abolish poverty."

They were all at it again, like dogs at a bone. Across the Babel James caught Jeff's gay grin at him.

By sheer weight Dickinson's voice boomed out of the medley.

"… just as Henry George says: 'Private ownership of land is the nether mill-stone. Material progress is the upper mill-stone. Between them, with an increasing pressure, the working classes are being ground.' We're just beginning to see the effect of private property in land. Within a few years.…"

"What we need is to get back to Democracy. Individualism has run wild.…"

"Trouble is we can't get anywhere under the Constitution. Every time we make a move—check. It was adopted by aristocrats to hold back the people and that's what it's done. Law—"

Apparently nobody got a chance to finish his argument. The Polish Jew broke in sharply. "Law! There iss no law."

"Plenty of it, Sobieski, Go out on the streets and preach your philosophic anarchy if you don't believe it. See what it will do to you. Law's a device to bolster up the strong and to hammer down the weak."

James had given a polite cynical indulgence to views so lost to reason and propriety. But he couldn't quite stand any more. He made a sign to Jeff and they adjourned to the next room.

"Your friends always so—so enthusiastic?" he asked with the slightest lift of his upper lip.

"Not always. They're a little excited to-night because Harshaw imprisoned those fourteen striking miners for contempt of court."

"Don't manufacture bombs here, do you?"

Jeff laughed. "We're warranted harmless."

James offered him good advice. "That sort of talk doesn't lead to anything—except trouble. Men who get on don't question the fundamentals of our social system. It doesn't do, you know. Take the constitution. Now I've studied it. A wonderful document. Gladstone said."

"Yes, I know what Gladstone said. I don't agree with him. The constitution was devised by men with property as a protection against those who had none."

"Why shouldn't it have been?"

"It should, if vested interests are the first thing to consider. In there"—with a smiling wave of his hand—"they think people are more important than things. A most unsettling notion!"

"Mean to say you believe all that rant they talk?"

"Not quite," Jeff laughed.

"Well, I'd cut that bunch of anarchists if I were you," his cousin suggested. "Say, Jeff, can you let me have fifty dollars?"

Jeff considered. He had been thinking of a new spring

overcoat, but his winter one would do well enough. From the office he could get an advance of the balance he needed to make up the fifty.

"Sure. I'll bring it to your rooms to-morrow night."

"Much obliged. Hate to trouble you," James said lightly. "Well, I won't keep you longer from your anarchist friends. Good-night."

CHAPTER 6

"The cure for the evils of Democracy is more
Democracy."

—De Tocqueville

THE REBEL HUMBLY ASSISTS AT THE UNVEILING
OF A HERO'S STATUE

Part 1

On the occasion when his cousin was graduated with the
highest honors from the law school of Verden University Jeff
sat inconspicuously near the rear of the chapel. James, as
class orator, rose to his hour. From the moment that he
moved slowly to the front of the platform, handsome and
impassive, his calm gaze sweeping over the audience while
he waited for the little bustle of expectancy to subside, Jeff
knew that the name of Farnum was going to be covered with
glory.

The orator began in a low clear voice that reached to the last
seat in the gallery. Jeff knew that before he finished its
echoes would be ringing through the hall like a trumpet call
to the emotions of those present.

William MacLeod Raine

It was not destined that Jeff should hear a word of that stirring peroration. His eye fell by chance upon a young woman seated in a box beside an elderly man whom he recognized as Peter C. Frome. From that instant he was lost to all sense perception that did not focus upon her. For he was looking at the dryad who had come upon him out of the ferns three years before. She would never know it, but Alice Frome had saved him from the weakness that might have destroyed him. From that day he had been a total abstainer. Now as he looked at her the vivid irregular beauty of the girl flowed through him like music. Her charm for him lay deeper than the golden gleams of imprisoned sunlight woven in her hair, than the gallant poise of the little head above the slender figure. Though these set his heart beating wildly, a sure instinct told him of the fine and exquisite spirit that found its home in her body.

She was leaning forward in her chair, her eyes fixed on James almost as if she were fascinated by his oratory. Her father watched her, a trifle amused at her eagerness. In her admiration she was frank as a boy. When Farnum's last period was rounded out and he made to leave the stage her gloved hands beat together in excited applause.

After the ceremonies were over James came straight to her. Jeff missed no detail of their meeting. The young lawyer was swimming on a tide of triumph, but it was easy to see that Alice Frome's approval was the thing he most desired. His cousin had never seen him so gay, so handsome, so altogether irresistible. For the first time a little spasm of envy shot through Jeff, That the girl liked James was plain enough. How could any girl help liking him?

The orator was so much the center of attention that Jeff postponed his congratulations till evening. He called on his cousin after midnight at his rooms. James had just returned from a class banquet where he had been the toastmaster. He was still riding the big wave.

"It's been a great day for me, Jeff," he broke out after his cousin had congratulated him. "I've earned it, too. For seven years I've worked toward this day as a climax. Did you see me talking to P. C. Frome and his daughter? I'm going to be accepted socially in the best houses of the city. I'll make them all open to me."

"I don't doubt it."

"And the best of it is that I've made my own success."

"Yes, you've worked hard," Jeff admitted with a little gleam of humor in his eyes. He would not remind his cousin that he had lent him most of the money to see him through law school.

"Oh, worked!" James was striding up and down the room to get rid of some of his nervous energy. "I've done more than work. I've made opportunities... grabbed them coming and going. Young as I am Verden expects big things of me. And I'll deliver the goods, too."

"What's the program?" Jeff asked, much amused.

"Don't know yet. I'm going into politics and I mean to get ahead. I'll make a big splash and keep in the public eye."

His cousin could not help laughing. "You always were a pretty good press agent for J. K. Farnum."

"Why shouldn't I be?"

"I don't know why you shouldn't. A man who gets ahead puts

himself in a position where he can bring about reforms."

"That's it exactly. I mean to make myself a power."

"Get hold of one good practical reform and back it. Pound away on it until the people identify you with it. Take direct legislation as your text, say. There's going to be a strong drift that way in the next ten years. Machines and bosses are going to be swept to the junk heap."

"How do you know?"

Jeff could give no adequate justification for the faith that was in him. It would be no answer to tell James that he knew the plain people of the state better than the politicians did. However, he mentioned a few facts.

"It's all very well for you to be a radical, but I have to conserve my influence," James objected. "I've got to be practical. If I were just going to be a reporter it would be different."

"Don't be too practical, James. You've got to have some vision if you're going to lead the people. Nobody is so blind to the future as practical politicians and business men." He stopped, smiling quizzically. "But you're the orator of the family. I don't want to infringe on your copyright. Only you have the personality to be a real leader. Get started right. Remember that America faces forward, and that we're going to move with seven league boots to better conditions."

James mused out loud. "If a man could be a Lincoln to save the people from industrial slavery it would be worth while."

Jeff did not laugh at his conceit. "Go to it. I'll promise you the backing of the *World*."

"What have you to do with the *World*?"

"Beginning with next Monday I'm to be managing editor."

"You!"

"Even so. Captain Chunn has bought the paper."

"Chunn, the man who made millions in a lucky strike in Alaska?"

"Same man."

James was still incredulous. "How did Chunn happen to pick you for the editor?"

"He's an old friend of mine. 'Member the day I had the fight with Ned Merrill. Captain Chunn was the man who stood up for me."

"And you've known him ever since?"

"I've always corresponded with him."

"Well, I'll be hanged. Talk about luck." James looked his cousin over with increased respect. He always took off his hat to success, but he had been so long accustomed to thinking of Jeff as a failure that he could not adjust his mind to the situation. "Why, you can't run a paper. Can you?"

Jeff smiled. "I told Captain Chunn he was taking a big chance."

"If he's as rich as they say he is he can afford to lose some money."

James took the news of his cousin's good fortune a little peevishly. He did not grudge Jeff's advancement, but he resented that it had befallen him to-day of all days. The promotion of the reporter took the edge off his own achievements.

Part 2

As James understood his own genius, it was as a statesman that he was fitted preeminently to shine. He had the urbanity, the large impassive manner, and the magnetic eloquence of the old-style congressman. All he needed was the chance.

With the passing months he grew more restless at the delay. There were moments in the night when he trembled lest some stroke of evil fate might fall upon him before he had carved his name in the niche of fame. To sit in an empty law office and wait for clients took more patience than he could summon. He wanted an opportunity to make speeches in the campaign that was soon to open. That he finally went to Big Tim himself about it instead of to his ward committeeman was characteristic of James K.

After he sent his card in the young lawyer was kept waiting for thirty-five minutes in an outer office along with a Jew peddler, a pugilist ward heeler, an Irish saloonkeeper, and a brick contractor. Naturally he was exceedingly annoyed. O'Brien ought to know that James K. Farnum did not rank with this riff-raff.

When at last James got into the holy of holies he found Big Tim lolling back in his swivel chair with a fat cigar in his mouth. The boss did not take the trouble to rise as he waved his visitor to a chair.

Farnum explained that he was interested in the political situation and that he was prepared to take an active part in the campaign about to open. The big man listened, watching him out of half shut attentive eyes. He had never yet seen a kid glove politician that was worth the powder to blow him up. Moreover, he had special reasons for disliking this one. His cousin was editor of the *World*, and that paper was

William MacLeod Raine

becoming a thorn in his side.

O'Brien took the cigar from his mouth. "Did youse go to the primary last night?' he asked.

James did not even know there had been one. He had in point of fact been at a Country Club dance.

"Can youse tell me what the vote of your precinct was at the last city election?"

The budding statesman could not.

"What precinct do youse live in?"

Farnum was not quite sure. He explained that he had moved recently.

Big Tim grunted scornfully. He was pleased to have a chance to take down the cheek of any Farnum.

"What do youse think you can do?"

"I can make speeches. I'm the best orator that ever came out of Verden University."

"Tommyrot! How do youse stand in your precinct? Can youse get the vote out to go down the line for us? That's what counts. Oratory be damned!"

James was pale with rage. The manner of the boss was nothing less than insulting.

"Then you decline to give me a chance, Mr. O'Brien?"

"I do not. In politics a man makes his own chance. He gets

along by being so useful we can't get along without him. See? He learns the game. You don't know the A B C of it. It's my opinion youse never will."

O'Brien's hard cold eye triumphed over him as a principal does over a delinquent schoolboy.

His vanity stung, the lawyer sprang to his feet. "Very well, Mr. O'Brien. I'll show you a thing or two about what I can and can't do."

For just an instant a notion flitted across Big Tim's mind that he might be making a mistake. He was indulging an ugly temper, and he knew it. This was a luxury he rarely permitted himself. Now he decided to "go the whole hog," as he phrased it to himself later. His lips set to an ugly snarl.

"It's like the nerve of ye to come to me. Want to begin at the top instid of at the bottom. Go to Billie Gray if youse want to have some wan learn youse the game. If you're any good he'll find it out."

James got himself out of the office with all the dignity of which he was capable. Go to Billie Gray, the notorious ballot box stuffer! Take orders from the little rascal who had shaved the penitentiary only because of his pull! James saw himself doing it. He was sore in every outraged nerve of him. Never before in his life had anybody sat and sneered at him openly before his eyes. He would show the big boss that he had been a fool to treat him so. And he would show P. C. Frome and Ned Merrill that he was a very valuable man.

How? Why, by fighting the corporations! Wasn't that the way that all the big men got their start nowadays as lawyers? As soon as they discovered his value Frome and his friends would be after his services fast enough. James was no

William MacLeod Raine

radical, but he believed Jeff knew what he was talking about when he predicted an impending political change, one that would carry power back from the machine bosses to the people. The young lawyer decided to ride that wave as far as it would take him. He would be a tribune of the people, and they in turn would make of him their hero. With the promised backing of the *World* he would go a long way. He knew that Jeff would fling him at once into the limelight. And he would make good. He would be the big speaker for the reform movement. Nobody in the state could sway a crowd as he could. James had not the least doubt about that. It was glory and applause he wanted, not the drudgery of dirty ward politics.

Part 3

Under Jeff's management the *World* had at once taken the leadership in the fight for political reform in the state. He made it the policy of the paper to tell the truth as to corruption both in and out of his own party. Nor would he allow the business office, as influenced by the advertisers, to dictate the policy of the paper. The result was that at the end of the first year he went to the owner with a report of a deficit of one hundred and twenty-five thousand dollars for the twelve months just ended.

Captain Chunn only laughed. "Keep it up, son. I've had lots of fun out of it. You've given this town one grand good shaking up. The whole state is getting its fighting clothes on. We've got Merrill and Frome scared stiff about their supreme court judges. Looks to me as if we were going to lick them."

The political campaign was already in progress. Hitherto the public utility corporations of Verden had controlled and practically owned the machinery of both parties. The *World* had revolted, rallied the better sentiment in the party to which it belonged, and forced the convention to declare for a reform platform and to nominate a clean ticket composed of men of character.

Jeff agreed. "I think we're going to win. The people are with us. The *World* is booming." It's the advertising troubles me. Frome and Merrill have got at the big stores and they won't come in with any space worth mentioning."

"Damn the big advertisers," exploded Chunn. "I've got two million cold and I'm going to see this thing out, son. That's what I told Frome last week when he had the nerve to have me nominated to the Verden Club. Wanted to muzzle me. Be a good fellow and quit agitating. That was the idea. I sent back word I'd stuck by Lee to Appomattox and I reckoned I was too old a dog to learn the new trick of deserting my flag."

"If you're satisfied I ought to be," Jeff laughed. "As for the advertising, the stores will come back soon. The managers all want to take space, but they are afraid of spoiling their credit at the banks while conditions are so unsettled."

"Oh, well. We'll stick to our guns. You fire'em and I'll supply the ammunition." The little man put his hand on Jeff's shoulder with a chuckle. "We're both rebels—both irrecon-cilables, son. I reckon we're going to be well hated before we get through with this fight."

"Yes. They're going about making people believe we're cranks and agitators who are hurting business for our own selfish ends."

"I reckon we can stand it, David." Chunn had no children of his own and he always called Jeff son or David. "By the way, how's that good looking cousin of yours coming out? I see you're giving his speeches lots of space."

A light leaped to the eyes of the younger man. "He's doing fine. James is a born orator. Wherever he goes he gets a big ovation."

Chunn grunted. "Humph! That'll please him. He's as selfish as the devil, always looking out for James Farnum."

"He wins the people, Captain."

"You talk every evening yourself, but I don't see reports of any of your speeches."

"I don't talk like James. There's not a man in the state to equal him, young as he is."

"Humph!"

Captain Chunn grumbled a good deal about the way Jeff was always pushing his cousin forward and keeping in the background himself. In his opinion "David" was worth a hundred of the other.

CHAPTER 7

"Spirits of old that bore me,
And set me, meek of mind,
Between great deeds before me,
And deeds as great behind,

Knowing Humanity my star
As forth of old I ride,
0 help me wear with every scar
Honor at eventide."

THE REBEL DISCOVERS THAT ADHESION IS A
PROPERTY OF MUD; ALSO THAT A SOLDIER MUST
SOMETIMES TURN HIS BACK AND BURN THE
BRIDGES BEHIND HIM

Part 1

The fight for the control of the state developed unpre-
cedented bitterness. The big financial interests back of the
political machines poured out money like water to elect a
ticket that would be friendly to capital. An eight-hour-day
bill to apply to miners and underground workers had been
passed by the last legislature and a supreme court must be
elected to declare this law unconstitutional. Moreover, a

United States senator was to be chosen, so that the personnel of the assembly was a matter of great importance.

Through the subsidized columns of the *Advocate* and the *Herald* all the venom of outraged public plunder was emptied on the heads of Jeff Farnum and Captain Chunn. They were rebels, blackmailers, and anarchists. Jeff's life was held up to public scorn as dissolute and licentious. He had been expelled from college and consorted only with companions of the lowest sort. A free thinker and an atheist, he wanted to tear down the pillars which upheld society. Unless Verden and the state repudiated him and his gang of trouble breeders the poison of their opinions would infect the healthy fabric of the community.

There was about Jeff a humility, a sort of careless generosity, that could take with a laugh a hit at himself. But in the days that followed he was often made to wince when good men drew away from him as from a moral pervert. Twice he was hissed from the stage when he attempted to talk, or would have been, if he had not quietly waited until the indignant protesters were exhausted. It amused him to see that his old college acquaintance "Sissie" Thomas and Billy Gray, the ballot box stuffer of the Second Ward, were among the most vehement of those who thus scorned him. So do the extremes of virtue and vice find common ground when the blasphemer raises his voice against intrenched capital.

The personal calumny of the enemy showed how hard hit the big bosses were, how beneath their feet they felt the ground of public opinion shift. It had been only a year since Big Tim O'Brien, boss of the city by permission of the public utility corporations, had read Jeff's first editorial against ballot box stuffing. In it the editor of the *World* had pledged that paper never to give up the fight for the people until such crookedness was stamped out. Big Tim had laughed until his paunch

William MacLeod Raine

shook at the confidence of this young upstart and in impudent defiance had sent him a check for fifty dollars for the Honest Election League.

Neither Big Tim nor the respectable buccaneers back of him were laughing now. They were fighting with every ounce in them to sweep back the wave of civic indignation the *World* had gathered into a compact aggressive organization.

Young Ned Merrill, who represented the interests of the allied corporations, had Big Tim on the carpet. The young man had not been out of Harvard more than three years, but he did not let any nonsense about fair play stand in his way. In spite of the clean-cut look of him—he was broad-shoul-dered and tall, with an effect of decision in the square cleft chin that would some day degenerate into fatness—Ned Merrill played the game of business without any compunctions.

"You're making a bad fight of it, O'Brien. Old style methods won't win for us. These crank reformers have got the people stirred up. Keep your ward workers busy, but don't expect them to win." He leaned forward and brought his fist down heavily on the desk. "We've got to smash Farnum—discredit him with the bunch of sheep who are following him."

"What more do youse want? We're callin' him ivery black name under Hiven."

Merrill shook his head decisively. "Not enough. Prove something. Catch him with the goods."

"If youse'll show me how?"

"I don't care how, You've got detectives, haven't you? Find out all about him, where he comes from, who his people were. Rake his life with a fine tooth comb from the day he was born. He's a bad egg. We all know that. Dig up facts to prove it."

Within the hour detectives were set to work. One of them left next day for Shelby. Another covered the neighborhoods where Jeff had lived in Verden. Henceforth wherever he went he was shadowed.

It was about this time that Samuel Miller lost his place in the city library on account of his political opinions. For more than a year he and Jeff had roomed together at a private boarding house kept by a Mrs. Anderson. Within twentyfour hours of his dismissal Miller was on the road, sent out by the campaign committee of his party to make speeches throughout the state.

Jeff himself was speaking nearly every night now that the day of election was drawing near. This, together with the work of editing the paper and the strain of the battle, told heavily on a vitality never too much above par. He would come back to his rooms fagged out, often dejected because some friend had deserted to the enemy.

One cold rainy evening he met Nellie Anderson in the hall. She had been saying good-bye to some friends who had been in to call on her.

"You're wet, Mr. Farnum," the young woman said.

"A little."

She stood hesitating in the doorway leading to the apartment of herself and her mother, then yielded shyly to a kindly impulse.

William MacLeod Raine

"We've been making chocolate. Won't you come in and have some? You look cold."

Jeff glimpsed beyond her the warm grate fire in the room. He, too, yielded to an impulse. "Since you're so good as to ask me, Miss Nellie."

She took charge of his hat and overcoat, making him sit down in a big armchair before the fire. He watched her curiously as she moved lightly about waiting on him. Nellie was a soft round little person with constant intimations of a childhood not long outgrown. Jeff judged she must be nineteen or twenty, but she had moments of being charmingly unsure of herself. The warm color came and went in her clear cheeks at the least provocation.

"Mother's gone to bed. She always goes early. You don't mind," she asked naively.

Jeff smiled. She was, he thought, about as worldly wise as a fluffy kitten. "No, I don't mind at all," he assured her.

Nor did he in the least. His weariness was of the spirit rather than the body, and he found her grace, her shy sweetness, grateful to the jaded senses. It counted in her favor that she was not clever or ultra-modern. The dimpling smiles, the quick sympathy of this innocent, sensuous young creature, drew him out of his depression. When he left the pleasant warmth of the room half an hour later it was with a little glow at the heart. He had found comfort and refreshment.

How it came to pass Jeff never quite understood, but it soon was almost a custom for him to drop into the living room to get a cup of chocolate when he came home. He found himself looking forward to that half hour alone with Nellie Anderson. Whoever else criticized him, she did not. The manner in which she made herself necessary to his material comfort was masterly. She would be waiting, eager to help him off with his overcoat, hot chocolate and sandwiches ready for him in the cozy living-room. To him, who for years had lived a hand-to-mouth boarding house existence, her shy wholesome laughter made that room sing of home, one which her personality fitted to a dot. She was always in good humor, always trim and neat, always alluring to the eye. And she had the pretty little domestic ways that go to the head of a bachelor when he eats alone with an attractive girl.

Their intimacy was not exactly a secret. Mrs. Anderson, who was rather deaf and admitted to being a heavy sleeper, knew that Jeff dropped in occasionally. He suspected she did not know how regularly, but she was one of that large class of American mothers who let their daughters arrange their own love affairs and would not have interfered had she known.

Once or twice it flashed upon Jeff that this ought not to go on. Since he had no intention of marrying Nell he must not let their relationship reach the emotional climax toward which he guessed it was racing. But his experience in such matters was limited. He did not know how to break off their friendship without hurting her, and he was eager to minimize the possibility of danger. His modesty made this last easy. Out of her kindness she was good to him, but it was not to be expected that so pretty a girl would fall in love with a man like him.

The most potent argument for letting things drift was his own craving for her. She was becoming necessary to him. Whenever he thought of her it was with a tender glow. Her soft long-lashed eyes would come between him and the editorial he was writing. A dozen times a day he could see a picture of the tilted little coaxing mouth. The gurgle of her laughter called to him for hours before he left the office.

He got into the habit of talking to her about the things that were troubling him—the tactics of the enemy, the desertion of friends, the dubious issue of the campaign. Curled up in a big chair, her whole attention absorbed in what he was saying Nellie made a good listener. If she did not show a full understanding of the situation, he could always sense her ready sympathy. Her naive, indignant loyalty was touching.

"I read what the *Advocate* said about you today," she told him one night, a tide of color in her cheeks. "It was horrid. As if anybody would believe it."

"I'm afraid a good many people do," he said gravely.

"Nobody who knows you," she protested stoutly.

"Yes, some who know me."

He let his eyes dwell on her. It was easy to see how undisciplined of life she was, save where its material aspects had come into impact with her on the economic side.

"None of your real friends."

"How many real friends has a man—friends who will stand by him no matter how unpopular he is?"

"I don't know. I should think you'd have lots of them."

He shook his head, a hint of a smile in his eyes. "Not many. They keep their chocolate and sandwiches for folks whose trolley do'esn't fly the wire."

"What wire?" she asked, her forehead knitted to a question.

"Oh, the wire that's over the tracks of respectability and

vested interests and special privilege."

She had been looking at him, but now her gaze went to the fire with that slow tilt of the chin he liked. Another color wave swept the oval of the soft cheeks.

"You've got more friends than you think," she said in a low voice.

"I've got one little friend I wouldn't like to lose."

She did not speak and his hand moved forward to cover hers. Instantly a wild and insurgent emotion tingled through him. He felt himself trembling and could not steady his nerves.

Without a word Nellie looked up and their eyes met. Something electric flashed from one to another. Her shy fear of him was adorable.

"Oh, don't, don't!" she murmured. "What will you think of me now?"

He had leaned forward and kissed her on the lips.

Jeff sprang to his feet, the muscles in his lean cheeks standing out. Some bell of warning was ringing in him. He was a man, young and desirous, subject to all the frailties of his sex, holding experiences in his past that had left him far from a puritan. And she was a woman, of unschooled impulses, with unsuspected banked passions, an innocent creature in whom primeval physical life rioted.

He moved toward the door, his left fist beating into the palm of his right hand. He must protect her, against himself—and against her innocent affection for him.

William MacLeod Raine

She fluttered past him, barring the way. Her cheeks were flaming with shame.

"You despise me. Why did I let you?" A sob swelled up into her soft round throat.

"You blessed lamb," he groaned.

"You're going to leave me. You—you don't want me for a friend any longer."

Her lips trembled—the red little lips that always reminded him of a baby's with its Cupid's bow. She was on the verge of breaking down. Jeff could not stand that. He held out his hands, intending to take hers and explain that he was not angry or disappointed at her. But somehow he found her in his arms instead, supple and warm, vital youth flowing in the soft cheeks' rich coloring and in the eyes quick and passionate with the tender abandon of her sex.

He set his teeth against the rush of desire that flooded him as her soft body clung to his. The emotional climax he had vaguely feared had leaped upon them like an uncaged tiger. He fought to stamp down the fires that blazed up in him. Time to think—he must have time to think.

"You don't despise me then," she cried softly, a little catch in her breath.

"No," he protested, and again "No."

"But you think I've done wrong."

"No. I've been to blame. You're a dear girl—and I've abused your kindness. I must go away—now."

"Then you—you do hate me," she accused with a quivering lip.

"No… no. I'm very fond of you."

"But you're going to leave me. It's because I've done wrong."

"Don't blame yourself, dear. It has been all my fault. I ought to have known."

Her hands fell from him. The life seemed to die out of her whole figure. "You do despise me."

Desire of her throbbed through him, but he spoke very quietly. "Listen, dear. There is nobody I respect more… and none I like so much. I can't tell you how… fond of you I am. But I must go now. You don't understand."

She bit her lip to repress the sobs that would come and turned away to hide her shame. Jeff caught her in his arms, kissed her passionately on the lips, the eyes, the soft round throat.

"You do… like me," she purred happily.

Abruptly he pushed her from him. Where were they drifting? He must get his anchors down before it was too late.

Somehow he broke away, leaving her there hurt and bewildered at his apparent fickleness, at the stiffness with which he had beaten back the sweet delight inviting them.

Jeff went to his rooms, his mind in a blind chaotic surge. He sat before the table for hours, fighting grimly to persuade himself he need not put away this joy that had come to him. Surely friendship was a good thing… and love. A man ought not to turn his back on them.

It was long past midnight when he rose, took his father's sword from the wall where it hung, and unsheathed it. A vision of an open fireplace in a log house rose before him, his father in the foreground looking like a picture of Stonewall Jackson. The kind brave eyes that were the soul of honor gazed at him.

"You damned scoundrel! You damned scoundrel!" Jeff accused himself in a low voice.

He knew his little friend was good and innocent, but he knew too she had inherited a temperament that made her very innocence a

anger to her. Every instinct of chivalry called upon him to protect her from the weakness she did not even guess. She had given him her kindness and her friendship, the dear child! It was up to him to be worthy of them. If he failed her he would be a creature forever lost to decency.

There was a sob in his throat as Jeff pushed the blade back into the worn scabbard and rehung the sword upon the wall. But the eyes in his lifted face were very bright. He too would keep his sword unstained and the flag of honor flying.

All through the next day and the next his resolution held. He took pains not to see her alone, though there was not an hour of the day when he could get away from the thought of her. The uneasy consciousness was with him that the issue was after all only postponed, that decisions of this kind must be made again and again so long as opportunity and desire go together. And there were moments of reaction when his will was like a rope of sand, when the longing for her swept over him like a great wave.

As Jeff slipped quietly into the hall the door of her room opened. Their eyes met, and presently hers fell. She was troubled and ashamed at what she had done, but plainly eager in her innocence to be forgiven.

Jeff spoke gently. "Nellie."

Her eyes suddenly filled with tears. "Aren't we ever going to be friends again?"

Through the open door he could see the fire glowing in the grate and the chocolate set on the little table. He knew she had prepared for his coming and how greatly she would be hurt if he rejected her advances.

"Of course we're friends."

"Then you'll come in, just for a few minutes."

He hesitated.

"Please," she whispered. "Or I'll know you don't like me any more."

Jeff followed her into the room and closed the door behind him.

William MacLeod Raine

Part 2

Two days before the election Big Tim's detective wired from Shelby, Tennessee, the outline of a story that got two front page columns in both the *Advocate* and the *Herald.* Jefferson Davis Farnum was the son of a thief, of a rebel soldier who had spent seven years in the penitentiary for looting the bank of which he was cashier. In addition to featuring the news story both papers handled the subject at length in their editorial columns. They wanted to know whether the people of this beautiful state were willing to hand over the Commonwealth to be plundered by the reckless gang of which this son of a criminal was the head.

The paper reached Jeff at his rooms in the morning. He had lately taken the apartments formerly occupied by his cousin, James moving to Mrs. Anderson's until after the election. The exchange had been made at the suggestion of the editor, who gave as a reason that he wanted to be close to his work until the winter was past. It happened that James was just now very glad to get a cheaper place. He was very short of funds and until after the election had no time for social functions. All he needed with a room was to sleep in it.

Jeff was still reading the story from Shelby when his cousin came in hurriedly. James was excited and very white.

"My God, Jeff! It's come at last. I knew it would ruin me some day," the lawyer cried, after he had carefully closed the door of the bedroom.

"It won't ruin you, James. Your name isn't mentioned yet. Perhaps it may not be. It can't hurt you, even if it is."

"I tell you it will ruin me both socially and politically. Once it gets out nobody will trust me. I'll be the son of a thief,"

James insisted wildly.

"You're the son of a man who made a slip and has paid for it," answered Jeff steadily. "Don't let your ideas get warped. This town is full of men who have done wrong and haven't paid for it."

"That's one of your fool socialist theories." James spoke sharply and irritably. "No man's guilty till the law says so. They haven't been in the penitentiary. He has. That's what damns me if it gets out."

Jeff laid a hand affectionately on his cousin's shoulder. "Don't you believe it for a moment. There's no moral distinction between the man who has paid and the man who hasn't paid for his sins toward society. There is good and there is bad in all of us, closely intertwined, knit together into the very warp and woof of our lives. We're all good and we're all bad."

It was with James a purely personal equation. He could not forget its relation to himself.

"My name is to be voted on at the University Club next month. I'll be blackballed to a dead certainty," he said miserably.

"Probably, if the story gets out. It's tough, I know." Jeff's eyes gleamed angrily. "And why should they? You're just as good a man to-day as you were yesterday. But there's nothing so fettering, so despicable as good form. It blights. Let a man bow down to the dead hand of custom and he can never again be true to what he thinks and knows. His judgment gets warped. Soon Madame Grundy does his thinking for him, along well-grooved lines."

"Oh, well! That's just talk. What am I to do?" James broke out nervously.

"I know what I would do in your case."

"What?"

"Come out with a short statement telling the exact facts. I'd make no apologies or long explanation. Just the plain story as simply as you can."

"Well, I'll not," the lawyer broke out. "Easy enough for you to say what I ought to do. Look at who my friends are—the Fromes and the Merrills and the Gilmans. Best set in town. I strained a point when I broke loose from them to take up this progressive fight. They'd cut me dead if a story like this came out."

"I daresay. Communities are loaded to the guards with respectable cowards. But if you stand on your own feet like a man they'll think more of you for it. Most of them will be glad to know you again inside of five years. For you're going to be successful, and people like the Merrills and the Gilmans bow down to success."

The lawyer shook his head doggedly. "I'm not going to tell a thing I don't have to tell. That's settled." He hesitated a moment before he went on. "I've got a reason why I want to stand well with the Fromes, Jeff. I'm not in a position to risk anything."

Jeff waited. He thought he knew that reason.

"I'm going to marry Alice Frome if I can."

"You've asked her." Jeff's voice sounded to himself as if it belonged to another man.

"No. Not yet. Ned Merrill's in the running. Strong, too. He's being backed by his father and old P. C. Frome. The idea is to consolidate interests by this marriage. But I've got a fighting chance. She likes me. Since I went into this political fight against her father she's taken pains to show me how friendly she feels. But if this story gets out—I'm smashed. That's all."

"Go to her. Tell her the truth. She'll stand by you," his cousin urged.

"You don't understand these people, Jeff. I do. Even if she wanted to stand by me she couldn't. They wouldn't let her. Right now I'm carrying all the handicap I can."

Jeff walked to the window and stood looking out with his hands in his pockets. The hum of the busy street rose to his ears, but he did not hear it. Nor did he see the motor cars whizzing past, the drays lumbering along, the thronged sidewalks of Powers Avenue. A door that had for years been ajar in his heart had swung to with a crash. The incredible folly of his dream was laid bare to him. Despised, distrusted and disgraced, there was no chance that he might be even a friend to her. She moved in another world, one he could not reach if he would and would not if he could. All that he believed in she had been brought up to disregard. Much that was dear to her he must hammer down so long as there was life in him.

But James—he had fought his way up to her. Why shouldn't he have his chance? Better—far better James than Ned Merrill. He had heard the echoes of a disgraceful story about that young man in his college days, the story of how he had trampled down a working girl for his pleasure. James was

William MacLeod Raine

clean and honorable... and she loved him. Jeff's mind fastened on that last as a thing assured. Had he not seen her with starry eyes fixed on her hero, held fast as a limed bird? She too was entitled to her chance, and there was a way he could give it to her.

He turned back to James, who was sitting despondently at the managing editor's desk, jabbing at the blotting sheet with a pencil.

Jeff touched the *Advocate* he still held in his hand. "Did you read this story carefully?"

"No. I just ran my eye down it. Why?"

"Whoever dug it up has made a mistake. He has jumped to the conclusion that I'm Uncle Robert's son. Why not let it go at that?"

His cousin looked up with a flash of eager hope. "You mean—"

"I might as well be hanged for a sheep as a lamb. Let it go the way they have it."

The lawyer's heart leaped, but he could not let this go without a protest. "No, I—I couldn't do that. It's awfully good of you, Jeff."

The managing editor smiled in his whimsical way. "My reputation has long been in tatters. A little more can't hurt it."

James conceded a reflective assent with a manner of impartiality. "Of course your friends wouldn't think any the less of you. They're not so—so—"

"respectable as yours," Jeff finished for him.

"I was going to say so hidebound."

"All the same, isn't it?"

"But it would be a sacrifice for you. I recognize that. And I'm not sure that I could accept it. I will have to think that over," the lawyer concluded magnanimously.

"You'll find it is best. But I think I would tell Miss Frome, even if I didn't tell anybody else. She has a right to know."

"You may depend upon me to do whatever is best about that."

James was hardly out of the office before Captain Chunn blew in like a small tornado. He was boiling with rage.

"What's this infernal lie about you being the son of a convict, David?" he demanded, waving a copy of the Herald.

"Sit down, Captain. I'll tell you the story because you're entitled to it. But I shall have to speak in confidence."

"Confidence! Dad burn it, what are you talking about? Are you trying to tell me that Phil Farnum was a thief and a convict?"

Jeff's steel-blue eyes looked straight into his. "Nothing so impossible as that, Captain. I'm going to tell you the story of his brother."

Jeff told it, but he and the owner of the *World* disagreed radically about the best way to answer the attack.

"Why must you always stand between that kid glove cousin of yours and trouble? Let him stand the gaff himself. It will do him good," Chunn stormed.

But Jeff had his way. The *World* made no denial of the facts charged. In a statement on the front page that covered less than three sticks he told the simple story of the defalcation of Robert Farnum. One thing only he added to the account given in the opposition papers. This was that during the past two years the shortage of the bank cashier had been paid in full to the Planters' First National at Shelby.

There were many forecasts as to what the effect of the Farnum story would be on the election returns. It is enough to say that the ticket supported by the *World* was chosen by a small majority. James was elected to the legislature by a plurality of fifteen hundred votes over his antagonist, a majority unheard of in the Eleventh District.

CHAPTER 8

Is not this the trouble with our whole man-made world, that the game is played with loaded dice? Against the poor, the weak and the unfortunate have the cards been stacked. A tremendous percentage is in favor of the crook, the scoundrel, the smug robber of industry by whom the hands are dealt.

Wealth, created by the many, is more and more flowing into the vaults of the few. Legislatures, Congress, the courts, all the machinery of government, answer to the crack of the whip wielded by Big Business. The creed of the allied plunderers is that he should take who has the power and he should keep who can.

Until we mutiny against the timidity of our times Democracy and Prosperity will be dreams. The poor and the parasite we shall have always with us.

In that new world which is to be MEN and not THINGS will be supreme, property a means and not an end. The heart of the world will be born anew under an economic reconstruction that will give freedom for individual development. For our social and industrial life will be founded not on a denial of God but on an affirmation of Brotherhood.

—From the Note Book of a Dreamer

William MacLeod Raine

THE HERO MEETS AND ADMIRES A MONA LISA
SMILE. HE IS TENDERED AN APOLOGY FOR
A PAST DISCOURTESY

Part 1

Came James Farnum down Powers Avenue carrying with buoyant dignity the manner of greatness that sat so well on him. His smile was warm for a world that just now was treating him handsomely. There could be no doubt that for a first term he was making an extraordinary success of his work in the legislature. He had worked hard on committees and his speeches had made a tremendous hit. Jeff had played him up strong in the world too, so that he was becoming well known over the state. That he had risen to leadership of the progressives in the House during his first term showed his quality. His ambition vaulted. Now that his feet were on the first rungs of the ladder it would be his own fault if he did not reach the top.

His progress down the busy street was in the nature of an ovation. Everywhere he met answering smiles that told of the people's pride in their young champion. Already James had discovered that Americans are eager for hero worship. He meant to be the hero of his state, the favorite son it would delight to honor. This was what he loved: the cheers for the victor, not the clash of the battle.

"Good morning, Farnum. What are the prospects?" It was Clinton Rogers, of the big shipbuilding firm Harvey & Rogers, that stopped him now.

"Still anybody's fight, Mr. Rogers." The young lawyer's voice fell a note to take on a frankly confidential tone, an accent of friendliness that missed the fatal buttonholing familiarity of the professional politician. "If we can hold our fellows together we'll win. But the Transcontinental is bidding high for votes—and there's always a quitter somewhere."

"Does Frome stand any chance?"

"It will be Hardy or Frome. The least break in our ranks will be the signal for a stampede to P. C. The Republicans will support him when they get the signal. It's all a question of our fellows standing pat."

"From what I can learn it won't be your fault if Hardy isn't elected. I congratulate you on the best record ever made by a ember in his first term."

"Oh, we all do our best," James answered lightly. "But I'm grateful for your good opinion. I hope I deserve it."

James could afford to be modest about his achievements so long as Jeff was shouting his praises through the columns of the *World* to a hundred thousand readers of that paper. What the shipbuilder had said pleased him mightily. For Clinton Rogers was one of the few substantial moneyed men of Verden who had joined the reform movement. Not a single member of the Verden Club, with the exception of Rogers, was lined up with those making the fight for direct legislation. Even those who had no financial interest in the Transcontinental or the public utility corporations supported that side from principle.

James himself had thought a long time before casting in his lot with the insurgents led by his cousin. He had made tentative approaches both to Frome and to Edward B. Merrill. Both of these gentlemen had been friendly enough, but James had made up his mind they undervalued his worth. The way to convince them of this was to take the field against them.

He smiled now as he swung along the avenue. Both Frome and Merrill—yes, and Big Tim too, for that matter!—knew by this time whether they had made a mistake in sizing him up as a raw college boy with his eye teeth not cut.

A passing electric containing two young women brought his gloved hand to his hat. The long slant eyes of the lady on the farther side swept him indolently. In answer to her murmured suggestion the girl who was driving brought the machine round in a half circle which ended at the edge of the curb in front of Farnum.

The lawyer's hat came off again with easy grace. The slim young driver leaned back against the cushions and merely smiled a greeting, tacitly yielding command of the situation to her cousin, an opulent young widow adorned demurely with that artistic touch of mourning that suggests a grief not inconsolable.

"Good morning, Miss Frome—Mrs. Van Tyle," James distributed impartially before turning to the latter lady. "Isn't this a day to be alive in? Who says it always rains in Verden?"

"I do—or nearly always. At least it finds no difficulty in giving a good imitation," returned the young woman addressed.

"A libel—I vow a libel," Farnum retorted gaily. "I was just going to hope you might be tempted to forget New York and Vienna and Paris to pay us a long visit. We're all hoping it. I'm merely the spokesman." He waved a hand to indicate the busy street black with humanity.

A hint of pleasant adventure quickened the eyes of the young widow who surveyed lazily his wellgroomed good looks. She judged him a twentieth century American emerging from straightened circumstances and eager to trample even the memory of it under foot.

"Did the Chamber of Commerce appoint you a committee to hope that I would impose on my relatives longer? Or was it resoluted at a mass meeting?" she asked with her Mona Lisa smile.

He laughed. "Well, no! I'm a self-appointed committee voicing a personal desire that has universal application. But if it would have more weight with you I'll have the Chamber take it up and get myself an accredited representative."

"So kind of you. But do you think the committee could do itself justice on the street curb?"

She had among other sensuous charms a voice attuned to convey slightest shades of meaning. James caught her half-shuttered smoldering glance and divined her a woman subtle and complex, capable of playing the world-old game of the sexes with unusual dexterity. The hint of challenging mystery in the tawny depths of the mocking eyes fired his imagination. She was to him a new find in women, one altogether different from those he had known. He had a curiosity to meet at close range this cosmopolitan heiress of such cultivation as Joe Powers' millions could purchase.

What Verden said of her he knew: that she was too free, too scornful, too independent of conventions. All the tabby cats whispered it to each other with lifted eyebrows that suggested volumes, the while they courted her eager and unashamed. But he had a feeling that perhaps Verden was not competent to judge. The standards of this town and of New York were probably vastly different. James welcomed the chance to enlarge his social experience. Promptly he accepted the lead offered.

"I'm sure it can't. To present the evidence cogently will take at least two hours. May I make the argument this evening, if it please the court, during a call?"

"But I understood you were too busy saving the state—from my father and my uncle by the way—to have time for a mere woman," she parried.

The good humor of her irony flattered him because it implied that she offered him a chance to cultivate her—he was not at all sure how much or how little that might mean—regardless of his political affiliations. Not many women were logical enough to accept so impersonally his opposition to the candidacy of an uncle and the plans of a father. "I AM busy," he admitted, "but I need a few hours' relaxation. It will help me to work more effectively to-morrow—against your father and your uncle," he came back with a smile that included them both.

Alice Frome took up the challenge gaily. "We're going to beat you. Father will be elected."

"Then I'll be the first to congratulate him," he promised. Turning to Mrs. Van Tyle, "Shall we say this evening?" he added.

"You're not afraid to venture yourself into the hands of the enemy," drawled that young woman, her indolent eyes daring him.

Again he studiously included them both in his answer. "I'm afraid all right, but I'm not going to let you know it. Did I hear you set a time?"

"If you are really willing to take the risk we shall be glad to see you this afternoon."

James observed that Alice Frome did not second her cousin's invitation. He temporized.

"Oh, this afternoon! I have an engagement, but I am tempted to forget it in remembering a subsequent one."

His smiling gaze passed to Alice and gave her another chance. Still she did not speak.

"The way to treat a temptation is to yield to it," the older cousin sparkled.

"In order to be done with it, I suppose. Very well. I yield to mine. This afternoon I will have the pleasure of calling at The Brakes."

Alice nodded a curt good-bye, but her cousin offered him a beautifully gloved hand to shake. A delightful tingle of triumph warmed him. The daughter of Big Joe Powers, the grim gray pirate who worked the levers of the great Trans-continental Railroad system, had taken pains to be nice to him. The only fly in the ointment of his self-satisfaction had been Alice Frome's reticence.

Why had she not shown any desire to have him call? He could guess at one reason. The campaign for the legislature and the subsequent battle for the senatorship had been bitter. Charges of corruption had been flung broadcast. A dozen detectives had been hired to get evidence on one side or the other. If he were seen going to The Brakes just now fifty rumors might be flying inside of the hour.

His guess was a good one. Alice drove the car forward several blocks without speaking, Valencia Van Tyle watching with good-humored contempt the little frown that rested on her cousin's candid face.

"I perceive that my uncompromising cousin is moved to protest," she suggested placidly.

"You ought not to have asked him, Val. It isn't fair to him or to father," answered Alice promptly. "People will talk. They will say father is trying to influence him unfairly. I wish you hadn't asked him till this fight is over."

"My dear Nora, does it matter in the least what people say?" yawned Valencia behind her hand.

"Not to you because you consider yourself above criticism. But it matters to me that two honest men should be brought into unjust obloquy without cause."

"My dear Hothead, they are big enough to look out for themselves."

"Nobody is big enough to kill slander."

"Nonsense, child. You make a mountain out of a mole hill. People WILL gossip. It really isn't of the least importance what they gabble about."

"Especially when you want to amuse yourself by making a fool of Mr. Farnum," retorted the downright Alice with a touch of asperity.

Valencia already half regretted having asked him. The chances were that he would prove a bore. But she did not choose to say so. "If I'm treading on your preserves, dear," she ventured sweetly.

"That's ridiculous," flushed Alice. "I only suggested that you wait till after the election before chaining him to your chariot wheels."

"You're certainly an *enfant terrible*, my dear," murmured the widow, with the little rippling laugh of cynicism her cousin found so annoying. "But that young man does need a lesson. He's eaten up with conceit of himself. Somebody ought to take him in hand."

"So you're going to sacrifice yourself to duty," scoffed Alice as she brought the electric to a stop under the porte-cochere of the Frome residence.

Mrs. Van Tyle folded her hands demurely. "It's sweet of you to see it that way, Alice."

Part 2

James turned in at the Century Building. In the elevator he met his cousin. Both of them were bound for the office of the candidate being supported by the progressives for the Senate.

"Anything new?" Jeff asked.

"A rumor that Killen has fallen by the wayside. Big Tim was with him for an hour last night at the Pacific."

"I've not been sure of Killen for quite a while. He's a weak sister."

"He'd better not go wrong if he expects to keep on living in this state," James imparted, a hard light in his eyes.

At the third floor they left the elevator and turned to the right under an arch bearing the sign Hardy, Elliott & Carson. Without knocking they passed into Hardy's private office.

Of the three men they found there it was plain that one was being pushed doggedly to bay. He was small and insignificant, with weak blinking eyes. Standing with his back to the wall, he moistened his lips with the tip of his tongue.

"Who says it?" he whined shrilly. "Who says I sold out?"

An apoplectic, bull-necked ruffian stood directly in front of him and sawed the air violently with a fat forefinger.

"I ain't sayin' it, Killen—I'm askin' if you have. What I say is that you'd better make your will before you vote for Frome. Make 'em pay fat, for by thunder! you'll be political junk, Mr. Sam Killen."

Killen, sweating agony, turned appealingly to Jeff. "I haven't said I was going to vote for Frome. Mr. Rawson's got no right to bulldoze me and I'm not going to stand it."

"The hell you ain't," roared Rawson, shaking his fist at the unhappy legislator. "I guess you'll stand the gaff till you explain."

"Just a moment, Bob," interrupted Jeff. "Let's get at the facts. Don't convict the prisoner till the evidence is in."

Rawson hobbled his wrath for the moment. "That's all right, Jeff. You ask Hardy. I'm giving you straight goods."

The keen-eyed, smooth-shaven man in a gray business suit who had been listening silently to the gathering storm contributed information briefly and impartially.

"Mr. Killen spent an hour last night with Big Tim at the Pacific Hotel."

"Sneaked in by the side entrance and took the elevator to the seventh floor. The deal was arranged in Room 743," added Rawson.

"You spied on me," burst from Killen's lips.

"Sure thing. And we caught you with the goods," sneered the red-faced politician.

"I'll not stand it. I'll not support a man that won't trust me."

"You won't, eh?" Rawson was across the floor in two jumps, worrying his victim as a terrier does a rat. "Forget it. You were elected to support R. K. Hardy, sewed up with a pledge tight and fast. We're not in the primer class, Killen. Don't get

William MacLeod Raine

a notion you're going to do as you damn please. You'll—vote—for—R.—K.—Hardy. Get that?"

"I refuse to be moved by threats, and I decline to discuss the matter further," retorted Killen with a pitiable attempt at dignity.

Rawson laughed with insulting menace. "That's a good one. I've sold out, but it's none of your business what I got. That what you mean?"

"You surely must recognize our right to an explanation, Killen," Jeff said gently.

"No, sir, I don't," flushed the little man with sullen bravado. "I ain't got a thing against you, but Rawson goes too far."

"I think he does," Jeff agreed. "Killen is all right. Gentlemen, suppose you let him and me talk it over alone. We can reach an agreement that is satisfactory."

Hardy's face cleared. This was not the first waverer Jeff had brought back into line, not the first by several. There was something compelling in his friendly smile and affectionate manner.

"I'm sure Mr. Killen intends only what is right. I'm content to leave the matter entirely with you and him," Hardy said.

Jeff turned to Rawson. "And you, old warhorse?"

"Have it your own way, but don't forget there's a nigger in the woodpile."

Jeff and Killen walked to the office of the latter, which was on the next floor of the Century Building, the legislator stiffening his will to resist the assaults he felt would be made upon it. But as soon as the door was shut Jeff surprised him by laying a hand on his shoulder.

"Tell me all about it, Sam."

Killen gasped. He got an impossible vision of young Farnum as his brother in trouble. "About what? I didn't say—"

"I've known for a week something was wrong. I couldn't very well ask you, but since I've blundered in you'd better let me help you if I can."

Killen was touched. His lip trembled. "It don't do any good to talk about things. I guess a fellow has to carry his own griefs. Nobody else is hunting for a chance to invest in them."

"What's a friend for?" Jeff wanted to know gently.

The little man gulped. "I guess I've got no friends. Anyhow they don't count when a fellow's in hard luck. It's every man for himself."

The younger man's smile was warm as summer sunshine. "Wrong guess, Sam. We're in this little old world to help each other when we can."

The wretched man drew the back of a trembling hand across his moist eyes. He inhaled a long sobbing breath and broke into apology for his weakness. "Haven't slept for a week except from trional. The back of my head pricks day and night. Can't think of anything but my troubles."

"Unload them on me," Jeff said lightly.

"It's that mortgage on my mill," Killen blurted out. "It falls due this month and I can't meet it. Things haven't been going well with me."

"Can't you get it renewed?"

"Through a dummy Big Tim has bought it up. He won't renew, unless—" Killen broke off, to continue in a moment: "And that ain't all. My little girl needs an operation awful badly. The doctor says she had ought to go to Chicago. I just can't raise the price."

"How much is the mortgage?"

"Three thousand," replied the man; and he added with a gust of weak despair, "My God, man! That mill's all I've got to keep bread in the mouths of my motherless children."

"I reckon Big Tim has offered to cancel the mortgage notes and give you about a thousand to go on," Jeff suggested casually.

Killen nodded. "It would put me on my feet again and give the kiddie her chance." The answer had slipped out naturally, but now the fear chilled him that he had been lured into making a confession. "I didn't say I was going to take it," he added hastily.

"You're quite safe with me, Killen," Jeff told him. He was wondering whether he could not get Captain Chunn to take over the mortgage.

"I'm not so much struck on Hardy myself," grumbled the legislator. "He's a rich man, just as Frome is. Six of one and half a dozen of the other, looks like to me."

"No, Killen. Frome represents the Transcontinental and the utility corporations. Hardy stands for the people. And you're pledged to support Hardy. You mustn't forget that."

"I ain't likely to forget that mortgage either," Killen came back drearily.

"I think I can arrange about having the mortgage renewed. Will that do?"

"Yes. We're going to have a good year in the lumber business. Probably in twelve months I could clear it off."

"Good! And about the little girl—she'll have her chance. I promise you that."

The mill man wrung his hand, tears in his eyes. "You're a white man, Jeff, and a dashed good friend. I tell you I'd hate like poison to go back on Hardy. A fellow can't afford to do a thing like that. But what else could I do? A fellow's got to stand by the children he brings into the world, ain't he?"

Farnum evaded with a smile this discussion of moral issues. "Well, you can stand by them and us, too, if I can fix up this mortgage proposition for you."

"When will you let me know?" asked Killen anxiously.

"Will to-morrow morning do? In James' office, say."

"I'll have to know before noon," Killen reminded him, flushing with embarrassment.

"If I can arrange to get the money—and I think I can—I'll let you know at eleven. Don't worry, Sam. It will be all right."

The legislator shook hands again. "I ain't going to forget what you're doing for me. No, sir!"

Jeff laughed his thanks easily. "That's all right. I reckon you would have done as much for me. Sam Killen isn't the man to throw his friends down."

"That's right," returned the other with a sudden valiant infusion of courage. "I stand pat. I'm not going to lie down before the Transcontinental. Not on your life, I ain't."

They were walking toward the outer door as Killen's speech overflowed. "The Transcontinental doesn't own this state yet. No, sir! Nor Frome and Merrill either. We'll show 'em—"

The valor of the big voice collapsed like a rent balloon. For the office door had opened to let in Big Tim O'Brien. His shrewd eyes passed with whimsical disgust over Killen and rested on Farnum.

The situation made for amusement, since Jeff knew that Big Tim had heard over the transom enough to show that Killen's vote had been recaptured for Hardy.

"You've stumbled on a red hot Hardy ratification meeting. Did you come to get into the bandwagon while there is time, Tim?" Jeff asked with twinkling eyes.

"No sinking ship for mine. I guess I wouldn't ratify yet a while if I were youse, Farnum."

He stood aside to let the editor of the *World* pass. Jeff laughed. "Go to it, Tim."

"I haven't got anything to say to you, Mr. O'Brien," the mill man announced with heightened color.

"Maybe I've got something to say to youse, Mr. Killen."

Jeff passed out smiling. "Well, I'll not interrupt you. See you to-morrow, Sam."

Big Tim sat down heavily in a chair and pulled from his vest pocket a fat black cigar.

"Smoke, Killen?"

"No, thanks." The legislator spoke with stiff dignity.

Big Tim looked at the other man and his paunch shook with the merriment that appeared to convulse him.

"What's the matter?" snapped the mill man.

"I'm laughin' at the things I see, Killen. Man, but you're an easy mar-rk."

"How?"

"Can't you see they're stringin' youse for a sucker?"

"No, I can't see it. I've made up my mind. I'm going to stand by Hardy."

"Fine! Now I'll tell youse one thing. We're goin' to elect Frome to-morrow." O'Brien rose as one who has no time for unprofitable talk. "Your friends have sold youse out. I'm going to call on one of thim right now."

"I don't believe it."

"Of course you don't." Tim's projecting balcony shook with the humor of it. "But you'll be convinced when they take your mill from youse, me boy. It's a frame-up—and you're the goat."

With which shot he took his departure, too shrewd to attempt any argument. He had left behind him a doubt. That was all he could do just now.

Before Tim was out of the building Killen was gumshoeing after him. He meant to find out whether O'Brien had been lying when he said he was going to call on one of his friends. Fifty yards behind him Killen followed, along Powers Avenue, down Pacific Street, to the Equitable Building. From the pilot of one of the elevators he learned that the big boss had got off at the seventh floor and gone straight into James Farnum's office.

His mind was instantly alive with suspicions tumbling over each other in chaotic incoherency. There was a deal of some kind on foot. Jeff's cousin was in it. Then Jeff must be playing him for a sucker. His teeth set with a snap.

Meanwhile Big Tim was having a heart to heart talk with James K. Farnum.

The young lawyer had risen in surprise at the entrance of O'Brien. The big fellow, laughing easily, had helped himself to a chair.

"Make yourself at home, Tim," he said jauntily.

"Anything I can do for you, Mr. O'Brien?" James asked with stiff dignity.

"Sure. Or I wouldn't be here. Sit down. I'll not bite ye."

The lawyer continued to stand.

"I've come to tell you that I'm a dammed fool, Mr. Farnum," the boss grinned.

James bowed slightly. He did not know what was coming, but he had no intention of committing himself to anything as yet.

"In ever lettin' youse get away from me. I mistook yez for a kid glove."

Big Tim gazed with palpable admiration at the cleancut figure, at the square cleft chin in the strong handsome face. It was his opinion this young man would go far, and that every step of the way would be in the interests of James K. Farnum. Shrewdly he guessed that the way to pierce that impassive front was through an appeal to vanity and to selfinterest.

James waited, alert and expressionless, but O'Brien, having made his apology, puffed in silence.

"I think you suggested some business that brought you," James reminded him.

"You've got in you the makings of a big man. Nothing on the coast to touch youse, Mr. Farnum. And I didn't see it. I was sore on your name. That was what was bitin' me. It's sure on Big Tim this time."

None of the triumph that flooded Farnum reached the surface.

"I think I don't quite understand," he said quietly.

"I'm eatin' humble pie because youse slipped wan over on me. You're the best campaign speaker in the state, bar none, boy as you are."

James could not keep his gratified smile down. "This heartfelt testimonial comes free, I take it," he pretended to mock.

"Come off with youse," O'Brien flung back good humoredly. "I'm not here to hand you booquets, but to talk business. Here's the nub of it, me boy. You need me, and I need you."

"I don't quite see how I need you, Mr. O'Brien."

"That's because you're young yet and don't know the game. Let me tell you this." The boss leaned forward, his hard eyes focused on Farnum. "You'll never get anywhere so long as youse trail with that reform bunch. It's all hot air and tomfool theory. Populism and socialism! Take my wor-rd for it, there's nothin' to 'em."

"I'm neither a populist nor a socialist, Mr. O'Brien."

"Coorse you're not. I can see that with wan eye shut. That's why I hate to see youse ruin yourself with them that are. I've no need to tell you that this country's run by business men and not cranks. Me, I'm a business man, and I run the city. P. C. Frome's a business man; so's Merrill. That's why they're on top. Old Joe Powers is a business man from first to last. You'll never get anywhere, me boy, until youse look at things from a business point of view."

If James was impressed he gave no sign of it. "Which means you want me to support P. C. for the Senate. Is that it?"

"I don't care whether you do or don't. We've got this fight won. But this is only the beginning. I can see that. Agitators and trouble breeders are busy iverywhere. Line up right and you've got a big future before you. Joe Powers himself has noticed your speeches. P. C. told me that last night."

For a moment the lawyer felt an exultant paeon of victory

beat in his blood. His imagination saw the primrose path of the future stretch before him in a golden glow. The surge of triumph passed and he was himself again, cool and wary. His eyes met Big Tim's full and straight. "I was elected to support Hardy. I expect to stay with him."

The political boss waved aside this declaration. "Sure. Of course you've got to VOTE for him. I've got too much horse sense to try to buy YOU. But after this election? Your whole future's not tied up with fool reformers, is it? Say, what's the matter with you havin' a talk with P. C.?"

"Oh, I'll talk with him. P. C. and I are good friends."

"When can you see him? Why not to-night?"

"No hurry, is there?" James paused an instant before he added: "I'm going to The Brakes this afternoon on a social call. If Frome happens to be at home we might talk then. So far as making a direct appointment with him, I wouldn't care to do that until the senatorial election is decided. You understand that I pledge myself to nothing."

"That's right," agreed Big Tim. "It don't do any harm to hear both sides of a proposition. I guess that cousin o' yours kind of hypnotized you. He's got more fool schemes for redeemin' this state. Far as I can see it don't need any redeemin'. It's loaded to the rails with prosperity and clippin' off its sixty miles an hour. I say, let well enough alone. Where youse keep your matches, Mr. Farnum? Thanks! Well, talk it over with P. C. I reckon you can get together. So long, me boy."

Not until he was safe in the street did the big boss of Verden allow his satisfaction expression.

"We've got him! We've got the boob hooked!" he told

himself exultantly.

A little man standing behind a showcase was watching him tensely.

CHAPTER 9

"Man is for woman made,
And woman made for man
As the spur is for the jade,
As the scabbard for the blade,
As for liquor is the can,
So man's for woman made,
And woman made for man."

THE HERO STUDIES THE MONA LISA SMILE IN ITS PROPER SETTING. INCIDENTALLY, HE MEETS AN EMPIRE BUILDER

Since James was not courting observation he took as inconspicuous a way as possible to The Brakes. He was irritably conscious of the incongruity of his elaborate afternoon dress with the habits of democratic Verden, which had been too busy "boosting" itself into a great city, or at least one in the making, to have found time to establish as yet a leisure class.

Leaving the car at the entrance to Lakeview Park, he cut across it by sinuous byways where madronas and alders isolated him from the twilit green of the open lawn. Though it was still early the soft winter dusk of the Pacific Northwest was beginning to render objects indistinct. This perhaps may have been the reason he failed to notice the skulking figure among the trees that dogged him to his destination.

James laughed at himself for the exaggerated precaution he took to cover a perfectly defensible action. Why shouldn't he visit at the house of P. C. Frome? Entirely clear as to his right, he yet preferred his call not to become a matter of public gossip. For he did not need to be told that there would be ugly rumors if it should get out that Big Tim had called at his office for a conference and he had subsequently been seen going to The Brakes. Dunderheads not broad enough to separate social from political intercourse would be quick to talk unpleasantly about it.

Deflecting from the path into a carriage driveway, he came through a woody hollow to the rear of The Brakes. The grounds were spacious, rolling toward the road beyond in a falling sweep of wellkept lawn. He skirted the green till he came to a "raveled walk that zig-zagged up through the grass, leaving to the left the rough fern-clad bluff that gave the place its name.

The man who let him in had apparently received his instructions, for he led Farnum to a rather small room in the rear of the big house. Its single occupant was reclining luxuriantly among a number of pillows on a lounge. From her lips a tiny spiral of smoke rose like incense to the ceiling. James was conscious of a little ripple of surprise as he looked down upon the copper crown of splendid hair above which rested the thin nimbus of smoke. He had expected a less intimate reception.

But the astonishment had been sponged from his face before Valencia Van Tyle rose and came forward, cigarette in hand.

"You did find time."

"Was it likely I wouldn't?"

"How should I know?" her little shrug seemed to say with an indifference that bordered on insolence.

James was piqued. After all then she had not opened to him the door to her friendship. She was merely amusing herself with him as a provincial *pis aller.*

Perhaps she saw his disappointment, for she added with a touch of warmth: "I'm glad you came. Truth is, I'm bored to death of myself."

"Then I ought to be welcome, for if I don't exorcise the devils of ennui you can now blame me."

"I shall. Try that big chair, and one of these Egyptians."

He helped himself to a cigarette and lit up as casually as if he had been in the habit of smoking in the lounging rooms of the ladies he knew. She watched him sink lazily into the chair and let his glance go wandering over the room. In his face she read the indolent sense of pleasure he found in sharing so intimately this sanctum of her more personal life.

The room was a bit barbaric in its warmth of color, as barbaric as was the young woman herself in spite of her super-civilization. The walls, done in an old rose, were gilded and festooned to meet a ceiling almost Venetian in its scheme of decoration. Pink predominated in the brocaded tapestries and in the rugs, and the furniture was a luxurious modern compromise with the Louis Quinze. There were flowers in profusion—his gaze fell upon the American Beauties he had sent an hour or two ago—and a disorder of popular magazines and French novels. Farnum did not need to be told that the room was as much an exotic as its mistress.

"You think?" her amused voice demanded when his eyes came back to her. "that the room seems made especially for you."

She volunteered information. "My uncle gave me a free hand to arrange and decorate it."

As he looked at her, smoking daintily in the fling of the fire glow, every inch the pampered heiress of the ages, his blood quickened to an appreciation of the sensuous charm of sex she breathed forth so indifferently. The clinging crepe-de-chine—except in public she did not pretend even to a conventional mourning for the scamp whose name she bore lent accent to her soft, rounded curves, and the slow, regular rise and fall of her breathing beneath the filmy lace promised a perfect fullness of bust and throat. He was keenly responsive to the physical allure of sex, and Valencia Van Tyle was endowed with more than her share of magnetic aura.

"You have expressed yourself. It's like you," he said with finality.

Her tawny eyes met his confident appraisal ironically. "Indeed! You know then what I am like?"

"One uses his eyes, and such brains as heaven has granted him," he ventured lightly.

"And what am I like?" she asked indolently.

"I'm hoping to know that better soon—I merely guess now."

"They say all women are egoists—and some men." She breathed her soft inscrutable ripple of laughter. "Let me hasten to confess, and crave a picture of myself."

"But the subject deserves an artist," he parried.

"He's afraid," she murmured to the fire. "He makes and unmakes senators—this Warwick; but he's afraid of a girl."

James lit a fresh cigarette in smiling silence.

"He has met me once—twice—no, three times," she meditated aloud. "But he knows what I'm like. He boasts of his divination and when one puts him to the test he repudiates."

"All I should have claimed is that I know I don't know what you are like."

"Which is something," she conceded.

"It's a good deal," he claimed for himself. "It shows a beginning of understanding. And—given the opportunity—I hope to know more." He questioned of her eyes how far he might go. "It's the incomprehensible that lures. It piques interest and lends magic. Behind those eyelids a little weary all the subtle hidden meaning of the ages shadows. The gods forbid that I should claim to hold the answer to the eternal mystery of woman."

"Dear me! I ask for a photograph and he gives me a poem," she mocked, touching an electric button.

"I try merely to interpret the poem."

She looked at him under lowered lids with a growing interest. Her experience had not warranted her in hoping that he would prove worth while. It would be clear gain if he were to disappoint her agreeably.

"I think I have read somewhere that the function of present-day criticism is to befog the mind and blur the object criticised."

He considered an answer, but gave it up when a maid appeared with a tray, and after a minute of deft arrangement disappeared to return with the added paraphernalia that goes to the making and consuming of afternoon tea.

James watched in a pleasant content the easy grace with which the flashing hands of his hostess manipulated the brew. Presently she flung open a wing of the elaborate cellaret that stood near and disclosed a gleaming array of cut-glass decanters. Her fingers hovered over them.

"Cognac?"

"Think I'll take my tea straight just as you make it."

"Most Western men don't care for afternoon tea. You should hear my father on the subject."

"I can imagine him." He smiled. "But if he has tried it with you I should think he'd be converted."

She laughed at him in the slow tantalizing way that might mean anything or nothing. "I absolve you of the necessity of saying pretty things. Instead, you may continue that portrait you were drawing when the maid interrupted."

"It's a subject I can't do justice."

She laughed disdainfully. "I thought it was time for the flattery. As if I couldn't extort that from any man. It's the A B C of our education. But the truth about one's self—the unpalatable, bitter truth—there's a sting of unexpected pleasure in hearing that judicially."

"And do you get that pleasure often?"

"Not often. Men are dreadful cowards, you know. My father is about the only man who dares tell it to me."

Farnum put down his cup and studied her. She was leaning back with her fingers laced behind her head. He wondered whether she knew with what effectiveness the posture set off her ripe charms—the fine modeling of the full white throat, the perfect curves of the dainty arms bare to the elbows, the daring set of the tawny, tilted head. A spark glowed in his eyes.

"Far be it from me to deny you an accessible pleasure, though I sacrifice myself to give it. But my sketch must be merely subjective. I draw the picture as I see it."

She sipped her tea with an air of considering the matter. "You promise at least a family likeness, with not an ugly wrinkle of character smoothed away."

"I don't even promise that. For how am I to know what meaning lurks behind that subtle, shadowy smile? There's irony in it—and scorn—and sensuous charm—but back of them all is the great enigma."

"He's off," she derided slangily.

"And that enigma is the complex YOU I want to learn. Of course you're a specialized type, a product of artistic hothouse propagation. You're so exquisite in your fastidious-ness that to be near you is a luxury. Simplicity and you have not a bowing acquaintance. One looks to see your most casual act freighted with intentions not obvious."

"The poor man thinks I invited him here to propose to him," she told the fire gravely, stretching out her little slippered feet toward it.

He laughed. "I'm not so presumptuous. You wouldn't aim at such small game. You would be quite capable of it if you wanted to, but you don't. But I'm devoured with curiosity to know why you asked me, though of course I shan't find out."

Her narrowed eyes swept him with amusement. "If I knew myself! Alice says it was to make a fool of you. I don't think she is right. But if she is I'm in to score a failure. You're too coolheaded and—" She stopped, her eyes sparkling with the daring of her unvoiced suggestion.

"Say it," he nodded.

"—and selfish to be anybody's fool. Perhaps I asked you just in the hope you might prove interesting."

He got up and stood with his arm on the mantel. From his superior height he looked down on her dainty insolent perfection, answering not too seriously the challenge of her eyes. No matter what she meant—how much or how little she was wonderfully attractive. The provocation of the mocking little face lured mightily.

"I am going to prove interested at any rate. Let's hope it may be a preliminary to being interesting."

"But it never does. Symptoms of too great interest bore one. I enjoy more the men who are impervious to me. Now there's my father. He comes nearer understanding me than anybody else, but he's quite adamantine to my wiles."

"I shall order a suit of chain armor at once."

"An unnecessary expense. Your emotions are quite under control," she told him saucily.

"I wish I were as sure."

"I thought you promised to be interesting," she complained.

"Now you're afraid I'm going to make love to you. Let me relieve your mind. I'm not."

"I knew you wouldn't be so stupid," she assured him.

"No objection to my admiring your artistic effect at a distance, as a spectator in a gallery?"

"I shall expect that," she rippled.

"Just as one does a picture too expensive to own."

"I suppose I AM expensive."

"Not a doubt of it. But if you don't mind I'll come occasionally to the gallery to study the masterpiece."

"I'll mind if you don't."

Voices were heard approaching along the hall. The portieres parted. The immediate effect on Farnum of the great figure that filled the doorway was one of masterful authority. A massive head crested a figure of extraordinary power. Gray as a mediaeval castle, age had not yet touched his gnarled strength. The keen steady eyes, the close straight lips, the shaggy eyebrows heavy and overhanging, gave accent to the rugged force of this grim freebooter who had reversed the law of nature which decrees that railroads shall follow civilization. Scorning the established rule of progress, he had spiked his rails through untrodden forests and unexplored canons to watch the pioneer come after by the road he had blazed. Chief among the makers of the Northwest, he yearly conceived and executed with amazing audacity enterprises that would have marked as monumental the life work of lesser men.

Farnum, rising from his seat unconsciously as a tribute of respect, acknowledged thus tacitly the presence of greatness in the person of Joe Powers.

The straight lips of the empire builder tightened as his eyes gleamed over the soft luxury of his daughter's boudoir. James would have been hard put to it to conceive any contrast greater than the one between this modern berserk and the pampered daughter of his wealth. A Hun or a Vandal gazing down with barbaric scorn on some decadent paramour of captured Rome was the most analogous simile Farnum's brain could summon. What freak of nature, he wondered, had been responsible for so alien an offspring to this ruthless builder? And what under heaven had the two in common except the blood that ran in both their veins?

Peter C. Frome, who had followed his brother-in-law into the room, introduced the young man to the railroad king.

The great man's grip drove the blood from Farnum's hand.

"I've heard about you, young man. What do you mean by getting in my way?"

The young man's veins glowed. He had made Joe Powers notice him. Not for worlds would he have winked an eyelash, though the bones of his hand felt as if they were being ground to powder.

"Do I get in your way, sir?" he asked innocently.

"Do you?" boomed the deep bass of the railroader. "You and that mad brother of yours."

"He's my cousin," James explained.

"Brother or cousin, he's got to get off the track or be run over. And you, too, with that smooth tongue of yours."

Farnum laughed. "Jeff's pretty solid. He may ditch the train, sir."

"No!" roared Powers. "He'll be flung into the ditch." He turned abruptly to Frome. "Peter, take me to a room where I can talk to this young man. I need him."

"'Come into my little parlor,' said the spider to the fly."

They wheeled as at a common rein to the sound of the young mocking voice. Alice Frome had come in unnoticed and was standing in the doorway smiling at them. The effect she produced was demurely daring. The long lines of her slender sylph-like body, the girlishness of her golden charm, were vigorously contradicted in their suggestion of shyness by the square tilted chin and the challenge in the dancing eyes.

"Alice," admonished her father with a deprecatory apology in his voice to his brother-in-law.

Powers knit his shaggy brows in a frown not at all grim. The young woman smiled back confidently. She could go farther with him than anybody else in the world could, and she knew it. For he recognized in her vigorous strength of fiber a kinship of the spirit closer than that between him and his own daughter. An autocrat to the marrow, it pleased him to recognize her an exception to his rule. Valencia was also an exception, but in a different way.

"Have you any remarks to make, Miss Frome?" he asked.

"Oh, I've made it," returned the girl unabashed. She turned to James and shook hands with him. "How do you do, Mr. Farnum? I see you are going to be tied to Uncle Joe's kite, too."

Was there in her voice just a hint of scorn? James did not know. He laughed a little uneasily.

"Shall I be swallowed up alive, Miss Frome?"

"You think you won't, but you will. He always gets what he wants."

For all the warmth and energy of youth in her there was a vivid spiritual quality that had always made a deep appeal to James. He sensed the something fine and exquisite she breathed forth and did reverence to it.

"And what does he want now?" the young man parried.

"He wants YOU."

"Unless you would like him yourself, Alice," her uncle countered.

The color washed into her cheeks. "Not just now, thank you. I was merely giving him a friendly warning."

"I'm awfully obliged to you. I'll be on my guard," laughed James.

He stepped across to the lounge to make his farewell to Mrs. Van Tyle.

"You'll come again," she said in a low voice.

"Whenever the gallery is open—if I am sent a ticket of admission."

"Wouldn't it be better to apply for a ticket and not wait for it to be sent?"

"I think it would—and to apply for one often."

"I am waiting, Mr. Farnum," interrupted Powers impatiently.

To the young man the suggestion sounded like a command. He bowed to Alice and followed the great man out of the room.

CHAPTER 10

Many business men of every community are respectable cowards. The sense of property fills them with a cramping timidity.

—From the Note Book of a Dreamer

SAFE AND SOUND BUSINESS RALLIES TO THE DEFENSE OF THE COUNTRY. THE REBEL, FRUSTRATED, PLANS FURTHER VILLAINIES

Part 1

When James reached his office next morning he found Killen waiting for him. One glance at the weak defiant face told him that the legislator was again in revolt. The lawyer felt a surge of disgust sweep over him. All through the session he had cajoled and argued the weak-kneed back into line. Why didn't Hardy do his own dirty work instead of leaving it to him to soil his hands with these cheap grafters?"

No longer ago than yesterday it had been a keen pleasure to feel himself so important a factor in the struggle, to know that his power and his personality were of increasing value to his side.

But to-day—somehow the salt had gone out of it. The value of the issue had dwindled, his enthusiasm gone stale. After all, what did it matter who was elected? Why should not the corporate wealth that was developing the country see that men were chosen to office who would safeguard vested interests? It was all very well for Jeff to talk about democracy and the rights of the people. But Jeff was an impracticable idealist. He, James, stood for success. Within the past twenty-four hours there had been something of a shift of standards for him.

His visit to The Brakes had done that for him. He craved luxury just as he did power, and the house on the hill had said the final word of both to him in the personalities of Joe Powers and his daughter. It had come home to him that the only way to satisfy his ambition was by making money and a lot of it. This morning, with the sharpness of his hunger rendering him irritable, he was in no mood to conciliate disaffectants to the cause of which he was himself beginning to weary.

"Well?" he demanded sharply of Killen.

"I've been looking for your cousin, but I can't find him. He was to have met me here later."

"Then I presume he'll be here when he said he would." The eyes of the lawyer were cold and hard as jade.

"You can tell him it won't be necessary for me to see him. I've made other arrangements," Killen said uneasily.

"You mean that you repudiate your agreement with him. Is that it?" Farnum's voice was like a whiplash.

"I've decided to support Frome. Fact is—"

136   William MacLeod Raine

"Oh, damn the facts! You made an agreement. You're going to sell out. That's all there is to it."

The young man's face was dark with furious disgust.

Killen flared up. "You better be careful how you talk to me, Mr. Farnum. I might want to know what Big Tim was doing in your office yesterday. I might want to know what business took you up to The Brakes by a mighty roundabout way."

James strode forward in a rage. "Get out of here before I throw you out, you little spying blackguard."

"You bet I'll get out," screamed the mill man. "Get clear out and have nothing more to do with your outfit. But I want to tell you that folks will talk a lot when they know how you and Big Tim fixed up a deal—" Killen, backing toward the door as he spoke, broke off to hasten his exit before the lawyer's threatening advance.

James slammed the door shut on him and paced up and down in an impotent fury of passion. "The dirty little blackleg! He'd like to bracket me in the same class as himself. He'd like to imply that I—By Heaven, if he opens his lying mouth to a hint of such a thing I'll horsewhip the little cad."

But running uneasily through his mind was an undercurrent of disgust—with himself, with Jeff, with the whole situation. Why had he ever let himself get mixed up with such an outfit? Government by the people! The thing was idiotic, mere demagogic cant. Power was to the strong. He had always known it. But yesterday that old giant at The Brakes had hammered it home to him. He did not like to admit even to himself that his folly had betrayed Hardy's cause, but at bottom he knew he should not have gone to The Brakes until after the election and that he ought never to have let Killen out of the office without an explanation. Yesterday he would have won back the man somehow by an appeal to his loyalty and his self-interest.

He must send word at once to Jeff and let him try to remedy the mischief.

His cousin, coming into the office with Rawson just as James took down the receiver of the telephone, noticed at once the disturbance of the latter.

James told his story. It was clear to him that he must anticipate Killen's disclosure of his visit to The Brakes and so draw the sting from it as far as possible. But his natural reluctance to shoulder blame made him begin with Killen's defection.

"I told you to let me deal with the little traitor," Rawson exploded.

"He was quite satisfied when I left him yesterday. They must have got at him again," Jeff suggested. "I left O'Brien with him. But I was dead sure of him."

James cleared his throat and began casually. "I expect the little beggar got suspicious when he saw Big Tim coming to my office."

"To your office?" Rawson cut in sharply.

The lawyer flushed, but his eyes met and quelled the incipient doubt in those of the politician. "Yes, he came to feel the ground. Of course I told him flatly where I stood. But Killen must have thought something was doing he wasn't in on. It seems he followed me to The Brakes yesterday afternoon when I called on Mrs. Van Tyle."

"Followed you to The Brakes. Good Lord!" groaned Rawson. "What in Mexico were you doing there?"

"Thought I mentioned that I was calling on Mrs. Van-Tyle," returned James stiffly.

"Wasn't that call a little injudicious under the circumstances, James?" contributed Jeff with his whimsical smile.

"I suppose I may call wherever I please."

"It was a piece of dashed foolishness, that's what it was. You say Killen saw you. The thing will fly like dust in the wind. It will be buzzed all over the House by this time and every man that wants to sell out will find a reason right there," stormed Rawson.

"Are you implying that I sold out?" demanded James icily.

Jeff put a conciliatory hand on his cousin's shoulder. "Of course he doesn't. He isn't a fool, James. But there's a good deal in what Rawson says. It was a mistake. The waverers will find in it their excuse for deserting. Of course Big Tim has been at them all night. We'll go right up to the House in your machine, Rawson. We haven't a moment to lose."

Rawson nodded. "It's dollars to doughnuts the thing is past mending, but it's up to us to see. If I can only get at Killen in time I'll choke the story in his throat. You wait here at the 'phone, Jeff, and I'll call you up if you're needed at this end of the line. Better have a taxi waiting below in case you need one. Come along, James."

If he did not get to Killen in time it was not Rawson's fault, for he made his car flash up and down Verden's hills with no regard to the speed limit. He swept it along Powers Avenue, dodging in and out among the traffic of the busy city like a halfback through a broken field after a kick. With a twist of the wheel he put the machine at the steep hill of Yarnell Way, climbed the brow of it, and plunged with a flying leap down the long incline to the State House.

James clung to the swaying side of the car as it raced down. It was raining hard, and the drops stung their faces like bird shot. Two hundred yards in front appeared a farm wagon, leaped toward them, and disappeared in the gulf behind. A dog barking at them from the roadside was for an instant and then was not. In their wake they left cursing teamsters, frightened horses, women and children scurrying for safety; and in the driver's seat Rawson sat goggle-eyed and rigid, swallowing the miles that lay in front of him.

The car took the last incline superbly and swung up the asphalt carriage way to a Yale finish at the marble stairway of the State House. Rawson was running up the steps almost before the machine had stopped. Farnum caught him at the elevator and a minute later they entered together the assembly room of the House.

One swift glance told Rawson that Killen was not in his seat, and as his eyes swept the room he noted also the absence of Pitts, Bentley, and Miller. Of the doubtful votes only Ashton and Reilly were present.

He flung a question anything of Bentley, Akers?"

"Mr. Bentley! Why, yes, sir. He was called to the telephone a few minutes ago and he left at once. Mr. Miller went with him, and Mr. Pitts."

"Were Ashton and Reilly here then?"

"No, sir. They came in a moment before you did."

Rawson drew Farnum to one side and whispered.

"Killen must have gone right from your room to Big Tim. They got the others on the phone. They must have been on that street car we met a mile back. There's just a chance to head 'em off. I'll chase back in my machine while you call up Jeff and have him meet the car as it comes in. Tell him not to let them out of his sight if he has to hold them with a gun. You keep an eye on Reilly and Ashton. Don't let anyone talk to them or get them on the phone. Better take them up to the library."

James nodded sulkily. He did not like Rawson's peremptory manner any the better because he knew his indiscretion had called it down upon him. What he had been unable to forget for the past hour was that if this break to Frome had happened yesterday it would have been he that gave the orders and Rawson who jumped to execute them. Now he had slipped back to second place.

He caught Jeff on the line and repeated Rawson's orders without comment of his own, after which he went back from the committee room, gathered up Reilly and Ashton, and took them on a pretext to the library.

It must have been nearly an hour later that a messenger boy handed James a note. It was a hasty scribble from Rawson.

Euchred, by thunder! Both Jeff and I missed them. Big Tim butted in with a car at Grover Street before we could make connections. Am waiting at the House for them. Don't bring A. & R. in till time to vote. FROME CAN'T WIN IF YOU MAKE THEM BOTH STICK.

James stuck the note in his pocket and flung himself with artificial animation into the story he was telling. Once or twice the others suggested a return to the House, but he always had just one more good story they must hear. Since only routine business was under way there was no urgency, and when at length they returned to the House chamber the clock pointed to five minutes to twelve.

Rawson and two or three of the staunchest Hardy men relieved Farnum of his charge in the cloak room and took care of the two doubtfuls. The seats of Bentley, Miller, Pitts and Killen were still vacant, and there was a tense watchfulness in the room that showed rumors were flying of a break in the deadlock.

Already the state senators were drifting in for the noon joint sessions, and along with them came presently the missing assemblymen flanked by O'Brien and Frome adherents.

The President of the Senate called the session to order and announced that the eleventh general assembly would now proceed to take the sixty-fourth ballot for the election of a United States Senator.

In an oppressive silence the clerk began to call the roll.

"Allan."

A raw-boned farmer from one of the coast counties rose and answered "Hardy."

"Anderson."

In broken English a fat Swede shouted, "Harty."

"Ashton."

"Hardy." The word fell hesitantly from dry lips. The man would have voted for the Transcontinental candidate had he dared, but he was not sure enough that the crucial moment was at hand and the pressure of his environment was too great.

"Bentley."

Three hundred eyes focused expectantly on the gaunt white-faced legislator who rose nervously at the sound of his name and almost inaudibly gulped the word "Frome."

A fierce tumult of rage and triumph rose and fell and swelled again. Bentley became the center of a struggling vortex of roaring humanity and found himself tossed hither and thither like a chip in a choppy sea.

It was many minutes before the clerk could proceed with the roll-call. When his name was reached James said "Hardy" in a clear distinct voice that brought from the gallery a round of applause sharply checked by the presiding officer. Killen gave his vote for Frome tremulously and shrank from the storm he had evoked. Rawson could be seen standing on his seat, one foot on the top of his desk, shaking his fist at him in purple apoplectic rage, the while his voice rose above the tumult, "You damned Judas! You damned little traitor!"

The presiding officer beat in vain with his gavel for quiet. Not until they had worn themselves to momentary exhaustion could the roll-call be continued.

Miller and Pitts voted for Frome and stirred renewed shouts of support and execration.

"Takes one more change to elect Frome. All depends on Reilly now," Rawson whispered hoarsely to Jeff. "If he sticks we're safe for another twenty-four hours."

But Reilly, knowing the decisive moment had come, voted for Frome and gave him the one more needed to elect. Pandemonium was loose at once. The Transcontinental forces surrounded him and fought off the excited men he had betrayed who tried to get at him to make him change his vote. The culminating moment of months of battle had come and mature men gave themselves to the abandon of the moment like college boys after a football game.

When at last the storm had subsided Ashton, who had seen several thousand dollars go glimmering because his initial came at the beginning of the alphabet instead of at the close, in the hope of still getting into the bandwagon in time moved to make the election unanimous. His suggestion was rejected with hoots of derision, and Frome made the conventional speech of acceptance to a House divided against itself.

Jeff joined his cousin as he was descending the steps to the lower hall. "Don't blame yourself, old man. It would have happened anyhow in a day or two. They were looking for a chance to desert. We couldn't have held them. Better luck next time."

James found cold comfort in such consolation. He was dissatisfied with the part he had played in the final drama. Instead of being the hero of the hour, he was the unfortunate whose blunder had started the avalanche. Yet he was gratified when Rawson said in effect the same thing as Jeff.

"And I'm going to have the pleasure of telling that damned little Killen what I think of him," the politician added with savage satisfaction.

"Don't blame him. He's only a victim. What we must do is to

change the system that makes it possible to defeat the will of the people through money," Jeff said.

"How are you going about it?" Rawson demanded incredulously.

"We'll go after the initiative and referendum right now while the people are stirred up about this treachery. The very men who threw us down will support us to try and square themselves. The bill will slip through as if it were oiled," Jeff prophesied.

"Oh, hang your initiative and referendum. I'm a politician, not a socialist reformer," grinned Rawson.

James said nothing.

Part 2

If the years were bringing Jeff a sharper realization of the
forces that control so much of life they were giving him too
the mellowness that can be in revolt without any surrender of
faith in men. He could for instance now look back on his
college days and appreciate the kindness and the patience of
the teachers whom he had then condemned. They had been
conformists. No doubt they had compromised to the pressure
of their environment. But somehow he felt much less like
judging men than he used to in the first flush of his
intellectual awakening. It was perhaps this habit of making
allowance for weakness, together with his call to the
idealism in them, that made him so effective a worker with
men.

He was as easy as an old shoe, but people sensed the steel in
him instinctively. In his quiet way he was coming to be a
power. For one thing he was possessed of the political
divination that understands how far a leader may go without
losing his following. He knew too how to get practical
results. It was these qualities that enabled him out of the
wreckage of the senatorial defeat to build a foundation of
victory for House Bill 77.

To bring into effect Jeff's pet measure of the initiative and
referendum necessitated an amendment to the state constitution, which must be passed by two successive legislative
assemblies and ratified by a vote of the people in order to
become effective. The bill had been slumbering in committee, but immediately after the senatorial election Jeff insisted
on having it brought squarely to the attention of the House.

His feeling for the psychological moment was a true one and
he succeeded by a skillful newspaper campaign in rallying
the people to his support. The sense of outrage felt at this

William MacLeod Raine

shameless purchase of a seat in the Senate, accented by a knowledge of its helplessness to avenge the wrong done it, counted mightily in favor of H. B. No. 77 just now. It promised a restoration of power to the people, and the clamor for its passage became insistent.

A good deal of quiet lobbying had been done for the bill, and the legislators who had sold themselves, having received all they could reasonably expect from the allied corporations, were anxious to make a show of standing for their constituents. Politicians in general considered the bill a "freak" one. Some who voted for it explained that they did not believe in it, but felt the people should have a chance to vote on it themselves. By a large majority it passed the House. Two days later it squeezed through the Senate.

Rawson, who had been persuaded half against his judgment to support the bill, lunched with Jeff that day.

"Now watch the corporations dig a grave for your little pet at the next legislature," he chuckled, helping himself to bread while he waited for the soup.

"They may. Then again they may not," Farnum answered. "We are ruled by political machines and corporations only as long as we let them. I've a notion the people are going to assert themselves at the next election."

"How are you going to make the will of the dear people effective with the assembly?" asked Rawson, amused.

"Make the initiative and referendum the issue of the campaign. Pledge the legislators to vote for it before nominating them."

"Pledge them?" grinned Rawson cynically. "Weren't they

pledged to support Hardy? And did they?"

"No, but they'll stick next time, I think."

"You're an incurable optimist, my boy."

"It isn't optimism this time. It's our big stick."

"Didn't know we had one."

"Do you remember House Bill 19?"

"No. What's that got to do with it?"

"It slipped through early in the session. Anderson introduced it. Nobody paid any attention to it because he's a back country Swede and his bill was very wordy. The governor signed it to-day. That bill provides for the recall of any public official, alderman or legislator if the people are not satisfied with his conduct."

The big man stared. "I thought it only applied to district road supervisors. Were you back of that bill, Jeff?"

"I had it drawn up and helped steer it through the committee, though I was careful not to appear interested."

"You sly old fox! And nobody guessed it had general application. None of us read the blamed thing through. You're going to use it as a club to make the legislators stand pat on their pledges."

"Yes."

"But don't you see how revolutionary your big stick is?" Rawson's smile was expansive. "Why, hang it, man, you're

　　　　William MacLeod Raine

destroying the fundamental value of representative government. It's a deliberate attack on graft."

"Looks like it, doesn't it?"

It was while Rawson was waiting for his mince pie piled with ice cream that he ventured a delicate question.

"Say, Jeff! What about James? Is he getting ready to flop over to the enemy?"

"No. Why do you ask that?"

"I notice he explained when he voted for House Bill 77 that he reserved the right to oppose it later. Said he hadn't made up his mind, but felt the people should be given a chance to express themselves on it."

Upon Farnum's face rested a momentary gravity. "I can't make James out lately. He's lost his enthusiasm. Half the time he's irritable and moody. I think perhaps he's been blaming himself too much for Hardy's defeat."

Rawson laughed with cynical incredulity. "That's it, is it?"

CHAPTER 11

"Faustina hath the fairest face,
And Phillida the better grace;
Both have mine eye enriched:
This sings full sweetly with her voice;
Her fingers make so sweet a noise;
Both have mine ear bewitched.
Ah me! sith Fates have so provided,
My heart, alas! must be divided."

THE HERO, ASSISTED BY THE MONA LISA SMILE, DEPLORES THE DEBILITATING EFFECTS OF MODERN CIVILIZATION

Part 1

With the adjournment of the legislature politics became a less absorbing topic of interest. James at least was frankly glad of this, for his position had begun to be embarrassing. He could not always stand with a foot in either camp. As yet he had made no break with the progressives. Joe Powers had given him a hint that he might be more useful where he was. But as much as possible he was avoiding the little luncheons at which Jeff and his political friends were wont to foregather. He gave as an excuse the rush of business that was swamping him. His excuse at least had the justification of truth. His speeches had brought him a good many clients and Frome was quietly throwing cases his way.

It was at one of these informal little noonday gatherings that Rawson gave his opinion of the legal ability of James.

"He isn't any great lawyer, but he never gives it away. He knows how to wear an air of profound learning with a large and impressive silence. Roll up the whole Supreme Court into one and it can't look any wiser than James K. Farnum."

Miller laughed. "Reminds me of what I heard last week. Jeff was walking down Powers Avenue with James and an old fellow stopped me to point them out. There go the best citizen and the worst citizen in this town, he said. I told him that was rather hard on James. You ought to have heard him. For him James is the hero of the piece and Jeff the villain."

"Half the people in this town have got that damn fool notion," Captain Chunn interrupted violently.

"More than half, I should say."

"Every day or two I hear about how dissipated Jeff used to be and how if it were not for his good and noble cousin he would have gone to the deuce long ago," Rawson contributed.

Chunn pounded on the table with his fist. "Jeff's own fault. Talk about durn fools! That boy's got them all beat clear off the map. And I'm dashed if I don't like him better for it."

"Move we change the subject," suggested Rawson. "Here comes Verden's worst citizen."

With a casual nod of greeting round the table Jeff sat down. "Any of you hear James' speech before the Chamber of Commerce yesterday? It was bully. One of his best," he said as he reached for the menu card.

Captain Chunn groaned. The rest laughed. Jeff looked round in surprise. "What's the joke?"

William MacLeod Raine

Part 2

It was a great relief to James, in these days when the complacency of his self-satisfaction was a little ruffled, to call
often on Valencia Van Tyle and let himself drift pleasantly
with her along primrose paths where moral obligations never
obtruded. Under the near-Venetian ceiling of her den, with
its pink Cupids and plump dimpled cherubs smiling down,
he was never troubled about his relation to Hardy's defeat.
Here he got at life from another slant and could always find
justification to himself for his course.

She had a silent divination of his moods and knew how to
minister indolently to them. The subtle incense of luxury that
she diffused banished responsibility. In her soft sensuous
blood the lusty beat of duty had small play.

But even while he yielded to the allure of Valencia Van
Tyle, admitting a finish of beauty to which mere youth could
not aspire, all that was idealistic in him went out to the
younger cousin whose admiration and shy swift friendship
he was losing. His vanity refused to accept this at first. She
was a little piqued at him because of the growing intimacy
with Valencia. That was all. Why, it had been only a month
or two ago that her gaze had been warm for him, that her
playful irony had mocked sweetly his ambition for service to
the community. Their spirits had touched in comradeship.
Almost he had caught in her eyes the look they would hold
for only one man on earth. The best in him had responded to
the call. But now he did not often meet her at The Brakes.
When he did a cool little nod and an indifferent word
sufficed for him. How much this hurt only James himself
knew.

One of the visible signs of his increasing prosperity was a
motor car, in which he might frequently be seen driving with

the daughter of Joe Powers, to the gratification of its owner and the envy of Verden. The cool indifference with which Mrs. Van Tyle ignored the city's social elite had aroused bitter criticism. Since she did not care a rap for this her escapades were frankly indiscreet. James could not really afford a machine, but he justified it on the ground that it was an investment. A man who appears to be prosperous becomes prosperous. A good front is a part of the bluff of twentieth century success. He did not follow his argument so far as to admit that the purchase of the car was an item in the expenses of a campaign by which he meant to make capital out of a woman's favor to him, even though his imagination toyed with the possibilities it might offer to build a sure foundation of fortune.

"You should go to New York," she told him once after he had sketched, with the touch of eloquence so native to him, a plan for a line of steamers between Verden and the Orient.

"To be submerged in the huddle of humanity. No, thank you."

"But the opportunities are so much greater there for a man of ability."

"Oh, ability!" he derided. "New York is loaded to the water line with ability in garrets living on crusts. To win out there a man must have a pull, or he must have the instinct for making money breed, for taking what other men earn."

She studied him, a good-looking, alert American, sheet-armored in the twentieth century polish of selfishness, with an inordinate appetite for success. Certainly he looked every inch a winner.

"I believe you could do it. You're not too scrupulous to look

William MacLeod Raine

out for yourself." Her daring impudence mocked him lightly.

"I'm not so sure about that." James liked to look his conscience in the face occasionally. "I respect the rights of my fellows. In the money centers you can't do that and win. And you've got to win. It doesn't matter how. Make good—make good! Get money—any way you can. People will soon forget how you got it, if you have it."

"Dear me! I didn't know you were so given to moral reflections." To Alice, who had just come into the room to settle where they should spend their Sunday, Valencia explained with mock demureness the subject of their talk. "Mr. Farnum and I are deploring the immoral money madness of New York and the debilitating effects of modern civilization. Will you deplore with us, my dear?"

The younger woman's glance included the cigarette James had thrown away and the one her cousin was still smoking. "Why go as far as New York?" she asked quietly.

Farnum flushed. She was right, he silently agreed. He had no business futtering away his time in a pink boudoir. Nor could he explain that he hoped his time was not being wasted.

"I must be going," he said as casually as he could.

"Don't let me drive you away, Mr. Farnum. I dropped in only for a moment."

"Not at all. I have an appointment with my cousin."

"With Mr. Jefferson Farnum?" Alice asked in awakened interest. "I've just been reading a magazine article about him. Is he really a remarkable man?"

"I don't think you would call him remarkable. He gets things done, in spite of being an idealist."

"Why, in spite of it?"

"Aren't reformers usually unpractical?"

"Are they? I don't know. I have never met one." She looked straight at Farnum with the directness characteristic of her. "Is the article in Stetson's Magazine true?"

"Substantially, I think."

Alice hesitated. She would have liked to pursue the subject, but she could not very well do that with his cousin. For years she had been hearing of this man as a crank agitator who had set himself in opposition to her father and his friends for selfish reasons. Her father had dropped vague hints about his unsavory life. The Stetson write-up had given a very different story. If it told the truth, many things she had been brought up to accept without question would bear study.

James suavely explained. "The facts are true, but not the inferences from the facts. Jeff takes rather a one-sided view of a very complex situation. But he's perfectly honest in it, so far as that goes."

"You voted for his bill, didn't you?" Alice asked.

"Yes, I voted for it. But I said on the floor I didn't believe in it. My feeling was that the people ought to have a chance to express an opinion in regard to it."

"Why don't you believe in it?"

Valencia lifted her perfect eyebrows. "Really, my dear, I

didn't know you were so interested in politics."

Alice waited for the young man's answer.

"It would take me some time to give my reasons in full. But I can give you the text of them in a sentence. Our government is a representative one by deliberate choice of its founders. This bill would tend to make it a pure democracy, which would be far too cumbersome for so large a country."

"So you'll vote against it next time to save the country," Alice suggested lightly. "Thank you for explaining it." She turned to her cousin with an air of dismissing the subject. "Well, Val. What about the yacht trip to Kloochet Island for Sunday? Shall we go? I have to 'phone the captain to let him know at once."

"If you'll promise not to have it rain all the time," the young widow shrugged with a little move. "Perhaps Mr. Farnum could join us? I'm sure uncle would be pleased."

Alice seconded her cousin's invitation tepidly, without any enthusiasm. James, with a face which did not reflect his disappointment, took his cue promptly. "Awfully sorry, but I'll be out of the city. Otherwise I should be delighted."

Valencia showed a row of dainty teeth in a low ripple of amusement. Alice flashed her cousin one look of resentment and with a sentence of conventional regret left the room to telephone the sailing master.

Farnum, seeking permission to leave, waited for his hostess to rise from the divan where she nestled.

But Valencia, her fingers laced in characteristic fashion back of her neck, leaned back and mocked his defeat with indolent amused eyes.

"My engagement," he suggested as a reminder.

"Poor boy! Are you hard hit?"

"Your flights of fancy leave me behind. I can't follow," he evaded with an angry flush.

"No, but you wish you could follow," she laughed, glancing at the door through which her cousin had departed. Then, with a demure impudent little cast of her head, she let him have it straight from the shoulder. "How long have you been in love with Alice? And how will you like to see Ned Merrill win?"

"Am I in love with Miss Frome?"

"Aren't you?"

"If you say so. It happens to be news to me."

"As if I believed that, as if you believed it yourself," she scoffed.

Her pretty pouting lips, the long supple unbroken lines of the soft sinuous body, were an invitation to forget all charms but hers. He understood that she was throwing out her wiles, consciously or unconsciously, to strike out from him a denial that would convince her. His mounting vanity drove away his anger. He forgot everything but her sheathed loveliness, the enticement of this lovely creature whose smoldering eyes invited. Crossing the room, he stood behind her divan and looked down at her with his hands on the back of it.

"Can a man care much for two women at the same time?" he

asked in a low voice.

She laughed with slow mockery.

Her faint perfume was wafted to his brain. He knew a besieging of the blood. Slowly he leaned forward, holding her eyes till the mockery faded from them. Then, very deliberately, he kissed her.

"How dare you!" she voiced softly in a kind of wonder not free from resentment. For with all her sensuous appeal the daughter of Joe Powers was not a woman with whom men took liberties.

"By the gods, why shouldn't I dare? We played a game and both of us have lost. You were to beckon and coolly flit, while I followed safely at a distance. Do you think me a marble statue? Do you think me too wooden for the strings of my heart to pulsate? By heaven, my royal Hebe, you have blown the fire in me to life. You must pay forfeit."

"Pay forfeit?"

"Yes. I'm your servant no longer, but your lover and your master—and I intend to marry you."

"How ridiculous," she derided. "Have you forgotten Alice?"

"I have forgotten everything but you—and that I'm going to marry you."

She laughed a little tremulously. "You had better forget that too. I'm like Alice. My answer is, 'No, thank you, kind sir.'"

"And my answer, royal Hebe, is this." His hot lips met hers again in abandonment to the racing passion in him.

"You—barbarian," she gasped, pushing him away.

"Perhaps. But the man who is going to marry you."

She looked at him with a flash of almost shy curiosity that had the charm of an untasted sensation. "Would you beat me?"

"I don't know." He still breathed unevenly. "I'd teach you how to live."

"And love?" She was beginning to recover her lightness of tone, though the warm color still dabbed her cheeks.

"Why not?" His eyes were diamond bright. "Why not? You have never known the great moments, the buoyant zest of living in the land that belongs only to the Heirs o Life."

"And can you guide me there?" The irony in her voice was not untouched with wistfulness.

"Try me."

She laughed softly, stepped to the table, and chose a cigarette. "My friend, you promise impossibilities. I was not born to that incomparable company. To be frank, neither were you. Alice, grant you, belongs there. And that mad cousin of yours. But not we two earth creepers. We're neither of us star dwellers. In the meantime"—she lit her Egyptian and stopped to make sure of her light every moment escaping more definitely from the glamor of his passion— "you mentioned an engagement that was imperative. Don't let me keep you from it."

CHAPTER 12

From The New Catechism

Question: What is the whole duty of man?

Answer: To succeed.

Q. What is success?

A. Success is being a Captain of Industry.

Q. How may one become a Captain of Industry?

A. By stacking in his barns the hay made by others while the sun shines.

Q. But is this not theft?

A. Not if done legally and respectably on a large scale. It is high finance.

THE REBEL AND THE UNDESIRABLE CITIZEN TALK TREASON. THE HERO HAS PRIVATE CONVERSE WITH A GREAT PIONEER OF CIVILIZATION

Part 1

Jeff never for a day desisted from his fight to win back for the people the self rule that had been wrested from them for selfish purposes by corporate greed. "Government by the people" was the watchword he kept at the head of his editorial column. Better a bad government that is representative than a good one emanating from the privileged few, he maintained with conviction.

To his office came one day Oscar Marchant, the little, half-educated Socialist poet, coughing from the exertion of the stairs he had just climbed. He had come begging, the consumptive presently explained.

"Remember Sobieski, the Polish Jew?"

Jeff smiled. "Of course. Philosophical anarchy used to be his remedy."

"Starvation is the one he's trying now," returned Marchant grimly. "He's had typhoid and lost his job. The rent's due and they'll be turned out tomorrow. He's got a wife and two kids."

Farnum asked questions briefly and pulled out his check book. "Tell Sobieski not to worry," he said as he handed over a check. "I'll send a reporter out there and we'll make an appeal through the *World*. Of course his own name won't be used. No one will know who it really is. We'll look out for him till he's on his feet again."

Marchant gave him the best he had. "You're a pretty good Socialist, even though you don't know it."

"Am I?"

"But you're blind as a bat. The things you fight for in the *World* don't get to the bottom of what ails us."

"We've got to forge the tools of freedom before we can use them, haven't we?"

"You're all for patching up the rotten system we've got. It will never do."

"Great changes are most easily brought about under the old forms. Men's minds in the mass move slowly. They can see only a little truth at a time."

"Because they are blinded by ignorance and selfishness. Get at bottom facts, Farnum. What's the one great crime?"

Without a moment's hesitation Jeff answered. "Poverty. All other crimes are paltry beside that."

Marchant cocked himself up on the window seat with his legs doubled under him tailor fashion. "Why?"

"Because it stamps out hope and love and aspiration, all that is fine and true in life."

"Exactly. Men ought to love their work. But how can they ove that which is always associated in their minds with a denial of justice? Is it likely that men will work better under a system whereby they are condemned in advance to failure than under one standing rationally for a just and fair division of the fruits of labor? I tell you, Farnum, under present conditions the Juggernaut of progress is forever wasting humanity."

"I've always thought it a pity that the mainsprings of work should be fear and greed instead of hope and love," Jeff agreed.

"Why is it that poverty coexists with wealth increasing so rapidly? Why is it that productive power has been so enormously developed without lightening the burdens of labor?"

Marchant's eyes were starlike in their earnestness. He had a passion for humanity that neither want nor disease could quench, and with it a certain gift of expression street oratory had brought out. Even in private conversation he had got into the way of declaiming. But Jeff knew he was no empty talker. All that he had he literally gave to the poor.

"Because the whole spirit of business life is wrong," Farnum responded.

"Of course it's wrong. It's a survival of the law of the jungle, of tooth and fang. Its motto is dog eat dog. We all work under the rule of get and grab. What's the result of this higgledypiggledy system? One man starves and another has indigestion. That's the trouble with Verden to-day. Some of us haven't enough and others have too much. They take from us what we earn. That's the whole cause of poverty. The Malthusian theory is all wrong. It's not nature, but man that is to blame."

Farnum knew the little Socialist was right so far. Here in Verden, under the forms of freedom, was the very essence of slavery. All the product of labor was taken from it except enough to sustain a mere animal existence. Something was wrong in a world where a man begs in vain for work to support his family. Given proper conditions, men would not rise by trampling each other down, but by lending a hand to the unfortunate. The effect of efficiency would be to make things easier for the weak. The reward of service would be more service.

"The principle of the old order is dead," Marchant went on, wagging his thin forefinger at Jeff. "The whole social fabric is made up of lies, compromises, injustice. The only reason it has hung together so long is that people have been trained to think along certain lines like show animals. But they're waking up. Look at Germany. Look at England. What the plutocrats call the menace of Socialism is everywhere. Now that every worker knows he is being robbed of what he earns, how long do you think he will carry the capitalistic system on his back? From the beginning of the world we have tried it. With what result? An injustice that is staggering, a waste that is appalling, an inhumanity that is deadening."

Jeff let a hand fall lightly on his shoulder. "Of course it's all wrong. We know that. But can you show me how to make it right, except out of the hearts of men growing slowly wiser and better?"

"Why slowly?" demanded Marchant. "Why not to-day while we're still alive to see the smiles of men and women and children made glad? You always want to begin at the wrong end. I tell you that you can't change men's hearts until you change the conditions under which they live."

"And I tell you that you can't change the conditions until you change men's hearts," Jeff answered with his wistful smile.

"Rubbish! The only way to change the hearts of most Plutocrats is to hit them over the head with a two-by-four. Smug respectability is in the saddle, and it knows it's right. We'll get nowhere until we smash this iniquitous system to smithereens."

"So you want to substitute one system for another. You think you can eliminate by legal enactment all this fatty degeneration of greed and selfishness that has incased our souls. I'm afraid it will be a slower process. We must free ourselves from within. I believe we are moving toward some sort of a socialistic state. No man with eyes in his head can help seeing that. But we'll move a step at a time, and only so fast as the love and altruism inside us can be organized into external law."

"No. You'll wake up some morning and find that this whole capitalistic organization has crumbled in the night, fallen to pieces from dry rot."

Jeff might not agree with him, but he knew that Marchant, dreamer and incoherent poet, his heart aflame with zeal for humanity, was far nearer the truth of life than the smug complacent Pharisees that fattened from the toil of the helpless many who could do nothing but suffer in dumb silence.

Part 2

As the months passed Jeff grew in stature with the people of the state. In spite of his energy he was always fair. The plain truth he felt to be a better argument than the tricks of a demagogue.

A rational common sense was to be found in all his advice. Add to this that he had no personal profit to seek, no political axe to grind, and was always transparent as a child. More and more Verden recognized him as the one most conspicuous figure in the state dedicated to uncompromising war against the foes of the Republic.

Those who knew him best liked his humility, his good humor, the gentleness that made him tolerant of the men he must fight. His poise lifted him above petty animosities, and the daily sand-stings of life did not disturb his serenity.

Everywhere his propaganda gained ground. People's Power Leagues were formed with a central steering committee at Verden. Politicians with their ears close to the ground heard rumbles of the coming storm. They began to notice that reputable business men, prominent lawyers not affiliated with corporations, and even a few educators who had shaken away the timidity of their class were lining up to support Jeff's freak legislation. It began to look as if one of those periodical uprisings of the people was about to sweep the state.

Big Tim found his ward workers met persistently by the same questions from their ordinarily docile following. "Why shouldn't we tie strings to our representatives so as to keep them from betraying us?... Why can't we make laws ourselves in emergency and kill bad laws the legislature makes?... What's the matter with taking away some of the power from our representatives who have abused it?"

In the city election O'Brien went down to defeat. Only frag-
ments of his ticket were saved from the general wreckage.
Next day Joe Powers wired James Farnum to join him
immediately at Chicago.

"I'm going to put you in charge of the political field out
there," the great man announced, his gray granite eyes
fastened on the young lawyer. "Ned Merrill won't do.
Neither will O'Brien. Between them they've made a mess of
things."

"I don't know that it is their fault, except indirectly. One of
those populistic waves swept over the city."

"Why didn't they know what was going to happen? Why
didn't they let me know? That's what I pay them for."

"A child could have foreseen it, but O'Brien wouldn't believe
his eyes. He's been giving Verden an administration with too
much graft. The people got tired of it."

"What were Merrill and Frome up to? Why did they permit
it?" demanded Powers impatiently.

"They were looking out for their franchises. To get the
machine's support they had to give O'Brien a free hand."

"If necessary you had better eliminate Big Tim. Or at least
put him and his gang in the background. Make the machine
respectable so that good citizens can indorse it."

James nodded agreement. "I've been thinking about that. The
thing can be done. A business men's movement from inside
the party to purify it. A reorganization with new men in

charge. That sort of thing."

"Exactly. And how about the state?"

"Things don't look good to me."

"Why not?"

"This initiative and referendum idea is spreading."

Powers drove his fist into a pile of papers on the desk. "Stop it. I give you carte blanche. Spend as much as you like. But win. What good is a lobby to me if those hare-brained farmers can kill every bill we pass through their grafting legislature?"

The possibilities grew on Farnum. "I'll send Professor Perkins of Verden University to New Zealand to prepare a paper showing the thing is a failure there. I'll have every town in the state thoroughly canvassed by lecturers and speakers against the bill. I'll bombard the farmers with literature."

"What about the newspapers?"

"We control most of them. At Verden only the *World* is against us."

"Buy it."

"Can't be bought. Its editorial columns are not for sale."

"Anything can be bought if you've got the price. Who owns it?"

"A Captain Chunn. He made his money in Alaska. My

cousin is the editor. He is the real force back of it."

"Does the paper have any influence?"

"A great deal."

"I've heard of your cousin. A crack-brained Socialist, I understand."

"You'll find he's a long way from that," James denied.

"Whatever he is, buy him," ordered Powers curtly.

The young man shook his head. "Can't be done. He doesn't want the things you have to offer."

"Every man has his price. Find his, and buy him."

James shook his head decisively. "Absolutely impossible. He's an idealist and an altruist."

Powers snorted impatiently. "Talk English, young man, and I'll understand you."

Farnum had heard Joe Powers was a man who would stand plain talk from those who had the courage to give it him. His cool eyes hardened. Why not? For once the old gray pirate, chief of the robber buccaneers who rode on their predatory way superior to law, should see himself as Jeff Farnum saw him.

"What I mean is that the things he holds most important can't be bought with dollars and cents. He believes in justice and fair play. He thinks the strong ought to bear the burdens of the weak.

He has a passion to uplift humanity. You can't understand him because it isn't possible for you to conceive of a man whose first thought is always for what is equitable."

"Just as I thought, a Socialist dreamer and demagogue," pronounced Powers scornfully.

"Merrill and Frome have been thinking of him just as you do." James waved his hand toward the newspaper in front of the railroad king. "With what result our election shows."

"Well, where does his power lie? How can you break it?" the old man asked.

"He is a kind of brother to the lame and the halt all over the state. Among the poor and the working classes he has friends without number. They believe in him as a patriot fighting for them against the foes of the country."

"Do you call me a foe of the country, young man?" Powers wanted to know grimly.

"Not I," laughed James. "Why should I quarrel with my bread and jam? If you had ever done me the honor to read any of my speeches you would see that I refer to you as a Pioneer of Civilization and a Builder for the Future. But my view doesn't happen to be universal. I was trying to show you how the man with the dinner pail feels."

"Who fills his dinner pails?"

James met his frown with a genial eye. "There's a difference of opinion about that, sir. According to the economics of Verden University you fill them. According to the *World* editorials it's the other way. They fill yours."

"Hmp! And what's your personal opinion? Am I a robber of labor?"

"I think that the price of any success worth while is paid for in the failure of others. You win because you're strong, sir. That's the law of the game. It's according to the survival of the fittest that you're where you are. If you had hesitated some other man would have trampled you down. It's a case of wolf eat wolf."

The old railroad builder laughed harshly. This was the first time in his experience that a subordinate had so analyzed him to his face.

"So I'm a wolf, am I?"

"In one sense of the word you're not that at all, sir. You're a great builder. You've done more for the Northwest than any man living. You couldn't have done it if you had been squeamish. I hold the end justifies the means. What you've got is yours because you've won it. Men who do a great work for the public are entitled to great rewards."

"Glad to know you've got more sense than that fool cousin of yours. Now go home and beat him. I don't care how you do it, just so that you get results. Spend what money you need. but make good, young man—make good."

"I'll do my best," James promised.

"All I demand is that you win. I'm not interested in the method you use. But put that cousin of yours out of the demagogue business if you have to shanghai him."

James laughed. "That might not be a bad way to get rid of him till after the election. The word would leak out that he had been bought off."

The old buccaneer's eyes gleamed. He was as daring a lawbreaker as ever built or wrecked a railroad. "Have you the nerve, young man?"

"When I'm working for you, sir," retorted James coolly.

"What do you mean by that?"

"If I've studied your career to any purpose, sir, one thing stands out pretty clear. You haven't the slightest respect for law merely as law. When it's on your side you're a stickler for it; when it isn't you say nothing, but brush it aside as if it did not exist. In either case you get what you want."

"I'm glad you've noticed that last point. Now we'll have luncheon." He smiled grimly. "I daresay you'll enjoy it no less because I stole it from the horny hand of labor, by your mad cousin's way of it."

"Not a bit," answered James cheerfully.

CHAPTER 13

"Must it be? Must we then
Render back to God again
This, His broken work, this thing
For His man that once did sing?"

—Josephine Prestor Peabody

"And listen! I declare to you that if all is as you say—and
I do not doubt it—you have never ceased to be virtuous in
the sight of God!"

—Victor Hugo

THE REBEL PROVES THAT HE IS LOST TO GOOD
FORM AND RESPECTABILITY BY STEPPING
BETWEEN A SINNER AND THE WAGES OF SIN, THUS
EVIDENCING TO THE PILLARS OF SOCIETY HIS
COMPLETE DEGENERATION

Part 1

Sam Miller came into Jeff's office one night as he was looking over the editorials. Farnum nodded abstractedly to him.

"Take a chair, Sam. Be through in a minute."

Presently Jeff pushed the galley proof to one side and looked at his friend. "Well, Sam?" Almost at once he added: "What's the matter?"

There were queer white patches on Miller's fat face. He looked like a man in hell. A lump rose in his throat. Two or three times he swallowed hard.

"It's—it's Nellie."

"Nellie Anderson?"

He nodded.

Jeff felt as if his heart had been drenched in icy water. "What about her?"

"She's—gone."

"Gone where?"

"We don't know. She left Friday. There was a note for her mother. It said to forget her, because she was a disgrace to her name."

"You mean—" Jeff did not finish his question. He knew what the answer was, and in his soul lay a reflection of the mortal sickness he saw in his friend's face.

Miller nodded, unable to speak. Presently his words came brokenly. "She's been acting strangely for a long time. Her mother noticed it.... So did I. Like as if she wasn't happy. We've been worried. I...I..." He buried his face in his arm on the table. "My God, I love her, Jeff. I have for years. If I'd only known… if she'd only told me."

Jeff was white as the galley proof that lay before him with the unprinted side up. "Tell me all about it, Sam."

Miller looked up. "That's all. We don't know where she's gone. She had no money to speak of."

"And the man?" Jeff almost whispered.

"We don't know who he is. Might be any one of the clerks at the Verden Dry Goods Company.

Maybe it's none of them. If I knew I'd cut his heart out."

The clock on the wall ticked ten times before Jeff spoke. "Did she go alone?"

"We don't know. None of the clerks are missing from the store where she worked. I checked up with the manager yesterday."

Another long silence. "They may have rooms in town here."

"Not likely." Presently Miller added miserably: "She's— going to be a mother soon. We found the doctor she went to see."

"You're sure she hasn't been married? Of course you've looked over the marriage licenses for the past year."

"Yes. Her name isn't on the list."

"Did she have money?"

"About fifteen dollars, we figure."

"That wouldn't take her far—unless the man gave her some. Have you been to a detective agency?"

"Yes."

"We'll put blind ads in all the papers telling her to come home. We'll rake the city and the state with a fine tooth comb. We're bound to hear of her."

"She's desperate, Jeff. If she's alone she'll think she has no friends. We've got to find her in time or—"

Jeff guessed the alternative. She might take the easy way out, the one which offered an escape from all her earthly troubles. Girls of her type often did. Nellie was made for laughter and for happiness. He had known her innocent as a sunbeam and as glad. Now that she was in the pit, facing disgrace and disillusionment and despair, the horror and the dread of existence to her would be a millstone round her neck.

The damnable unfairness of it took. Jeff by the throat. Was it her fault that she had inherited a temperament where passions lurked unsuspected like a banked fire? Was she to blame because her mother had brought her up without warning, because she had believed in the love and the honor of a villain? Her very faith and trust had betrayed her. Every honest instinct in him cried out against the world's verdict, that she must pay with salt tears to the end of her life while the scoundrel who had led her into trouble walked gaily to fresh conquests.

Cogged dice! She had gone forth smiling to play the game of life with them, never dreaming that the cubes were loaded. He remembered how once her every motion sang softly to him like music, with what dear abandon she had given herself to his kisses. Her fondness had been a thing to cherish, her innocence had called for protection. And her chivalrous lover had struck the lightness forever from her soul.

For long he never thought of her without an icy sinking of the heart.

William MacLeod Raine

Part 2

Weeks passed. Sam Miller gave his whole time to the search for the missing girl. Jeff supplied the means; in every way he could he encouraged him and the broken mother. For a thousand miles south and east the police had her description and her photograph. But no trace of her could be found. False clews there were aplenty. A dozen haggard street-walkers were arrested in mistake for her. Patiently Sam ran down every story, followed every possibility to its hopeless end.

The weeks ran into months. Mrs. Anderson still hoped drearily. Every night the light in the hall burned now till daybreak. And every night she wept herself to sleep for that her one ewe lamb was lost in a ravenous world.

Tears were for the night. Wan smiles for the day, when she and Sam, drawn close by a common grief, met to understand each other with few words. He was back again at his work as curator of the museum at the State House, a place Jeff had secured for him after the election.

Outside of Nellie's mother the one friend to whom Sam turned now was Jeff. He came for comfort, to sit long hours in the office while Farnum did his night work. Sometimes he would read; more often sit brooding with his chin in his hands. When the midnight rush was past and Jeff was free they would go together to a restaurant.

Afterwards they would separate at the door of the block where Jeff had his rooms.

Part 3

Yet when Jeff found her it was not Sam who was with him, but Marchant. They had been to see Sobieski about a place Captain Chunn had secured for him as a night watchman of the shipbuilding plant of which Clinton Rogers was part owner. The Pole had mounted his hobby and it had been late when they got away from his cabin under the viaduct.

Just before they turned into lower Powers Avenue from the deadline below Yarnell Way, Marchant clutched at the sleeve of his friend.

"See that woman's face?" he asked sharply.

"No."

Jeff was interested at once. For during the past months he had fallen into a habit of scanning the countenance of any woman who might be the one they sought.

"She knew you. I could see fear jump to her eyes."

"We'll go back," Jeff decided instantly.

"She's in deep water. Death is written on her face."

Already Jeff was swinging back, almost on the run. But she had gone swallowed up in the darkness of the night. They listened, but could hear only the steady splashing of the rain. While they stood hesitating the figure of a woman showed at the other end of the alley and was lost at once down Pacific Avenue.

Jeff ran toward the lights of the other avenue, but before he reached it she had again disappeared. Marchant joined him a few moments later. The little socialist leaned against the wall to steady himself against the fit of coughing that racked him.

"Nuisance... this... being a lunger... What's it all... about, Jeff?"

"I know her. We'll cover the waterfront. Take from Coffee Street up. Don't miss a wharf or a boathouse. And if you find the girl don't let her get away."

The editor crossed to the Pacific & Alaska dock, his glance sweeping every dark nook and cranny that might conceal a huddled form. Out of a sodden sky rain pelted in a black night.

He was turning away when an empty banana crate behind him crashed down from a pyramid of them. Jeff whirled, was upon her in an instant before she could escape.

She was shrinking against the wall of the warehouse, her face a tragic mask in its haggard pallor, a white outline clenched hard against the driving rain. One hand was at her heart, the other beat against the air to hold him back.

"Nellie!" he cried.

"What do you want? Let me alone! Let me alone!" She was panting like a spent deer, and in her wild eyes he saw the hunted look of a forest creature at bay.

"We've looked everywhere for you. I've come to take you home."

"Home!" Her strange laughter mocked the word. "There's no home for folks like me in this world."

"Your mother is breaking her heart for you. She thinks of nothing else. All night she keeps a light burning to let you know."

She broke into a sob. "I've seen it. To-night I saw it—for the last time."

"It is pitiful how she waits and waits," he went on quietly. "She takes out your dresses and airs them. All the playthings you used when you were a little girl she keeps near her. She—"

"Don't! Don't!" she begged.

"Your place is set at the table every day, so that when you come in it may be ready."

At that she leaned against the crates and broke down utterly. Jeff knew that for the moment the battle was won. He slipped out of his rain coat and made her put it on, coaxing her gently while the sobs shook her. He led her by the hand back to Pacific Avenue, talking cheerfully as if it were a matter of course.

Here Marchant met them.

"I want a cab, Oscar," Jeff told him.

While he was gone they waited in the entrance to a store that sheltered them from the rain.

Suddenly the girl turned to Jeff. "I—I was going to do it to-night," she whispered.

He nodded. "That's all past now. Don't think of it. There are good days ahead—happy days. It will be new life to your mother to see you. We've all been frightfully anxious."

She shivered, beginning to sob once more. Not for an instant had he withdrawn the hand to which she clung so desperately.

"It's all right, Nellie. . .All right at last. You're going home to those that love you."

"Not to-night—not while I'm looking like this. Don't take me home to-night," she begged. "I can't stand it yet. Give me to-night, please. I…"

She trembled like an aspen. Jeff could see she was exhausted, in deadly fear, ready to give way to any wild impulse that might seize her. To reason with her would do no good and might do much harm. He must humor her fancy about not going home at once. But he could not take her to a rooming house and leave her alone while her mind was in this condition. She must be watched, protected against herself. Otherwise in the morning she might be gone.

"All right. You may have my rooms. Here's the cab."

Jeff helped her in, thanked Marchant with a word, got in himself, and shut the door. They were driven through streets shining with rain beneath the light clusters. Nellie crouched in a corner and wept. As they swung down Powers Avenue they passed motor car after motor car filled with gay parties returning from the theaters. He glimpsed young women in furs, wrapped from the cruelty of life by the caste system in which wealth had incased them. Once a ripple of merry laughter floated to him across the gulf that separated this girl from them.

A year ago her laughter had been light as theirs. Life had

been a thing beautiful, full of color. She had come to it eagerly, like a lover, glad because it was so good.

But it had not been good to her. By the cluster lights he could see how fearfully it had mauled her, how cruelly its irony had kissed hollows in her young cheeks. All the bloom of her was gone, all the brave pride and joy of youth—gone beyond hope of resurrection. Why must such things be? Why so much to the few, so little to the many? And why should that little be taken away? He saw as in a vision the infinite procession of her hopeless sisters who had traveled the same road, saw them first as sweet and carefree children bubbling with joy, and again, after the *World* had misused them for its pleasure, haggard, tawdry, with dragging steps trailing toward the oblivion that awaited them. Good God, how long must life be so terribly wasted? How long a bruised and broken thing instead of the fine, brave adventure for which it was meant?

Across his mind flashed Realf's words:

"Amen!" I have cried in battle-time,
When my beautiful heroes perished;
The earth of the Lord shall bloom sublime
By the blood of his martyrs nourished.
"Amen!" I have said, when limbs were hewn
And our wounds were blue and ghastly
The flesh of a man may fail and swoon
But God shall conquer lastly.

Part 4

As Jeff helped her from the cab in front of the block where he lived a limousine flashed past. It caught his glance for an instant, long enough for him to recognize his Cousin James, Mrs. Van Tyle and Alice Frome. The arm which supported Nellie did not loosen from her waist, though he knew they had seen him and would probably draw conclusions.

The young woman was trembling violently.

"My rooms are in the second story. Can you walk? Or shall I carry you?" Farnum asked.

"I can walk," she told him almost in a whisper.

He got her upstairs and into the big armchair in front of the gas log. Now that she had slipped out of his rain coat he saw that she was wet to the skin. From his bedroom he brought a bathrobe, pajamas, woolen slippers, anything he could find that was warm and soft. In front of her he dumped them all.

"I'm going down to the drug store to get you something that will warm you, Nellie. While I'm away change your clothes and get into these things," he told her.

She looked up at him with tears in her eyes. "You're good."

A lump rose in his heart. He thought of those evenings before the grate alone with her and of the desperate fight he had had with his passions. Good! He accused himself bitterly for the harm that he had done her. But before her his smile was bright and cheerful.

"We're all going to be so good to you that you'll not know us. Haven't we been waiting two months for a chance to spoil you?"

"Do you... know?" she whispered, color for an instant in her wan face.

"I know things aren't half so bad as they seem to you. Dear girl, we are your friends. We've not done right by you. Even your mother has been careless and let you get hurt. But we're going to make it up to you now."

A man on the other side of the street watched Jeff come down and cross to the drug store. Billie Gray, ballot box stuffer, detective, and general handy man for Big Tim O'Brien, had been lurking in that entry when Jeff came home. He had sneaked up the stairs after them and had seen the editor disappear into his rooms with one whom he took to be a woman of the street. Already a second plain clothes man was doing sentry duty. The policeman whose beat it was sat in the drug store and kept an eye open from that quarter.

To the officer Jeff nodded casually. "Bad weather to be out all night in, Nolan."

"Right you are, Mr. Farnum."

The editor ordered a bottle of whiskey and while it was being put up passed into the telephone booth and closed the door behind him. He called up Olive 43I.

Central rang again and again.

"Can't get your party," she told him at last.

"You'll waken him presently. Keep at it, please. It's very important."

At last Sam Miller's voice answered. "Hello! Hello! What is it?"

"I've found Nellie.... Just in time. thank God. . .She's at my rooms.... Have Mrs. Anderson bring an entire change of clothing for her.... Yes, she's very much exhausted. I'll tell you all about it later.... Come quietly. She may be asleep when you get here."

Jeff hung up the receiver, paid for the whiskey, and returned to his rooms. He did not know that he had left three good and competent witnesses who were ready to take oath that he had brought to his rooms at midnight a woman of the half world and that he had later bought liquor and returned with it to his apartment.

Billie Gray thumped his fist into his open palm. "We've got him. We've got him right. He can't get away from it. By Gad, we've got him at last!"

Jeff found Nellie wrapped in his bathrobe in the big chair before the gas log. Her own wet clothes were out of sight behind a screen.

"You locked the door when you went out," she charged.

"Some of my friends might have dropped in to see me," he explained with his disarming smile.

But he could see in her eyes the unreasoning fear of a child that has been badly hurt. He had locked the door on the outside. She was going to be dragged home whether she wanted to go or not. Dread of that hour was heavy on her soul. Jeff knew the choice must be hers, not his. He spoke quietly.

"You're not a prisoner, of course. You may go whenever you like. I would have no right to keep you. But you will hurt me very much if you go before morning."

"Where will you stay?" she asked.

"I'll sleep on the lounge in this room," he answered in his most matter of fact voice.

While he busied himself preparing a toddy for her she began to tell brokenly, by snatches, the story of her wanderings. She had gone to Portland and had found work in a department store at the notion counter. After three weeks she had lost her place. Days of tramping the streets looking for a job brought her at last to an overall factory where she found employment. The foreman had discharged her at the end of the third day. Once she had been engaged at an agency as a servant by a man, but as soon as his wife saw her Nellie was told she would not do. Bitter humiliating experiences had befallen her. Twice she had been turned out of rooming houses. Jeff read between the lines that as her time drew near some overmastering impulse had drawn her back to Verden. Already she was harboring the thought of death, but she could not die in a strange place so far from home. Only that morning she had reached town.

After she had retired to the bedroom Jeff sat down in the chair she had vacated. He heard her moving about for a short time. Presently came silence.

It must have been an hour and a half later that Sam and Mrs. Anderson knocked gently on the door.

"Cars stopped running. Had to 'phone for a taxi," Miller whispered.

The agitation of the mother was affecting. Her fingers twitched with nervousness. Her eyes strayed twenty times in five minutes toward the door behind which her daughter slept. Every little while she would tip-toe to it and listen breathlessly. In whispers Jeff told them the story, answering a hundred eager trembling questions.

Slowly the clock ticked out the seconds of the endless night. Gray day began to sift into the room. Mrs. Anderson's excursions to the bedroom door grew more frequent. Some-times she opened it an inch or two. On one of these occasions she went in quickly and shut the door behind her.

"Good enough. They don't need us here, Sam. We'll go out and have some breakfast," Jeff proposed.

On the street they met Billie Gray. He greeted the editor with a knowing grin. "Good morning, Mr. Farnum. How's every-thing? Fine and dandy, eh?"

Jeff looked at him sharply. "What the mischief is he doing here?" he asked Miller by way of comment.

All through breakfast that sinister little figure shadowed his thoughts. Gray was like a stormy petrel. He was surely there for no good, barring the chance of its being an accident. Both of them kept their eyes open on their way back, but they met nobody except a policeman swinging his club as he leaned against a lamp post and whistled the Merry Widow waltz.

But Farnum was not satisfied. He cautioned both Sam and Mrs. Anderson to say nothing, above all to give no names or explanation to anybody. A whisper of the truth would bring reporters down on them in shoals.

"You had better stay here quietly to-day," their host advised.

"I'll see you're not disturbed by the help. Sam will bring your meals in from a restaurant. I'd say stay here as long as you like, but it can't be done without arousing curiosity, the one thing we don't want."

"No, better leave late to-night in a taxi," Sam proposed.

"Better still, I'll bring around Captain Chunn's car and Sam can drive you home. We can't be too careful."

So it was arranged. Mrs. Anderson left it to them and went back into the bedroom where her wounded lamb lay.

About midnight Jeff stopped a car in front of the stairway. The two veiled women emerged, accompanied by Sam. They were helped into the tonneau and Miller took the driver's seat. Just as the machine began to move a little man ran across the street toward them.

Jeff's forearm went up suddenly and caught him under the chin. Billie Gray's head went back and his heels came up. Farnum was on him in an instant, ostensibly to help him up, but really to see he did not get up too quickly. As soon as the automobile swung round the corner Jeff lifted him to his feet.

"Sorry. Hope I didn't hurt you," he smiled.

"Smart trick, wasn't it?" snarled the detective. "Never mind, Mr. Farnum. We've got your goat right."

"Again?" Jeff asked with pleasant impudence.

"Got you dead to rights this trip." Gray fired another shot as he turned away. "And we'll find out yet who your lady friends are. Don't you forget it."

But Billie had overlooked a bet. He had been in the back of the drug store getting a drink when Sam and Mrs. Anderson arrived. The policeman on guard had not connected the coming of these with Jeff. None of the watchers knew that Jeff had not been alone with the girl all night.

Part 5

Sam called on Jeff two days later.

"I want you to come round to-night at seven-fifteen. We're going to be married," he explained.

The newspaper man's eye met his in a swift surprise. "You and Nellie?"

"Yes." Miller's jaw set. "Why not? YOU'RE not going to spring that damned cant about—"

"I thought you knew me better," his friend interrupted.

Miller's face worked. "I'll ask your pardon for that, Jeff. You've been the best friend she has. Well, we've thrashed it all out. She fought her mother and me two days; didn't think it right to let me give my name to her, even though she admits she has come to care for me. You can see how she would be torn two ways. It's the only road out for her and the baby that is on the way, but she couldn't bring herself to sacrifice me, as she calls it. I've hammered and hammered at her that it's no sacrifice. She can't see it; just cries and cries."

"Of course she would be unusually sensitive; Her nerves must be all bare so that she shrinks as one does when a wound is touched."

"That's it. She keeps speaking of herself as if she were a lost soul. At last we fairly wore her out. After we are married her mother and she will take the eight o'clock for Kenton. Nobody there knows them, and she'll have a chance to forget."

"You're a white man, Sam," Jeff nodded lightly. But his eyes

William MacLeod Raine

were shining.

"I'm the man that loves her. I couldn't do less, could I?"

"Some men would do a good deal less."

"Not if they looked at it the way I do. She's the same Nellie I've always known. What difference does it make to me that she stumbled in the dark and hurt herself—except that my heart is so much more tender to her it aches?"

"If you hold to that belief she'll live to see the day when she is a happy woman again," the journalist prophesied.

"I'm going to teach her to think of it all as only a bad night-mare she's been through." His jaw clinched again so that the muscles stood out on his cheeks. "Do you know she won't say a word—not even to her mother—about who the villain is that betrayed her? I'd wring his coward neck off for him," he finished with a savage oath.

"Better the way it is, Sam. Let her keep her secret.. The least said and thought about it the better."

Miller looked at his watch. "Perhaps you're right. I've got to go to work. Remember, seven-fifteen sharp. We need you as a witness. Just your business suit, you understand. No present, of course."

The wedding took place in the room where Jeff had been used to drinking chocolate with his little friend only a year before. It was the first time he had been here since that night when the danger signal had flashed so suddenly before his eyes. The whole thing came back to him poignantly.

It was a pitiful little wedding, with the bride and her mother in tears from the start. The ceremony was performed by their friend Mifflin, the young clergyman who had a mission for sailors on the waterfront. Nobody else was present except Marchant, the second witness.

As soon as the ceremony was finished Sam put Nellie and her mother into a cab to take them to their train. The other three walked back down town.

As Jeff sat before his desk four hours later, busy with a tax levy story, Miller came in and took a seat. Jeff waved a hand at him and promptly forgot he was on earth until he rose and put on his coat an hour later.

"Well! Did they get off all right?" he asked.

Miller nodded absently. Ten minutes later he let out what he was thinking about.

"I wish to God I knew the man," he exploded.

Jeff looked at him quietly. "I'm glad you don't. Adding murder to it wouldn't help the situation one little bit, my friend."

William MacLeod Raine

CHAPTER 14

Only the man who is sheet-armored in a triple plate of selfishness can be sure that weak hands won't clutch at him and delay his march to success.

—From the Note Book of a Dreamer

THE HERO, CONFRONTED WITH AN UNPLEASANT POSSIBILITY, PROVES HIS GREATNESS BY RISING SUPERIOR TO SENTIMENT

Part 1

James came down to the office one morning in his car with a smile of contentment on his handsome face. It had been decided that he was to be made speaker of the House after the next election, assuming that he and his party were returned to power. Jeff and the progressives were to stand back of him, and he felt sure that after a nominal existence the standpatters would accept him. He intended by scrupulous fair play to win golden opinions for himself. From the speakership to the governor's chair would not be a large step. After that—well, there were many possibilities.

He did not for a moment admit to himself that there was

anything of duplicity in the course he was following. His intention was to line up with the progressives during the campaign, to win his reelection on that platform, and to support a rational liberal program during the session. He would favor an initiative and referendum amendment not so radical as the one Jeff offered, a bill that would not cripple business or alarm capital. As he looked at it life was a compromise. The fusion of many minds to a practical result always demanded this. And results were more important than any number of theories.

As James passed into his office the stenographer stopped him with a remark.

"A man has been in twice to see you this morning, Mr. Farnum."

"Did he leave his name?"

"No. He said he would call again."

James passed into his private office and closed the door.

A quarter of an hour later his stenographer knocked. "He's here again, Mr. Farnum."

"Who?"

"The man I told you of."

"Oh!" James put down the brief he was reading. "Show him in."

A figure presently stood hesitating in the doorway. James saw an oldish man, gray and stooped with a rather wistful lost-dog expression on his face.

"What can I do for you, sir?" he questioned.

"Don't you know me?" the stranger asked with a quaver in his voice.

The lawyer did not, but some premonition of disaster clutched at his heart. He rose swiftly and closed the door behind his caller.

A faint smile doubtful of its right touched the weak face of the little old man. "So you don't know your own father— boy!"

A sudden sickness ran through the lawyer and sapped his strength. He leaned against the desk uncertainly. It had come at last. The whole world would learn the truth about him. The Merrills, the Fromes, Valencia Van Tyle—all of them would know it and scorn him.

"What are you doing here?" James heard himself say hoarsely.

"Why, I—I—I came to see my son."

"What for?"

Before so harsh and abrupt a reception the weak smile went out like a blown candle.

"I thought you'd be glad to see me—after so many years."

"Why should I be glad to see you? What have you ever done for me but disgrace me?"

Tears showed in the watery eyes. "That's right. It's gospel truth, I reckon."

"And now, when I've risen above it, so that all men respect me, you come back to drag me down."

"No—no, I wouldn't do that, son."

"That's what you'll do. Do you think my friends will want to know a man who is the son of a convict? I've got a future before me. Already I've been mentioned for governor. What chance would I have when people know my father is a thief?"

"Son," winced the old man.

"Oh, well! I'm not picking my words," James went on with angry impatience. "I'm telling you the facts. I've got enemies. Every strong man has. They'll smash me like an empty eggshell."

"They don't need to know about me. I'll not do any talking."

"That's all very well. Things leak out," James grumbled a little more graciously. "Well, you better sit down now you're here. I thought you were living in Arkansas."

"So I am. I've done right well there. And I thought I'd take a little run out to see you. I didn't know but what you might need a little help." He glanced aimlessly around the well-furnished office. "But I expect you don't, from the looks of things."

"If you think I've got money you're wrong," James explained. "I'm just starting in my profession, and of course I owe a good deal here and there. I've been hard pressed ever since I left college."

His father brightened up timidly. "I owe you money. We can

William MacLeod Raine

fix that up. I've got a little mill down there and I've done well, though it was hard sledding at first."

James caught at a phrase. What do you mean?"

"Owe me money!"

"I knew it must be you paid off the shortage at the Planters' National. When I sent the money it was returned. You'd got ahead of me. I was THAT grateful to you, son."

The lawyer found himself flushing. "Oh, Jeff paid that. He was earning money at the time and I wasn't. Of course I intended to pay him back some day."

"Did Jeff do that? Then you and he must be friends. Tell me about him."

"There's not much to tell. He's managing editor of a paper here that has a lot of influence. Yes. Jeff has been a staunch friend to me always. He recognizes that I'm a rising man and ought to be kept before the public."

"I wonder if he's like his father."

"Can't tell you that," his son replied carelessly. "I don't remember Uncle Phil much. Jeff's a queer fellow, full of Utopian notions about brotherhood and that sort of thing. But he's practical in a way. He gets things done in spite of his softheadedness."

There was a knock at the door. "Mr. Jefferson Farnum, sir."

James considered for a second. "Tell him to come in, Miss Brooks."

The lawyer saw that the door was closed before he introduced Jeff to his father. It gave him a momentary twinge of conscience to see his cousin take the old man quickly by both hands. It was of course a mere detail, but James had not yet shaken hands with his father.

"I'm glad to see you, Uncle Robert," Jeff said.

His voice shook a little. There was in his manner that hint of affection which made him so many friends, the warmth that suggested a woman's sympathy, but not effeminacy.

The ready tears brimmed into his uncle's eyes. "You're like your father, boy. I believe I would have known you by him," he said impulsively.

"You couldn't please me better, sir. And what about James—would you have known him?"

The old man looked humbly at his handsome, distinguished son. "No, I would never have known him."

"He's becoming one of our leading citizens, James is. You ought to hear him make a speech. Demosthenes and Daniel Webster hide their heads when the Honorable James K. Farnum spellbinds," Jeff joked.

"I've read his speeches," the father said unexpectedly. "For more than a year I've taken the *World* so as to hear of him."

"Then you know that James is headed straight for the Hall of Fame. Aren't you, James?"

"Nonsense! You've as much influence in the state as I have, or you would have if you would drop your fight on wealth."

"Bless you, I'm not making a fight on wealth," Jeff answered with good humor. "It's illicit wealth we're hammering at. But when you compare me to James K. I'll have to remind you that I'm not a silver-tongued orator or Verden's favorite son."

The father's wistful smile grew bolder. Somehow Jeff's arrival had cleared the atmosphere. A Scriptural phrase flashed into his mind as applicable to this young man. Thinketh no evil. His nephew did not regard him with suspicion or curiosity. To him he was not a sinner or an outcast, but a brother. His manner had just the right touch of easy deference youth ought to give age.

"Of course you're going to make us a long visit, Uncle Robert."

The old man's propitiating gaze went to his son. "Not long, I reckon. I've got to get back to my business."

"Nonsense! We'll not let you go so easily. Eh, James?"

"No, of course not," the lawyer mumbled. He was both annoyed and embarrassed.

"I don't want to be selfish about it, but I do think you had better put up with me, Uncle. James is at the University Club, and only members have rooms there. We'll let him come and see you if he's good," Jeff went on breezily.

James breathed freer. "That might be the best way, if it wouldn't put you out, Jeff."

"I wouldn't want to be any trouble," the old man explained.

"And you won't be. I want you. James wants you, too, but he can't very well arrange it. I can. So that's settled."

In his rooms that evening Jeff very gently made clear to his uncle that Verden believed him to be his son.

"If you don't mind, sir, we'll let it go that way in public. We don't want to hurt the political chances of James just now. And there are other things, too. He'll tell you about them himself probably."

"That's all right. Just as you say. I don't want to disturb things."

"I adopted you as a father about a year ago without your permission. It won't do for you to give me away now," the nephew laughed.

Robert Farnum nodded without speaking. A lump choked his throat. He had found a son after all, but not the one he had come to meet.

William MacLeod Raine

Part 2

At the ensuing election the progressives swept the state in spite of all that the allied corporations could do. James was returned to the legislature with an increased majority and was elected speaker of the House according to program. His speech of acceptance was the most eloquent that had ever been heard in the assembly hall. The most radical of his party felt that the committees appointed by him were in their personnel a little too friendly to the vested interests of Verden, but the *World* took the high ground that he could render his party no higher service than absolute fair play, that the bills for the rights of the people ought to pass on their merits and not by tricky politics.

Never before had there been seen at the State House a lobby like the one that filled it now. The barrel was tapped so that the glint of gold flowed through the corridors, into committee rooms, and to out of the way corners where legislators fought for their honor against an attack that never ceased. Sometimes the corruption was bold. More often it was insidious. To see how one by one men hitherto honest surrendered to bribery was a sight pathetic and tragic.

The Farnum cousins were the centers around whom the reformers rallied. James directed their counsels in the House and Jeff pounded away in the *World* with vital trenchant editorials and news stories. Every day that paper carried to the farthest corner of the state bulletins of the battle. Farmers and miners and laboring men watched its roll of honor to see if the local representatives were standing firm. As the weeks passed the fight grew more bitter. Now and again men fell by the wayside disgraced. But the pressure from their constituents was so strong that Jeff believed his bill would go through.

His friends forced it through the committee and pushed it to a vote. House Bill 33, as the initiative and referendum amendment was called, passed the lower legislative body with a small majority. The pool rooms offered five to four that it would carry in the senate.

It was on the night of the twenty-first of December that the amendment passed the House. On the morning of the twenty-third the *Herald* sprang a front page sensation. It charged that the editor of the *World* had ruined a girl named Nellie Anderson at a house where he had boarded and that she had subsequently disappeared. It featured also a story of how he had been seen to enter his rooms at midnight with a woman of the street, who remained there until morning reveling with him. Attached to this were the affidavits of two detectives, a police officer, and the druggist who had furnished the liquor.

The story exploded like a bomb shell in the camp of the progressives. Rawson tried at once without success to get Jeff on the telephone. He was not at the office, nor had he reached his rooms at all after leaving the *World* building on the previous night. None of his friends had seen or heard of him.

The afternoon papers had a sensation of their own. Jefferson Farnum had left Verden secretly without leaving an address. Evidently he had been given a hint of the exposure that was to be made of his life and had decamped rather than face the charges.

Rumor had a hundred tales to tell. The waverers at the State House chose to believe that Jeff had sold them out and fled with his price. It was impossible to deny the stories of his immorality, since it happened that Sam Miller, the only man who knew the whole story, was far up in the mountains arranging for a shipment of Rocky Mountain sheep to the state museum. Farnum's friends could only affirm their faith in him or surrender. Some gave way, some stood firm. The lobbyists and the opposition went about with confident, "I-told-you-so" smiles writ large on their faces. Within a few days it became apparent that the reform bill would be defeated in the senate. Its fate had been so long tied up with the people's belief in Jeff that with his collapse the general opinion condemned it to defeat. Its friends hung back, unwilling to risk a vote as yet.

The situation called for a leader and developed one. James Farnum stepped into the breach and took command. In a ringing speech he called for a new alignment. He would yield to none in the devotion he had given to House Bill Number 33. But it needed no prophet to see that now this amendment was doomed. Better half a loaf than no bread. He was a practical man and wanted to see practical results. Rather than see the will of the people frustrated he felt that House Bill I7 should be passed. While not an ideal bill it was far better than none. The principle of direct legislation at least would be established.

H. B. No. I7 was brought hurriedly out of committee. It had been introduced as a substitute measure to defeat the real reform. According to its provision legislation could be initiated by the people, but to make it valid as a law the legislature had to approve any bill so passed. The people could advise. They could not compel.

The speech of the speaker of the House precipitated a bitter fight. The more eager friends of H. B. No. 33 accused him of treachery, but many felt that it was the best possible practical politics under the circumstances. For weeks the issue hung in doubt, but gradually James gathered adherents among both progressives and conservatives. It became almost a foregone conclusion that H. B. No. I7 would pass.

CHAPTER 15

"Old Capting Pink of the Peppermint,
Though kindly at heart and good,
Had a blunt, bluff way of a-gittin' 'is say
That we all of us understood.

When he brained a man with a pingle spike
Or plastered a seaman flat,
We should 'a' been blowed but we all of us knowed
That he didn't mean nothin' by that.

I was wonderful fond of old Capting Pink,
And Pink he was fond o' me,
As he frequently said when he battered me head
Or sousled me into the sea."

—Wallace Irwin

BULLY GREEN PRESERVES DISCIPLINE AND THE
REBEL LEARNS TO SAY "SIR"

Part 1

On the night of the twenty-second of December Jeff left the
World building and moved down Powers Avenue to the all

William MacLeod Raine

night restaurant he usually frequented. The man who was both cook and waiter remembered afterwards that Farnum called for coffee, sausage, and a waffle.

Before the editor left the waffle house it was the morning of the twenty-third. He had never felt less sleepy. Nor did a book and a pipe before his gas log seem quite what he wanted. The vagabond streak in him was awake, the same potent wanderlust that as a boy had driven him to the solitude of the forests and the hills. This morning it sent him questing down Powers Avenue to that lower town where the derelicts of the city floated without a rudder.

A cold damp mist had crept up from the water front and enwrapped the city so that its lights showed like blurred moons. Some instinct took him toward the wharves. He could hear the distant cough of a tug as it fussed across the bay, and as he drew near the big Transcontinental wharves of Joe Powers the black hulk of a Japanese liner rose black out of the gray fog shadow. But the freighters, the coasters, tramps that went hither and thither over the earth wherever fat cargoes lured them—they were either swallowed in the mist or shadowed to a ghost-like wraith of themselves so tenuous that all detail was lost in the haze.

Jeff leaned on a pile and let his imagination people the harbor with the wandering children of the earth who had been drawn from all its seafaring corners to this Mecca of trade. He knew that here were swarthy little Japanese with teas and silks, dusky Kanakas with copra, and Alaskan liners carrying gold and returning miners. There would be brigs from Buenos Ayres and schooners that had nosed into Robert Louis Stevenson's magic South Sea islands. Puffy London steamers, Nome and Skagway liners condemned long since on the Atlantic Coast, queer rigged hybrids from Rio and other South American ports, were gorging themselves with lumber or wheat or provisions according to their needs. Here truly lay before him the romance of the nations.

The sound of a stealthy footfall warned him of impending danger. He whirled, and faced three men who were advancing on him. A vague suspicion that had oppressed him more than once in the past week leaped to definite conviction in his brain. He was the victim of a plot to waylay—perhaps to murder him. One of these men was a huge Swede, another a swarthy Italian with rings in his ears. He had seen them before, lurking in the shadows of an alley outside the *World* building. Last night he had come out from the office with Jenkins, which no doubt had saved him for the time. This morning he had played into the hands of these men, had obligingly wandered down to the waterfront where they could so easily conceal murder in a tide running out fast.

Strangely enough he felt no fear; rather a fierce exultant drumming of the blood that braced him for the struggle. His eyes swept the wharf for a weapon and found none.

"What do you want?" he demanded sharply.

The man in command ignored his question. "Stand by and down him."

The Italian crouched and leaped. Jeff's fist caught him fairly between the eyes. He went down like a log, rolled over once and lay still. The others closed instantly with Farnum and the three swayed in a fierce silent struggle.

Both of his attackers were more powerful than Jeff, but he was far more active. The darkness, too, aided him and hampered them. The Swede he could have managed, for the fellow was awkward as a bear. But the leader stuck to him like a burr. They went down together over a cleat in the flooring, rolling over and over each other as they fought.

Somehow Jeff emerged out of the tangle. He dragged himself to his knees and hammered with his fist at an upturned face beside him. Battered, bleeding, and winded, he got to his feet and shook off the hands that reached for him. Dodging past, he lurched along the wharf like a drunken man. The Italian had gathered himself to his knees. When Jeff came opposite him he dived like a football tackle and threw his arms around the moving legs. The newspaper man crashed heavily down to unconsciousness.

When Farnum opened his eyes upon a world strangely hazy he found himself lying in a row boat, his head bolstered by a man's knees.

"Drink this, mate," ordered a voice that seemed very far away.

The neck of a bottle was thrust between his lips and tilted so that he could not escape drinking.

"That dope'll hold him for a while, Say, Johnny Dago, put your back into them oars," he heard indistinctly.

Faintly there came to him the slap of the waves against the side of the boat. These presently died rhythmically away.

It was daylight when he awakened again. His throbbing head slowly definitized the vile hole in which he lay as the forecastle of a ship. Gradually the facts sifted back to him. He recalled the fight on the wharf and the drink in the boat. In this last he suspected knockout drops. That he had been shanghaied was beyond suspicion.

Laboriously he sat up on the side of his bunk and in doing so became aware of a sailor asleep in the crib opposite. His stertorous breathing stirred a doubt in Jeff's mind. Perhaps the crimps had taken him too.

The ship was rolling a good deal, but by a succession of tacks Jeff staggered to the scuttle and climbed the hatchway to the deck. A wintry sun was shining, and for a few moments he stood blinking in the light.

She was a three-masted schooner and was plunging forward into the choppy seas outside the jaws of the harbor. He whiffed the salt tang of the air and tasted the flying spray. An ebb tide was lifting the vessel forward on a freshening wind, and trim as a greyhound she slipped through the cat's-paws.

A thickset, powerful figure paced to and fro on the quarter-deck, occasionally bellowing an order in a tremendous voice like the roar of a bull. He was getting canvas set for the fresh breeze of the open seas that was catching him astern, and the sailors were jumping to obey his orders. The pounding sails and the singing cordage, the rattling blocks and the whipping ropes, would have told Jeff they were scudding along fast, even if the heeling of the schooner and its swift forward leaps had not made it plain.

"By God, Jones, she's walking," he heard the captain boom across to the mate.

Just then a figure cut past him and made straight for the captain. Farnum recognized in it the sailor whom he had left asleep in the forecastle and even in that fleeting glance was aware of the man's livid fury. Up the steps he went like a wild beast.

"What kind of a boat is this?" he panted hoarsely.

William MacLeod Raine

The captain turned toward him. His eyes were shining wickedly, but his voice was ominously suave and honeyed. "This boat, son, is a threemasted schooner, name of *Nancy Hanks*, Master Joshua Green, bound for the Solomon Islands with a cargo of Oregon fir."

"I've been shanghaied. This is a nest of crimps," the man screamed.

Joshua Green's salient jaw came forward. "Been shanghaied, have you? And we're a nest of crimps, are we? Son, the less I hear of that line of talk the better. Put that in your pipe and smoke it."

The man turned loose a flood of profanity and swore he would rot in hell before he would touch a rope on that ship.

Out went Green's great gnarled fist. The seaman shot back from the quarterdeck and struck a pile of rope below. He was up again and down again almost quicker than it takes to tell. Three times he hit the planks before he lay still.

The captain stood over him, his eyes blazing. He looked the savage, barbaric slavedriver he was.

"Me, I'm Bully Green, and don't you forget it. Been shang-haied, have you? Not going to touch a rope? Then, by thunder, you white-livered beachcomber, a rope will touch you till you're flayed. Get this in your coconut. You'll walk chalk, you lazy son of a sea cook, or I'll haze you till you wish you'd never been born." He punctuated his remarks with vigorous kicks. "Bully Green runs this tub, strike me dead if he don't. Now you hump for'ard and clap a hand to them sheets. Walk, you shanghaied Dutchman!"

The sailor crawled away, completely cowed. For one day he

had had more than enough. The captain watched him for a moment, his great jaw thrust grimly out. Then, as on a pivot, he whirled toward Jeff.

"Come here, you! Step lively, Sport!"

Farnum wondered whether he was about to undergo an experience similar to that of the sailor. "Do you want to know what kind of a ship this is?"

"No, sir. I'm perfectly satisfied about that," smiled his victim.

"Got no opinions you want to hand out free, son?"

"Think I'll keep them bottled."

"Say 'sir,' Sport!"

"Yes, sir," answered Farnum, his quiet eyes steady and unafraid.

"When I give an order you expect to jump?"

"Jump isn't the word."

"Sir!" thundered Green, and "Sir" the newspaper man corrected himself.

"Got no story to spiel about being shanghaied, son?"

"Would it do any good, sir?"

"Not unless you're aching to get what that son of a Dutchman got. See here, sport! You walk the chalk line, and Bully Green and you'll get along fine. I'm a lamb, I am, when I'm not riled. But get gay—and you'll have a hectic time. I'll rough you till you're shark-food. Get that through your teeth?"

"Yes, sir."

"Now you trot down to the fo'c'sle and dive into them slops you find there. You got just three minutes to do the dress-suit act."

Jeff, as he passed below, could hear the great bull voice roaring orders to the men. "Set y'r topsails! Jam 'er down hard, Johnnie Dago! Stand by, you lubbers!... Now then, easy does it... easy!"

Within the allotted three minutes Farnum had climbed into the foul oilskin coat and tarry breeches he found below and was ready for orders.

"Clap on to that windlass, sport! No loafing here.... Hump y'rself. D'ye hear me? Hump?"

Jeff threw his one hundred and fifty pounds of bone and muscle against the crank of the windlass. Some men would have fought first as long as they could stand and see. Others would have begged, argued, or threatened. But Jeff had schooled himself to master impulses of rage. He knew when to fight and when to yield. Nor did he give way sullenly or passionately. It was an outrage—highhanded tyranny—but at the worst it was a magnificent adventure. As he flung his weight into the crank he smiled.

Part 2

Before the trade winds the *Nancy Hanks* foamed along day after day, all sails set, making excellent time. But for his anxiety as to the effect his disappearance would have upon the political situation, Jeff would have enjoyed immensely the wild rough life aboard the schooner. But he could not conceal from himself the interpretation of his absence the machine agents would scatter broadcast. He foresaw a reaction against his bill and its probable defeat.

The issue was on the knees of chance. The fact that could not be obliterated was that he had been wiped from the slate until after the legislature would adjourn. For every hour was carrying him farther from the scene of action.

His only hope was that the *Nancy Hanks* might put in at the Hawaiian Islands, from which place he might get a chance to write, or, better still, to cable the reason of his absence. Captain Green himself wiped out this expectation. He jocosely intimated to Farnum one afternoon that he had no intention of calling the Islands.

"When we get through this six months' cruise you'll be a first-rate sailorman, son, and you'll get a sailorman's wages," he added genially.

The shanghaied man met his eye squarely. "I think I could arrange to draw on Verden for a thousand dollars if you would drop me at the Islands."

"Not for twenty thousand. You're going to stay with us till we get to the Solomon Islands, and don't you forget it."

Bully Green had taken rather a fancy to this amiable young man who had taken so sensible a view of the little

William MacLeod Raine

misadventure that had befallen him, but of course business was business. He had been paid to keep him out of the way and he intended to fulfil the contract.

"Here I'm educatin' you, makin' an able-bodied seaman out of you, son. You had ought to be grateful," he grinned.

"Oh, I am," Jeff agreed with a twinkle.

But Captain Green had reckoned without the weather. The *Nancy Hanks* drifted into three days of calm and sultry heat. At the end of the third day she began to rock gently beneath a murky sky.

"Dirty weather," predicted the mate, the same who had assisted at the shanghaing. "When you see a satin sea turn indigo and that peculiar shade in the sky you want to look out for squalls," he explained to Jeff.

It came on them in a rush. The sun went out of a black sky like a blown candle and the sea began to whip itself to a froth. The wind quickened, boomed to a roar, and sent the schooner heeling to a squall across the leaden waters. The open sea closed in on them. Before they could get in sail and make secure the sheets ripped with a scream, braces parted and the topmasts snapped off. The *Nancy* went pitching forward into the yawning deeps with drunken plunges from which it seemed she would never emerge. Great combing seas toppled down and pounded the decks, while the sailors clung to stays or whatever would give them a hold.

The squall lasted scarce an hour, but it left the schooner dismantled. Her sheets were in ribbons, her topmasts and bowsprit gone. There was nothing for it but a crippled beat toward the Islands.

Four days later she made an offing in the harbor at Honolulu just as a liner was nosing her way out.

Bully Green ranged up beside Farnum and cast a speculative eye on him.

"Sport, I had ought to iron you and keep you in the fo'c'sle until we leave here. It's the only square thing to do."

Jeff's gaze was on the advancing steamer. She was scarce two hundred yards away now and he could plainly read the name painted on her side. She was the *Bellingham* of Verden.

"I don't see the necessity, sir," he answered.

"I reckon you do, son. Samuel Green stands by his word to a finish. Now I've promised to keep you safe, and you can bet your last dollar I'm a-going to do it."

His prisoner turned from the rail against which he was leaning to the captain. Pinpoints of light were gleaming in the big eyes.

"How much safer do you want me than this?"

Green expectorated at a chip in the water and shifted his quid. "You've got brains, son. No telling what you might try to do. But see here. You're no drunken beachcomber. I know a gentleman when I see one. Gimme your word you'll not try to skip out or send a message back to the States and I'll go easy on you. I'm so dashed kindhearted, I am, that—"

Jeff leaped to the rail, stood poised an instant, and dived into the blue Pacific.

"Well, I'll be " Bully Green interrupted himself to roar an order to lower a boat.

CHAPTER 16

A young man left his father's house to see the world. Everywhere he found busy human beings. Cities were rising toward the skies, seas and plains were being lined with traffic, school, mill and office hummed with life. He wondered why men were so busy and what they were trying to do.

He went to a railroad director and asked: "Why are you building railroads?" "For profits," was the answer. But a laborer beckoned him aside and whispered: "No—we are making the *World* one neighborhood. East is now next door to West, and all peoples dwell in one continuing city."

The young man went to the boss of a labor union. "Why," he asked, "do you spend your days breeding discontent and leading strikes?" "Why?" repeated the leader fiercely, "that the workers receive more pay for shorter hours." "No," whispered a laborer, "we are teaching the *World* the sacred value of human beings. We are learning how to be brotherly —how to stand up for each other.

—James Oppenheim

William MacLeod Raine

UNDER STRANGE CIRCUMSTANCES THE REBEL
MAKES HIS BOW TO POLITE SOCIETY. TAKING
AN APPLE AS A TEXT, HE PREACHES ON
THE RISE OF ADAM

Part 1

"Man overboard!"

Somebody on the liner sang it out. Instantly there was a rush
of passengers to the side. From the schooner a boat was
being lowered and manned.

"I see him. He's swimming this way. I believe he's trying to
escape," one slender young woman cried.

"Nonsense, Alice! He fell overboard and he's probably so
frightened he doesn't know which way he is swimming."
This suggestion was from the beautiful blonde with bronze
hair who stood beside her under a tan parasol held by a
fresh-faced globetrotter.

"Don't you believe it, Val. Look how he's cutting through the
water. He's trying to reach us. Oh, I hope they won't get him.
Somebody get a rope to throw out."

"By Jove, you're right, Miss Alice," cried the Englishman.
"It's a race, and it's going to be a near thing." He disappeared
and was presently back with a rope.

"Come on! Come on!" screamed the passengers to the
swimmer.

"He's ripping strong with that overhead stroke. Ye gods, it's
close!" exclaimed the Britisher.

It was. The swimmer reached the side of the ship not four yards in front of the pursuing boat. He caught at the trailing rope and began to clamber up hand over hand, while the Englishman, a man standing near, and Alice Frome dragged him up.

The mate of the Nancy Hanks, standing up in the boat, caught at his foot and pulled. The man's hold loosened on the rope. He slid down a foot, steadied himself. Suddenly the left leg shot out and caught the grinning mate in the mouth. He went over backward into the bottom of the boat. Before he could extricate himself from the tangle his fall had precipitated, the dripping figure of the swimmer stood safely on the deck of the *Bellingham.*

In his wet foul slops the man was a sight to draw stares. The cabin passengers moved back to give him a wide circle, as men do with a wet retriever.

"What does this mean, my man?" demanded the captain of the *Bellingham,* pushing forward. He was a big red-faced figure with a heavy roll of fat over his collar.

"I have been shanghaied, sir. From Verden. I'm the editor of the *World* of that city."

"That's a lie," proclaimed the mate of the *Nancy Hanks* , who by this time had reached the deck. "He's a nutty deckswabber we picked up at 'Frisco."

"Why, it's Mr. Farnum," cried a fresh young voice from the circle.

The rescued man turned. His eyes joined those of a slim golden girl and he was struck dumb.

William MacLeod Raine

"You know this man, Miss Frome?" the captain asked.

"I know him by sight." She stepped to the front. "There can't be any doubt about it. He's Mr. Farnum of Verden, the editor of the *World.*"

"You're quite sure?"

"Quite sure, Captain Barclay. My cousin knows him, too."

The captain turned to Mrs. Van Tyle. She nodded languidly.

Barclay swung back to the mate of the *Nancy Hanks.* "I know your kind, my man, and I can tell you that I think the penitentiary would be the proper place for you and your captain, with my compliments to him."

"Better come and pay 'em yourself, sir," sneered the mate.

"Get off my deck, you dirty crimp," roared the captain. "Slide now, or I'll have you thrown off."

Mr. Jones made a hurried departure. Once in the boat, he shook his fist at Barclay and cursed him fluently.

The captain turned away promptly. "Mr. Farwell, if you'll step this way the steward will outfit you with some clothes. If they don't fit they'll do better than those togs you're wearing."

The English youth came forward with a suggestion. "Really, I think I can do better than that for Mr. Far—" He hesitated for the name.

"Farnum," supplied the owner of it.

"Ah! You're about my size, Mr. Farnum. If you don't mind, you know, you're quite welcome to anything I have."

"Thank you very much."

"Very well. Mr. Farwell—Farnum, I mean—shake hands with Lieutenant Beauchamp," and with the sense of duty done the worthy captain dismissed the new arrival from his mind.

Jeff bowed to Miss Frome and followed his broad-shouldered guide to a cabin. He was conscious of an odd elation that had not entirely to do with a brave adventure happily ended. The impelling cause of it was rather the hope of a braver adventure happily begun.

Part 2

"By Jove, I envy you, Mr. Farnum. Didn't know people bucked into adventures like that these tame days. Think of actually being shanghaied. It's like a novel. My word, the ladies will make a lion of you!"

The Englishman was dragging a steamer trunk from under his bed. It needed no second glance at his frank boyish face to divine him a friend worth having. Fresh-colored and blue-eyed, he looked very much the country gentleman Jeff had read about but never seen. It was perhaps by the gift of race that he carried himself with distinction, though the flat straight back and the good shoulders of the cricketer contri-buted somewhat, too. Jeff sized him up as a resolute, clean-cut fellow, happily endowed with many gifts of fortune to make him the likable chap he was.

Beauchamp threw out some clothes from a steamer trunk and left the rescued man alone to dress. Ten minutes later he returned.

"Expect you'd like an interview with the barber. I'll take you round. By the way, you'll let me be your banker till you reach Verden?"

"Thank you. Since I must."

From the barber shop the Englishman took him to the dining saloon. "Awfully sorry you can't sit at our table, Mr. Farnum. It's full up. You're to be at the purser's."

Jeff let a smile escape into his eyes. "Suits me. I've been at the bos'n's for several weeks."

"Beastly outrage. We'll want to hear all about it. Miss

Frome's tremendously excited. Odd you and she hadn't met before. Didn't know Verden was such a big town."

"I'm not a society man," explained Jeff. "And it happens I've been fighting her father politically for years. Miss Frome and Mrs. Van Tyle are about the last people I would be likely to meet."

From his seat Jeff could see the cousins at the other end of the room. They were seated near the head of the captain's table, and that officer was paying particular attention to them, perhaps because the *Bellingham* happened to be one of a line of boats owned by Joe Powers, perhaps because both of them were very attractive young women. They were types entirely outside Farnum's very limited experience. The indolence, the sheathed perfection, the soft sensuous allure of the young widow seemed to Jeff a product largely of her father's wealth. But the charm of her cousin, with its sweet and mocking smile, its note of youthful austerity, was born of the fine and gallant spirit in her.

Beauchamp sat beside Miss Frome and the editor observed that they were having a delightful time. He wondered what they could be talking about. What did a man say to bring such a glow and sparkle of life into a girl's face? It came to him with a wistful regret for his stolen youth that never yet had he sat beside a young woman at dinner and entertained her in the gay adequate manner of Lieutenant Beauchamp. James could do it, had done it a hundred times. But he had been sold too long to an urgent world of battle ever to know such delights.

Part 3

After dinner Jeff lost no time in waiting upon Miss Frome to thank her for her assistance. It was already dark. When he found her it was not in one of the saloons, but on deck. She was leaning against the deck railing in animated talk with Beauchamp, the while Mrs. Van Tyle listened lazily from a deck chair.

"I like the way that red head of his came bobbing through the water," Beauchamp was saying. "Looks to me as if he would take a lot of beating. He's no quitter. Since I haven't the pleasure of knowing Mr. Powers or Senator Frome, I think I'll back Farnum to win."

"It's very plain you don't know Joe Powers. He always wins," contributed his daughter blandly.

"But Mr. Farnum is a remarkable man just the same," Alice added. Then, with a little cry to cover her flushed embarrassment: "Here he is. We do hope you're a little deaf, Mr. Farnum. We've been talking about you."

"You may say anything you like about me, Miss Frome, except that I'm not grateful for the lift aboard you gave me this afternoon," Jeff answered.

He found himself presently giving the story of his adventure. He did not look at Alice, but he told the tale to her alone and was aware of the eagerness with which she listened.

"But why should they want to kidnap you? I don't see any reason for it," Alice protested.

A shadowy smile lay in the eyes of Mrs. Van Tyle. "Mr. Farnum is in politics, my dear."

A fat pork packer from Chicago joined the group. "I've been thinking about the sharks, Mr. Farnum. You played in great luck to escape them."

"Sharks!" Jeff heard the young woman beside him give a gasp. In the moonlight her face showed white.

"These waters are fairly infested with them," the Chicagoan explained. "We saw two this morning in the harbor. It was when the stewards threw out the scraps. They turned over on their—"

"Don't!" cried Alice Frome sharply.

The petrified horror on the vivid mobile face remained long as a sweet memory to Jeff. It had been for him that she had known the swift heart clutch of terror.

William MacLeod Raine

Part 4

Farnum, pacing the deck as he munched at an apple, heard himself hailed from the bridge above. He looked up, to see Alice Frome, caught gloriously in the wind like a winged Victory. Her hair was parted in the middle with a touch of Greek simplicity and fell in wavy ripples over her temples beneath the jaunty cap. She put her arms on the railing and leaned forward, her chin tilted to an oddly taking boyish piquancy.

"I say, give a fellow a bite."

By no catalogue of summarized details could this young woman have laid claim to beauty, but in the flashing play of her expression, the exquisite golden coloring, one could not evade the charm of a certain warm witchery, of the passionate beat of innocent life. The wonder of her lay in the sparkle of her inner self. Every gleam of the deep true eyes, every impulsive motion of the slight supple body, expressed some phase of her infinite variety. Her flying moods swept her from demure to daring, from warm to cool. And for all her sweet derision her friends knew a heart full of pure, brave enthusiasms that would endure.

"I don't believe in indiscriminate charity," Jeff explained, and he took another bite.

"Have you no sympathy for the deserving poor?" she pleaded. "Besides, since you're a socialist, it isn't your apple any more than it is mine. Bring my half up to me, sir."

"Your half is the half I've already eaten. And if you knew as much as you pretend to about socialism you'd know it isn't yours until you've earned it."

Her eyes danced. He noticed that beneath each of them was a sprinkle of tiny powdered freckles. "But haven't I earned it? Didn't I blister my hands pulling you aboard?"

He promptly shifted ground. "We're living under the capitalistic system. You earn it and I eat it," he argued. "The rest of this apple is my reward for having appropriated what didn't belong to me."

"But that's not fair. It's no better than stealing."

"Sh—h! It's high finance. Don't use that other word," he whispered. "And what's fair hasn't a thing to do with it. It's my apple because I've got it."

"But—"

He waved her protest aside blandly. "Now try to be content with the lot a wise Providence has awarded you. I eat the apple. You see me eat it.

That's the usual division of profits. Don't be an agitator, or an anarchist."

"Don't I get even the core?" she begged.

"I'd like to give it to you, but it wouldn't be best. You see I don't want to make you discontented with your position in life." He flung what was left of the apple into the sea and came up the steps to join her.

Laughter was in the eyes of both, but it died out of hers first.

"Mr. Farnum, is it really as bad as that?" Before he could find an answer she spoke again. "I've wanted for a long time to talk with some one who didn't look at things as we do. I mean as my father does and my uncle does and most of my friends. Tell me what you think of it—you and your friends."

"That's a large order, Miss Frome. I hardly know where to begin."

"Wait! Here comes Lieutenant Beauchamp to take me away. I promised to play ring toss with him, but I don't want to go now." She led a swift retreat to a spot on the upper deck shielded from the wind and warmed by the two huge smokestacks. Dropping breathless into a chair, she invited him with a gesture to take another. Little imps of mischief flashed out at him from her eyes. In the adventure of the escape she had made him partner. A rush of warm blood danced through his veins.

"Now, sir, we're safe. Begin the propaganda. Isn't that the word you use? Tell me all about everything. You're the first real live socialist I ever caught, and I mean to make the most of you."

"But I'm unfortunately not exactly a socialist."

"An anarchist will do just as well."

"Nor an anarchist. Sorry."

"Oh, well, you're something that's dreadful. You haven't the proper bump of respect for father and for Uncle Joe. Now why haven't you?"

And before he knew it this young woman had drawn from him glimpses of what life meant to him. He talked to her of the pressure of the struggle for existence, of the poverty that lies like a blight over whole sections of cities, spreading disease and cruelty and disorder, crushing the souls of its victims, poisoning their hearts and bodies. He showed her a world at odds and ends, in which it was accepted as the natural thing that some should starve while others were waited upon by servants.

He made her see how the tendency of environment is to reduce all things to a question of selfinterest, and how the great triumphant fact of life is that love and kindness persist. Her interest was insatiable. She poured questions upon him, made him tell her stories of the things he had seen in that strange underworld that was farther from her than Asia. So she learned of Oscar Marchant, coughing all day over the shoes he half-soled and going out at night to give his waning life to the service of those who needed him. He told her— without giving names—the story of Sam Miller and his wife, of shop girls forced by grinding poverty to that easier way which leads to death, of little children driven by want into factories which crushed the youth out of them.

Her eyes with the star flash in them never left his face. She was absorbed, filled with a strange emotion that made her lashes moist. She saw not only the tragedy and waste of life, but a glorious glimpse of the way out. This man and his friends set the common good above their private gain. For them a new heart was being born into the world. They were no longer consumed with blind greed, with love of their petty selves. They were no longer full of cowardice and distrust and enmity. Life was a thing beautiful to them. It was flushed with the color of hope, of fine enthusiasms. They might suffer. They might be defeated. But nothing could extinguish the joy in their souls. They walked like gods, immortals, these brothers to the spent and the maimed. For they had found spiritual values in it that made any material profit of small importance. Alice got a vision of the great truth that is back of all true reforms, all improvement, all progress.

"Love," she said almost in a whisper, "is forgetting self."

Jeff lost his stride and pulled up. He thought he could not have heard aright. "I beg your pardon?"

"Nothing. I was just thinking out loud. Go on please."

But she had broken the thread of his talk. He attempted to take it up again, but he was still trying for a lead when Alice saw Mrs. Van Tyle and Beauchamp coming toward them.

She rose. Her eyes were the brightest Jeff had ever seen. They were filled with an ardent tenderness. It was as if she were wrapped in a spiritual exaltation.

"Thank you. Thank you. I can't tell you what you've done for me."

She turned and walked quickly away. To be dragged back to the commonplace at once was more than she could bear. First she must get alone with herself, must take stock of this new emotion that ran like wine through her blood. A pulse throbbed in her throat, for she was in a passionate glow of altruism.

"I'm glad of life—glad of it—glad of it!" she murmured through the veil she had lowered to screen her face from observation.

It had come to her as a revelation straight from Heaven that there can be no salvation without service. And the motive back of service must be love. Love! That was what Jesus had come to teach the world, and all these years it had warped and mystified his message.

She felt that life could never again be gray or colorless. For there was work waiting that she could do, service that she could give. And surely there could be no greater happiness than to find her work and do it gladly.

CHAPTER 17

All sorts of absurd assumptions pass current as fixed and non-debatable standards. We might be free, and we tie ourselves to the slavery of rutted convention. Afraid of ideas, we come to no definite philosophy of life that is the result of clear and pellucid thinking.

We must get rid of our bonds, but only in order to take on new ones. For our convictions will shackle us. The difference is that then we shall be servants of Truth and not of dead Tradition.

—From the Note Book of a Dreamer

THE CHAPERONE EXPLAINS THAT THE REBEL IS IMPOSSIBLE AND THE CHAPERONED BEGS LEAVE TO DIFFER

Part 1

"And why mustn't I?" Alice demanded vigorously.

Her cousin regarded her with indolent amusement. "My dear, you are positively the most energetic person I know. It is refreshing to see with what interest you enter into a discussion."

Miss Frome, very erect and ready for argument, watched her steadily from the piano stool of their joint sitting room. "Well?"

"I didn't say you mustn't, my dear. I know better than to deal in imperatives with Miss Alice. What I did was mildly to suggest that you are going rather far. It's all very well to be civil, but—" Mrs. Van Tyle shrugged her shoulders and let it go at that. She was leaning back in an easychair and across its arm her wrist hung. Between the fingers, polished like old ivory to the tapering pink nails, was a lighted cigarette.

"Why shouldn't I be—pleasant to him? I like him." Her color deepened, but the eyes of the girl did not give way. There was in them a little flare of defiance.

"Be pleasant to him if you like, and if it amuses you. But—" Again Valencia stopped, but after a puff or two at her cigarette she added presently: "Don't get too interested in him."

"I'm not likely to," Alice returned with a touch of scorn. "Can't I like a man and admire him without wanting to marry him? I think that's a hateful way to look at it."

"It's your interpretation, not mine," Mrs. Van Tyle answered with perfect good humor. "Of course you couldn't want to marry him under any circumstances. His station in life—his anarchistic ideas—his reputation as a confirmed libertine— all of them make the thought of such a thing impossible."

Miss Frome's mind seized on only one of the charges. "I don't believe it. I don't believe a word of it. Anybody can throw mud—and some of it is bound to stick. He's a good man. You can see that in his face."

"You can perhaps. I can't." Valencia studied her beneath a droop of eyelids behind which she was very alert. "Those things aren't said about a man unless they are true. Moreover, it happens we don't have to depend on hearsay."

"What do you mean?"

"Do you remember that night we saw the Russian dancers?"

"Yes."

"On the way home our car passed him. He was helping a woman out of a cab in front of the building where he rooms. She was intoxicated, and—his arm was round her waist."

"I don't believe it. It was somebody else," the young woman flamed.

"His cousin recognized him. So did I."

"There must be some explanation. I'll ask him."

"Ask him!" Valencia's level eyebrows lifted "Really, I don't think that will do. Better quietly eliminate him."

"You mean treat him as if he were guilty when, I am sure he is not."

Mrs. Van Tyle's little laugh rippled out. "You're quite dramatic about it, my dear. The man's of no importance. He's a *poseur*, a demagogue, and one with a vicious streak in him. I understand, of course, that you're interested only because he different from the other men you know. That merely a part of his pose."

"I'm sure it isn't."

"You're romantic, my dear. I'll admit his arrival on this ship was dramatic. No doubt you're imagining him a knight going back to save gallantly a day that is lost. He's only a politician, and so far as I can understand they are almost all a bad lot."

"Including Father and Uncle Joe and Ned Merrill?" Alice asked acidly.

"They are not politicians, but business men. They are in politics merely to protect their interests. But I didn't intend to start a discussion about Mr. Farnum. I ask you to remember that as your chaperone I'm here to represent your father. Would he wish you to be friendly with this man?"

Alice was silent. What her father would think was not a matter of doubt.

"The man's impossible," Mrs. Van Tyle went on pleasantly. "And it's just as well to be careful. Not that I'm very prudish myself. But if you're going to marry Ned Merrill—"

She had struck the wrong note. Like a flash Alice answered.

"I'm not. That's definitely decided."

"Really! I thought it was rather arranged," Valencia smiled blandly.

It was all very well for Alice to protest, but in the end she would be a good girl and do as she was told. Not that her cousin objected to her having a little fling before the fatal day. But why couldn't the girl do her flirting with Beauchamp instead of with this wild socialist?

Valencia reflected that at any rate she had done her duty.

Part 2

Jeff was tramping the deck, his hands in his coat pockets, waiting for the trumpeter to fling out the two bars of music that would summon him to breakfast. He walked vigorously? drawing in deep breaths of the salt sea air. His thoughts were of Alice Frome. He was a lover, and in his imagination she embodied all things beautiful. Her charm flowed through him, pierced him with delight. When he heard music his mind flew to her. It voiced the rhythm of her motions and the sound of her warm laughter. The sunshine but reflected the golden gleams of light in her wavy hair.

As he swung round the smoking saloon Jeff came face to face with Alice. He turned and caught step with her. The coat she wore came to her ankles, but it could not conceal her light, strong tread nor the long lines of the figure that gave her the grace of a captured wood nymph.

"Only five hundred miles from Verden. By night we ought to be in wireless communication," he suggested.

Her glance flashed at him. "You'll be glad to get home."

"I will and I won't. There's work for me to do there. But it's the first real vacation I ever had in my life that lasted over a week. You can't think how I've enjoyed it."

"So have I. More than anything I can remember." They stopped to look at a steamer which lay low on the distant horizon line. After they had fallen into step again she continued at the point where they had been interrupted: "And after we reach home? Are you going to come and see me? Are you going to let me meet your friends, those dear people who are giving themselves to make life less hideous and harsh for the weak? Shall I meet Mr. Mifflin... and Mr.

Miller and your little Socialist poet? Or are you going to desert me?"

He smiled a little at her way of putting it, but he was troubled none the less. "Are you sure that your way is our way? One can give service on the Hill just as much as down in the bottoms. There's no moral grandeur in rags or in dirt. Isn't your place with your friends?"

"Haven't I a right to take hold of life for myself at first hand? Haven't I a right to know the truth? What have I done that I should be walled off from all these people who earn the bread I eat?"

"But your friends... your father..."

Her ironic smile derided him. "So after all you haven't the courage of your convictions. Because I'm Peter C. Frome's daughter I'm not to have the right to live."

"No, it's your right to take hold of life with both hands. But surely you must live it among your own people."

"I've got to learn how to live it first, haven't I?

Most of my friends are not even aware there a problem of poverty. They thrust the thought of it from them. Our wealthy class has no social consciousness. Take my father. He thinks the submerged are lost because they are thriftless and that all would be right if they wouldn't drink. To him they are just a waste product of civilization.

"But can you study the life of the people without growing discontented with the life you must lead?"

"There is a divine discontent, you know. I've got to see

things for myself. Why should all my opinions, my faith, be given to me ready-made. Why must I live by a formula I have never examined? If it isn't true I want to know it. And if it is true I want to know it." She had been looking straight before them toward the rising sun but now her gaze swept round on him. "Don't blame yourself for giving me new thoughts. I suppose all new ideas are likely to make trouble. But I've been working in this direction for years. Ever since I've been a little girl my heresies have puzzled my father. Meeting you has shown me a short cut. That's all."

Something she had said recalled to him a fugitive memory.

"Do you know, I think I saw you once when you were a little bit of a thing?"

"Where?"

"On the doorstep of your old place. I was rather busy at the time fighting Edward Merrill."

She stopped, looking at him in surprise. "Were you that boy?"

"I was that boy."

"You fought him to help a little ragged girl. She was a foreigner."

"I've forgotten why I fought him. The reason I remember the occasion is that I met then for the first time two of my friends."

She claimed a place immediately. "Who was the other one?"

"Captain Chunn."

Presently she bubbled into a little laugh. "How did the fight come out? My nurse dragged me into the house."

"Don't remember. I know the school principal licked me next day. I had been playing hookey."

They made another turn of the deck before she spoke again.

"So we're old acquaintances, and I didn't know it. That was nearly eighteen years ago. Isn't it strange that after so long we should meet again only last week?"

Jeff felt the blood creep into his face. "We met once before, Miss Frome."

"Oh, on the street. I meant to speak."

"So did I."

"When?"

With his eyes meeting hers steadily Jeff told her of the time she had found him in the bushes and mistaken him for a sick man. He could see that he had struck her dumb. She looked at him and looked away again.

"Why do you tell me this?" she asked at last in a low voice.

"It's only fair you should know the truth about me."

They tramped the circuit once more. Neither of them spoke. The trumpeter's bugle call to breakfast rang out.

At the bow she stopped and looked down at the waters they were furrowing. It was a long time before she raised her head and met his eyes. The color had whipped into her cheeks, but she put her question steadily.

"Are you telling me. . . that I must lose my friend?"

"Isn't that for you to say?"

"I don't know." She faltered for words, but not the least in her intention. "Are you—what I have always heard you are?"

"Can you be a little more definite?" he asked gently.

"Well—dissipated! You're not that?"

"No. I've trodden down the appetite. I'm a total abstainer."

"And you're not. . . those worse things that the papers say?"

"No."

"I knew it." Triumph rang in her voice. She breathed a generous trust. To know him for a true man it was necessary only to look into his fearless eyes set deep in the thin tanned face. It was impossible for anything unclean to survive with his humorous humility and his pervading sympathy and his love of truth. "I didn't care what they said. I knew it all the time."

Her sweet faith was a thing to see with emotion. He felt tears scorch the back of his eyes.

"The thing you know is bad enough."

"Oh, that! That is nothing… now. It doesn't matter."

Lieutenant Beauchamp emerged from a saloon and bore down upon them.

"Mrs. Van Tyle has sent me to bring you to breakfast, Miss Frome. Mornin', Mr. Farnum."

"And I'm ready for it, We've been round the deck ever so many times. Haven't we, Mr. Farnum?"

She nodded lightly to Jeff and walked away with the Englishman. The sunshine of her warm vitality was like quicksilver in Farnum's veins. What a gallant spirit, at once delicate and daring, dwelt in that vivid slender form! A snatch of Chesterton came to his mind:

> Her face was like an open word
> When brave men speak and choose,
> The very colors of her coat
> Were better than good news.
>
> "It is the hour of man: new purposes,
> Broad shouldered, press against the world's slow gate;
> And voices from the vast eternities
> Publish the soul's austere apostolate.
>
> Man bursts the chains that his own hands have made;
> Hurls down the blind, fierce gods that in blind years
> He fashioned, and a power upon them laid
> To bruise his heart and shake his soul with fears."

—Edwin Markham.

CHAPTER 18

THE PILLARS OF SOCIETY ARE GIVEN AN ILLUSTRATION OF A ROORBACK

Part 1

Rawson sat in the rotunda of the Pacific Hotel in desultory conversation with Captain Chunn, Hardy and Rogers. He brought his clenched hand down on the padded leather arm of the big chair.

"They'll jam it through to-morrow. That's what they'll do. James K. Farnum's been playing mighty pretty politics and he has got the votes to deliver the goods."

Hardy nodded as he knocked the ash from his cigar. "Now that it's all over we can see James K.'s trail easily enough. He meant to defeat the initiative and referendum amendment, and he meant to do it without losing his popularity. He's done it too. Jeff's disappearance made it certain our bill wouldn't go through. James jumps in with a hurrah and passes one that isn't worth the powder to blow it up. But he's going to claim it as a great victory for the people—and if I know that young man he'll get away with his bluff. Yet it's certain as taxes that he's been working for Joe Powers all the time."

"I wouldn't put it past him to have engineered some deal to get rid of his cousin," Chunn suggested.

Rawson shook his head. "No. Not respectable enough for James. And he's not fool enough to run his head into a trap. But I'd bet my head Big Tim gave him a tip it was to be pulled off. J. K. had to know. Otherwise he wouldn't have been in a position to play the game for them. But he didn't know any details—just a suggestion. Enough to wise him without making him responsible."

"And the play he's been making in the papers. Offering a reward for information about Jeff, insisting publicly that he has absolute confidence in his cousin's integrity while he shakes his head in private. If you want my opinion, that young man is a whited sepulchre. I never did believe in him."

Rogers turned to Captain Chunn with an incredulous smile. "But you still believe in Jeff. Frankly, it looks to me like a double sell out."

The old Confederate's eyes gleamed. "Sir, I've known that boy since he was a little tad. He's never told me a lie. He's square as they make them."

"I used to believe in his cousin James, too," Rogers commented.

"Oh, James! He's another proposition." Rawson's voice was sour with disgust. "He just naturally looked to see where his bread was buttered. He's as selfish as the devil for all that suave, cordial way of his. Right from the first his idea has been to make a big personal hit. And he figured out he could do it easier with Joe Powers back of him than against him. James K. is the smoothest fraud on the Pacific Coast. But Jeff—why, every hair of his head is straight. He's one out of a million, believe me."

"You've said it," Chunn agreed.

Rogers smiled across at them. "He's left a lot of good friends behind him anyhow. But it's strange he could drop off the earth without a soul knowing about it."

"The men who murdered him know about it," Rawson answered significantly.

Captain Chunn shook his head. "No, that boy will turn up yet."

"But not in time to save us. We're licked. There's not one chance in a million for us. That's the discouraging feature of it, to be sold out after we had won our fight."

Rawson agreed with Hardy. "Yes, we're licked. Even if Jeff were to show up, with all these stories against him, we wouldn't be able to stem the tide now."

"Mister Raw-w-son—Mister Raw-w-son." The singsong voice of a bellhop echoed through the rotunda.

Captain Chunn's walking stick flagged the lad and brought him sliding across the polished floor.

"Telegram for Mr. Rawson."

The big politician ripped it open and ran his eyes rapidly over the yellow slip. From his lips burst a sudden oath of surprise.

"By Jupiter, the miracle's happened. Jeff is alive and on his way here. He's sent me a wireless from out at sea somewhere."

"What!" Captain Chunn let out a whoop of joy.

"Listen here." Rawson read aloud his message. "'Shanghaied on schooner *Nancy Hanks*. Escaped at Honolulu. Back in Verden to-night. Keep up the fight.'"

"Didn't I say Jeff was alive? Didn't I say he would come back and beat those robbers yet?" the owner of the *World* demanded.

"Don't get excited. It may be a fake." This from Hardy, who was almost as much moved himself.

"Fake nothing! We'll go down to the telegraph office and make sure it's 0. K. Won't this make a bully story for the *World* 'Shanghaied' in big letters across the top, and underneath a red hot roast of the old city hall gang's methods of trying to defeat the will of the people." Rawson laughed aloud as his imagination pictured the story.

The old soldier's eyes gleamed. "I'll run twice as many copies as usual. We'll plaster the state with them, calling for mass meetings everywhere to insist on the legislature passing our bill."

"Go easy, gentlemen," advised Rogers. "If it's true we hold a trump card, but we want to play it mighty carefully so as to make it carry as much dynamite as possible."

The company could give no information more definite than that the message had come from the *Bellingham,* which was still a couple of hundred miles out at sea.

In view of the value of the news from a strategic slant his friends succeeded in keeping the lid on Captain Chunn's enthusiasm until the party was safe aboard a fast yacht steaming out of the harbor to meet the *Bellingham.* The old Confederate's first impulse had been to run an extra immediately, but he was argued out of it.

"We don't want to go off half cocked. We've got a beautiful comeback if we play it right. That is, if Jeff's got any proof. But we better wait and let Jeff run the newspaper end of it, Captain."

This was Hardy's view, and it was indorsed by the others.

"Another thing. This story has got to come just like an explosion on James K. Farnum's supporters. We've got to sweep them right back to our bill. Now if we break the force of it by giving them warning that swarm of lobbyists will get busy and stay busy all night," Rawson added.

Jim Dunn, the star reporter of the *World,* was hurriedly summoned by telephone. Chunn explained to the city editor that Dunn and the staff photographer were needed to cover a big story, but of what the story was no mention was made to the office. As soon as Dunn and Quillen reached the wharf the *Fly by Night* shot out of the dock.

Part 2

In the wintry afternoon sunlight Beauchamp and Alice were playing a match of shuffleboard against Jeff and the daughter of a Honolulu missionary. The game had reached an exciting and critical stage when they noticed that the ship was no longer quivering from the throb of the engines.

"A steam yacht, probably from Verden," the ship purser remarked to the first mate as they passed.

The players gave up their game to watch the boat that was being lowered from the deck of a yacht close at hand. Into it stepped five men in addition to the crew. Presently Jeff, leaning against the rail, borrowed the glasses of a man near. After Alice had looked she handed them to Farnum.

He gave a little exclamation of surprise.

"I beg your pardon?" the girl beside him murmured.

"They are my friends, Miss Frome. Come to meet me, I expect. The little man in gray with one arm is Captain Chunn."

She was all excitement at once. "Then they must have received your message?"

"Probably."

Jeff was the first man to meet Captain Chunn as he walked up the steps. The gray little man gave a whoop of joy.

"David!"

Their hands gripped.

Rawson fell on Farnum from behind and pounded him jubilantly. Instantly the editor was the center of a group of eager, urgent wellwishers.

Alice explained to Captain Barclay what it was all about and stood back smiling while questions and answers flew back and forth.

"What about our bill?" Jeff inquired as soon as the first hubbub had quieted.

"Dead as a door nail. Your cousin has substituted H. B. I7. They will pass it to-morrow or the next day."

A swift sickness ran through Farnum. "James gone back on us?"

"That's what. He's double-crossed us." Rawson snapped the words out bitterly.

"Why—why—surely not James." Jeff's mind groped for some possible explanation.

"Says our bill was lost anyhow and it was a question of getting through Garman's bill or none."

"But Garman's bill was framed by Ned Merrill. It doesn't give us anything."

Rawson nodded grimly. "That's the idea. We're to get nothing, but it's to be wrapped up like a Christmas present so as to fool us."

"And isn't there any chance at all for our bill?"

"Just this one chance." Rawson leaned forward and spoke in

a low voice, driving his hand down on the deck railing. "That you've got a charge of dynamite up your sleeve to throw into their camp. If you can't stampede them we're down and out."

Jeff and his allies presently moved away together to hold a conference of ways and means. The boat crew pulled back to the yacht. The engines began to throb once more. The *Bellingham* gathered momentum and was soon plunging forward at full speed.

William MacLeod Raine

Part 3

With a queer little surge of pride in him Alice watched Jeff and his friends move away. They depended on him. Unless he could save it their fight was lost. To her he was a prophet of the better civilization that would some day rise on the ruins of an Individualism grown topheavy. But he was neither a dreamer nor a weakling. His idealism was sane and practical, and he would fight to the last ditch when he must.

And this was another strange thing about him, that though his democracy was a faith, vital and ardent, it was tempered with the liberal spirit. He could make allowances; held no grudges, would laugh away insults at which another man would have raged. Out of her very limited experience Alice decided that he was a great man. That he was so warm and human with it all was one of his seizing charms. No boy could have been more interested in winning the shuffleboard game than he.

The fat pork packer from Chicago came wheezing toward her. He took the steamer chair beside Alice and jerked his head toward the spot where Jeff had disappeared.

"Now if you want my notion, Miss Frome, that's the kind of a man that breeds anarchy. I've seen his paper. He fills it full of stuff that makes the workingman discontented with his lot. A trouble maker, that's what he is. Stops the wheels of industry. Gets in the road of the boosters to croak hard times."

Alice observed the thick rolls of purple fat that bulged over his collar.

"Progress now," he went on. "I'm for progress. Develop the country. That gives work to the laborers and keeps them contented. But men like Farnum are always hampering development by annoying capital. Now that's foolish because capital employs labor."

The young woman suggested another possibility. "Or else labor employs capital."

"What!" The fat little man sat bolt upright in surprise. "I guess you never heard your Uncle Joe Powers talk any such foolishness." He snorted indignantly. "Hmp! The best friend labor has got is capital. If I had the say so I'd crush every labor union—for the good of the working people themselves."

Alice decided that the mental indigestion of the rich sat heavily upon him. She felt her temper rising and took advantage of the approach of Beauchamp to leave quickly.

"Oh, Lieutenant! Have you seen Valencia?"

The Englishman showed surprise. It happened that Alice had at that moment a view of Mrs. Van Tyle stretched on a deck chair some thirty feet away.

Miss Frome hurried him along. Presently, with a low laugh, she explained. "I wanted to get away from him. Carelessly, I dropped a new idea there. It's likely to go off. You know how dangerous they are."

"To people who haven't many. Had it anything to do with making money?"

"Not directly."

"Then you needn't be alarmed on our stout friend's account. He's immune to all ideas not connected with that subject."

The double blast of a trumpet invited them to dinner down stairs.

Part 4

Dunn was sitting in the smoking room writing his story of the kidnapping when a ruddy young Englishman stopped opposite him.

"You're Mr. Dunn, are you not? Reporter for the *World?*"

"Yes." The newspaper man looked him over with a swift, trained attention.

"A young lady would like to see you for a few minutes. She is interested in this shanghaing of Mr. Farnum."

Dunn's black gimlet eyes searched Beauchamp's face.

"All right. Glad to see her." Dunn's story was being trans-ferred to his pocket as he rose.

He followed his guide to the ladies' writing room. A slender young woman was standing in front of the bookcase. She turned as they entered. Beauchamp introduced the reporter to her, but Dunn failed to catch the name of this rather remarkable looking young lady.

"You are to write the story of Mr. Farnum's adventure?" she asked.

The reporter's eyes narrowed very slightly. "What story?"

"The account of the shanghaing. Oh, I know all about it. Have you all the facts?"

"I'll be glad to hear what you know, Miss—"

She answered his hesitation by mentioning her name.

Dunn grew more wary. "Miss Alice Frome, daughter of Senator Frome?"

"Yes."

"Anything you have to say I'll be pleased to hear, Miss Frome."

To his surprise she broke through the hedge of reserve he had withdrawn behind.

"You distrust me. You think because I'm Senator Frome's daughter that I must be against Mr. Farnum. Is that it?"

"I didn't say that," he sparred.

"I'm not against him. It's because I'm anxious to see him win that I want to be sure he has given you the whole story."

"Why shouldn't he give me the whole story?"

"Because he isn't the kind to boast. Did he tell you about the sharks?"

"Or how Miss Frome helped pull him aboard just in time to save him from the crimps?"

The reporter's eyes gleamed. "What's that?" he snapped quickly.

"And all about the race from the schooner to the *Bellingham,* It was the most exciting thing I ever saw."

"Great guns! What's the matter with Jeff Farnum? He didn't say a word about that—missed the cream of the story."

Alice smiled. "I thought perhaps he might have."

"He said he saw a chance to swim across to the *Bellingham*. That made a pretty good story. But sharks—and the shanghaiers chasing him—and a young lady helping to haul him aboard to safety—and that young lady Miss Alice Frome! Say, this is the biggest story that ever broke in Verden. If I fall down on it I'm a dead one sure enough."

"You think it will help Mr. Farnum's fight for his bill?"

"Help it. Say, I'd give fifty dollars to see James K. Farnum's face when he reads the *World* tomorrow morning. The town will go right up in the air. Hundreds of telegrams are going to pour in to members of the assembly from their constituents. We'll make a Yale finish of this yet."

"It's lucky Miss Frome recognized Mr. Farnum. Otherwise I suppose he would have been sent back to the *Nancy Hanks*."

"Oh, Miss Frome recognized him? Jeff said one of the passengers did. He couldn't remember who."

"I don't suppose my name is necessary to the story. Just say a young woman on board," Alice suggested.

Dunn's black eyes questioned her. "Are you for us, Miss Frome?"

She smiled. "I'm for you."

"Against Senator Frome and Mr. Powers?"

"I think the bill ought to be passed. I'm not against anybody."

"Well, I'll tell you this. It will help the story a lot to have you in it. Some people might say we framed the whole thing up. But with Senator Frome's daughter starring in it."

"Oh, no, Mr. Farnum's the star."

"Well, you're the leading lady. Don't you see how it helps? Clinches the whole thing as genuine. It's as good as putting the Senator himself on the stand as a witness for us. We've just got to have you."

"It will really help, you think?"

"No question."

"Very well."

"And photographs. You'll stand for one, of course."

"Now really I don't see "

"They can't get back of a photograph. It carries conviction. Of course we've got pictures of you at the office, Miss Frome. But I want to play fair with you. Besides, I want them to show the ship setting."

She laughed. "Don't worry. Your enterprising photographer caught me twice before I knew it. And he got one of my cousin, Mrs. Van Tyle. She doesn't know it, though."

"Good boy, Quillen. Now, if you'll begin at the beginning, Miss Frome, I'll listen to your story.

When she had finished his eyes were gleaming. "It's the biggest scoop I ever got in on. Sounds too good to be true."

Part 5

At Gillam's Point Jeff and his friends, with Dunn and Quillen, left the *Bellingham* on the launch which brought the pilot. They caught the fast express a half hour later and reached Verden shortly after midnight. His hat drawn down over his eyes and muffied to the ears in an ulster so that he might not be recognized, Farnum took a cab with Captain Chunn, Dunn and Quillen for the office of the World. He slipped into the building and his private room unnoticed by any member of the staff.

Dunn presently brought to him Jenkins, the make-up man.

"Rip your front page to pieces. We've got the story of a life time," Captain Chunn exploded.

Jenkins opened his eyes and grinned at Jeff. "That's what Jim tells me. Have you got the proof to hang the thing on Big Tim?"

"I've got a letter he wrote to Captain Green of the *Nancy Hanks*. It's on city hall stationery of the last administration."

"Funny he used that paper."

"Someone usually makes a slip in putting a deal of this kind through."

"And the letter?"

"Just a line, signed with O'Brien's initials. 'The terms agreed on are satisfactory.' I found the letter in Green's cabin. As I thought I might make use of it I helped myself."

"Bully! We'll run a fac-simile of it on the front page."

"Dunn's story covers the whole affair. I don't like some features of it, but our friends say it ought to be run as it stands. I've written three columns of editorial stuff dealing with the situation. And here's a story calling for a mass meeting in front of the State House to-morrow morning."

"You'll speak to the people?"

"I'll say a few words. Hardy and Rawson will be the speakers."

"Pity we've lost your cousin. He'd stir them up."

The muscles stood out on Jeff's lean jaw. James was a subject he could not yet discuss. "We're nailing the No Compromise flag to our masthead, Jenkins. We've got to prevent them from forcing through Garman's bill to-morrow. After that every day will be in our favor. Unless I'm mistaken the state will waken up as it never has before. The people will see how nearly they've been euchred out of what they want."

Jenkins came bluntly to another point. "This story would carry a lot more weight if those charges made against your character by the other papers had been answered."

"Then we'll answer them."

The night editor looked at him dubiously. "They've got four affidavits to back their story."

"Only four?" A gay smile was dancing in Jeff's eyes.

"Both the *Herald* and the *Advocate* have been playing it strong. Every day they rehash the story and challenge a denial."

"It will all be free advertising for us if we can make them eat crow."

"If we can!" Jenkins did not see how any effective answer was possible and he knew that in the present state of public opinion an unsupported bluff would be fatal.

"How would this do for a starter?"

Jeff handed him two typewritten sheets. The night editor read them through. He looked straight at Jeff.

"Can you back this up?"

"I can."

"But—what about those affidavits?"

Farnum grinned. "We'll take care of them when we come to them."

"It's your funeral," Jenkins admitted.

The whole front page of the *World* next morning was filled with the Farnum story. As part of it there were interviews with Alice Frome, with Captain Barclay, and with other passengers. The deadly note from O'Brien to Green of the *Nancy Hanks* occupied the place usually held by the cartoon. Beneath it, exactly in the center of the page, was a leaded box with the caption "A Challenge." It ran as follows:

The editor of the *World* does not think his reputation important enough to protect it at the expense of a woman. Yet he denies absolutely the import of the charges made by the *Herald* and the *Advocate*. That the matter may be forever set at rest the *World* challenges the papers named to a searching investigation. It proposes:

(1) That the names of five representative citizens of Verden be submitted to Governor Hawley by each of the three papers, and that from this number be select a committee of five to sift thoroughly the allegations;

(2) That the meetings of the committee be held in secret, no members of the press being admitted, and that those composing it pledge themselves never to divulge the names of any witnesses who may appear to give evidence;

(3) That the *Herald,* the *Advocate,* and the *World* severally agree to print on the front page for a week the findings of the committee as soon as received and exactly as received, without any editorial or other comment whatsoever.

By the decision of this committee Jefferson Farnum pledges himself to abide. If found guilty, he will at once resign from the editorial charge of the *World* and will leave Verden forever.

CHAPTER 19

The practical man is the man who knows what can't be done. When he begins to let hope take the place of information in this regard, he becomes a conservative. When prejudice takes the place of hope, the mere conservative graduates into a tory, or a justice of the supreme court. It's all a matter of the chemistry of substitution.

—Dr.G.L. Knapp

THE SAFE MAN FURNISHES DIVERSION

Part 1

For once the machine had overplayed its hand. Caught unexpectedly by Jeff's return, no effective counter attack was possible. Dunn's story in the *World* swept the city and the state like wildfire. It was a crouched dramatic narrative and its effect was telling. From it only one inference could be drawn. The big corporations, driven to the wall, had attempted a desperate coup to save the day. It was all very well for Big Tim to file a libel suit. The mind of the public was made up.

The mass meeting at the State House drew an enormous

　　　William MacLeod Raine

crowd, one so great that overflow meetings had to be held. Every corridor in the building was full of excited jostling people. They poured into the gallery of the Senate room and packed the rear of the floor itself. Against such a demonstration the upper house did not dare pass the Garman bill immediately. It was held over for a few days to give the public emotion a chance to die. Instead, the resentment against machine and corporate domination grew more bitter. Stinging resolutions from the back counties were wired to members who had backslidden. Committees of prominent citizens from up state and across the mountains arrived at Verden for heart-to-heart talks with the assemblymen from their districts.

At a hurried meeting of the managers of the public utilities companies it was decided that the challenge of the *World* must be accepted. For many who had believed in the total depravity of Jefferson Farnum were beginning to doubt. Unless the man's character could be impeached successfully the day was lost. And with four witnesses against him how could the trouble maker escape?

The committee of investigation consisted of Senator Frome; Clinton Rogers, the shipbuilder; Thomas Elliott, a law partner of Hardy; James Moran, a wholesale wheat shipper, and the leading clergyman of Verden. It sat behind locked doors, adjourning from one office to another to obtain secrecy.

For the defense appeared as witnesses Marchant, Miller, Mrs. Anderson and Nellie. To doubt the truth of the young wife's story was impossible. The agony of shyness and shame that flushed her, the simple broken words of her little tragedy, bore the stamp of minted gold. It was plain to see that she was a victim of betrayal, being slowly won back to love of life by her husband and her child.

The committee in its report told the facts briefly without giving names. Even P. C. Frome could find no excuse for not signing it.

The effect was instantaneous. On this one throw the machine had staked everything. That it had lost was now plain. In a day Jeff was the hero of Verden, of the state at large. His long fight for reform, the dramatic features of the shanghaing and his return, the collapse of the charges against his character, all contributed to lift him to dizzy popularity. He was the very much embarrassed man of the hour.

All the power of the Transcontinental, of the old city hall gang, of the money that had been spent to corrupt the legislature, was unable to roll back the tide of public deter- mination. White-faced assemblymen sneaked into offices at midnight to return the bribe money for which they dared not deliver the goods. Two days after the report of the investigating committee Jeff's bill passed the Senate. Within three hours it was signed by Governor Hawley. That it would be ratified by a vote of the people and so become a part of the state constitution was a foregone conclusion.

Jeff and his friends had forged the first of the tools they needed to rescue the government of the state from the control of the allied plunderers.

Part 2

In the days following her return to Verden Alice Frome devoured the newspapers as she never had before. They were full of the dramatic struggle between Jeff Farnum and the forces which hitherto had controlled the city and state. To her the battle was personal. It centered on the attacks made upon the character of her friend and his pledge to refute them.

When she read in the *Advocate* the report of the committee Alice wept. It was like her friend, she thought, to risk his reputation for some poor lost wanderer of the streets. Another man might have done it for the girl he loved or for the woman he had married. But with Jeff it would be for one of the least of these. There flashed into her mind an old Indian proverb she had read. "I met a hundred men on the road to Delhi, and they were all my brothers." Yes! None were too deep sunk in the mire to be brothers and sisters to Jeff Farnum.

Ever since her return Alice had known herself in disgrace with her father and that small set in which she moved. Her part in the big *World* story had been "most regrettable." It was felt that in letting her name be mentioned beside that of one who was a thoroughly disreputable vagabond she had compromised her exclusiveness and betrayed the cause of her class. Her friends recalled that Alice had always been a queer girl.

Her father and Ned Merrill agreed over a little luncheon at the Verden Club that girls were likely to lose themselves in sentimental foolishness and that the best way to stop such nonsense was for one to get married to a safe man. Pending this desirable issue she ought to be diverted by pleasant amusements.

The safe man offered to supply these.

Part 3

The farthest thing from Merrill's thoughts had been to discuss with her the confounded notions she had somehow absorbed. The thing to do, of course, was to ignore them and assume everything was all right. After all, of what importance were the opinions of a girl about practical things?

How the thing cropped up he did not afterward remember, but at the thirteenth green he found himself mentioning that all reformers were out of touch with facts. They were not practical.

The smug finality of his verdict nettled her. This may or may not have been the reason she sliced her ball, quite unnecessarily. But it was probably due to her exasperation at the wasted stroke that she let him have it.

"I'm tired of that word. It means to be suicidally selfish. There's not another word in the language so abused."

"Didn't catch the word that annoys you," the young man smiled.

"Practical! You used it yourself. It means to tear down and not build up, to be so near-sighted you can't see beyond your reach. Your practical man is the least hopeful member of the community. He stands only for material progress. His own, of course!"

"You sound like a Farnum editorial, Alice."

"Do I?" she flashed. "Then I'll give you the rest of it. He—your practical man—is rutted to class traditions. This would not be good form or respectable. That would disturb the existing order. So let's all do nothing and agree that all's well

William MacLeod Raine

with the world."

Merrill greeted this outburst with a complacent smile. "It's a pretty good world. I haven't any fault to find with it—not this afternoon anyhow."

But Alice, serious with young care and weighted with the problems of a universe, would have none of his compliments.

"Can't you see that there's a—a " She groped and found a fugitive phrase Jeff had once used—"a want of adjustment that is appalling?"

"It doesn't appall me. I believe in the survival of the fittest."

Her eyes looked at him with scornful penetration. They went through the well-dressed, broad-shouldered exterior of him, to see a suave, gracious Pharisee of the modern world. He believed in the God-of-things-as-they-are because he was the man on horseback. He was a formalist because it paid him to be one. That was why he and his class looked on any questioning of conditions as almost atheistic. They were born to the good things of life. Why should they doubt the ethics of a system that had dealt so kindly with them?

She gave him up. What was the use of talking about such things to him? He had the sense of property ingrained in him. The last thing he would be likely to do was to let any altruistic ideas into his head. He would play safe. Wasn't he a practical man?

She devoted herself to the game. To see her play was a pleasure to the eye. The long lines and graceful curves of her supple young body never appeared to better advantage than at golf. Her motions showed the sylvan freedom of the woods. Ned Merrill appreciated the long, light tread of her, the harmony of movement as of a perfect young animal, together with the fine spiritual quality that escaped her personality so unconsciously.

At the fifteenth hole he continued her education. "This country is founded upon individualism. It stands for the best chance of development possible to all its citizens. When you hamper enterprise you stop that development."

She took him up dryly. "I see. So you and father and Uncle Joe have developed your individualism at the expense of a million other people's. You have gobbled up franchises, forests, ore lands, coal mines, and every other opportunity worth having. As a result you're making them your slaves and crushing out all individuality."

"Not at all. We're really custodians for the people. We administer these things for their benefit because we are more fit to do it."

"How do you know you are?"

"The very fact that we have succeeded in getting what we have is evidence of it."

"All I can see is that our getting it and keeping it—you and I and Uncle Joe and a thousand like us—is responsible for all the poverty in the world. We're helping to make it every time we eat a dinner we didn't work to get."

Alice made a beautiful approach that landed her ball within four feet of the hole. Presently Merrill joined her.

"That was a dandy shot," he told her, and watched Alice hole out. "I don't agree with you. For instance, I work as hard as other men."

"But you're not working for the common good."

His impatience reached words. "That sort of talk is nonsense, Alice. I don't know what has come over you of late."

She smiled provokingly and changed the subject. Why argue with him? The slant with which they got at things was different. Like her father, he had the mental rigidity that is death to open-mindedness.

Briskly she returned to small talk. "You're only three up."

Part 4

On their way back to the club house the safe man recurred to one phase of their talk.

"You ought not to need any telling as to why I work, Alice."

She shot one swift annoyed glance at him. When Ned Merrill tried the sentimental she liked him least.

"Oh, all men like to work, I suppose. Uncle Joe says it's half the fun of life."

"Most men work for some woman. I'm working for you," he told her solenmly.

A little giggle of laughter floated across to him.

"What are you laughing about?" he demanded.

"Oh, the things I notice. Just now it's you, Ned."

"If you'll explain the joke."

"You wouldn't understand it. Dear me, what are you so stiff about?"

Merrill brought things to an issue. "Look here, Alice! What's the use of playing fast and loose? I'd like to know where we're at."

"Would you?"

"Yes, I would. You know all about the arrangement just as well as I do. I haven't pushed you. I've stood back and let you have your good times. Don't you think it's about time for us to talk business?"

"Just as soon as you like, Ned."

"Well, then, let's announce it."

"That we're not engaged to be married and never will be! Is that what you want to announce?"

He flushed angrily. "What's the use of talking that way? You know it has been arranged for years."

"I'm not going through with it. I told Father so. The thing is outrageous," she flamed.

"I don't see why. Our people want it. We are fond of each other. I never cared for any girl but you."

"Let's stick to the business reasons, Ned."

"Hang it, you're so acid about it! I do care for you "

Her dry anger spurted out. "That's unfortunate, since I don't care for you."

"I know you do. Just now you're vexed at me."

"Yes, I am," she admitted, nodding her head swiftly. "But it doesn't make any difference whether I am or not. I've made up my mind. I'm not going through with it."

"You promised."

"I didn't, not in so many words. And I was pushed into it. None of you gave me a fair chance. But I'll not go on with it."

"But, why?"

"Because I'm an American girl, and here we don't have to marry to amalgamate business interests. I won't do it. I'd rather be " She gave a little shrug of her shoulders. The passion died out of her voice. "Oh, well! No need getting melodramatic about it. Just the same, I won't do it. My mind's made up."

"A pretty figure I'll cut, after all these years," he complained sulkily. "Everyone will know you jilted me."

Alice turned to him, mischief sparkling in her eyes. "I wouldn't stand it if I were you. Show your spunk."

He stared. "What do you mean?"

"Why don't you jilt ME?"

"Jilt you?"

Her head went up and down in a dozen little nods of affirmation. "Yes. Marry Pauline Gillam. You know you'd like to, but you haven't had the courage to give me up. Now that you've got to give me up anyhow—"

"I'm very much obliged, Miss Frome. But I don't think it will be necessary for you to select another wife for me."

"Have you been married once. I didn't know it."

"You know what I mean?" He was stiff as a poker.

"I believe I do." She was in a perfectly good humor again now. "But you better take my advice, Ned. Think what a joke it will be on me. Everybody will say you could have had me."

"We'll not discuss the subject if you please."

Nevertheless Alice knew that she had dropped a seed on good ground.

CHAPTER 20

Now poor Tom Dunstan's cold,
Our shop is duller;
Scarce a tale is told,
And our talk has lost the old
Red-republican color!

* * * * *

'She's coming, she's coming!' said he;
'Courage, boys I wait and see!
'FREEDOM'S AHEAD!'

—Robert Buchanan

THE HERO IS LURED TO AN ADVENTURE INTO THE
UNCONVENTIONAL AND HEARS MUCH THAT IS
PAINFUL TO A WELL-REGULATED MIND

Near the close of a fine spring afternoon James Farnum and
Alice Frome were walking at the lower end of Powers
Avenue. In the conventional garb he affected since he had
become a man of substance the lawyer might have served as
a model of fashion to any aspiring youth. His silk hat, his
light trousers, the double-breasted coat which enfolded his

William MacLeod Raine

manly form, were all of the latest design. The weather, for a change, was behaving itself so as not to soil the chaste glory of Solomon thus displayed. There had been rain and would be more, but just now they passed through a dripping world shot full of sunlight.

"Of course I'm no end flattered at being allowed to go with you. But I'm dying of curiosity to know where we are going."

The young woman gave James her beguiling smile. "We're going to call on a sick man. I'm taking you along as chaperon. You needn't be flattered at all. You're merely a convenience, like a hat pin or an umbrella."

"But I'm not sure this is proper. Now as your chaperone—"

"You're not that kind of a chaperon, Mr. Farnum. You haven't any privileges. Nothing but duties. Unless it's a privilege to be chosen. That gives you a chance to say something pretty."

They crossed Yarnell Way. James, looking around upon the wrecks of humanity they began to meet, was very sure that he did not enjoy this excursion. An adventure with Miss Frome outside of the conventions was the very thing he did not want. What in the world did the girl mean anyhow? Her vagaries were beginning to disturb her relatives. So much he had gathered from Valencia.

Before he had got as far as a protest Alice turned in to the entrance of a building and climbed a flight of stairs. She pushed a button. A woman of rather slatternly appearance came to the door.

"Good afternoon, Mrs. Maloney. I've come to see how Mr.

Marchant is."

The landlady brushed into place some flying strands of hair. "Well, now, Miss Frome, he's better to-day. The nurse is with him. If you'll jist knock at the door 'twill be all right."

While they were in the passage James interposed an objection. "My dear Miss Frome, I really don't think—"

She interrupted brightly. "I'm glad you don't. You're not expected to, you know. I'm commanding this expedition. Yours not to answer why. Yours but to do and die." And she knocked on the door of the room at which they had stopped.

It was opened by a nurse in uniform. James observed that she, too, like Mrs. Maloney, brightened at sight of the visitor.

"Mr. Marchant will be pleased to see you, Miss Frome."

He was. His gladness illuminated the white face through the skin of which the cheek bones appeared about to emerge. A thin blue-veined hand shot forward to meet hers.

"Oh, comrade, but I'm glad to meet you."

"I think you know Mr. Farnum."

The man propped up in bed nodded a little grin at the lawyer. "We've met. It was years ago in Jeff's rooms."

"Oh—er—yes. Yes, I remember."

Presently Jeff and Sam Miller dropped in to see the invalid. From chance remarks the lawyer gathered that the little cobbler had brought himself so low by giving his overcoat one bitter night to a poor girl he had found shivering in

　　　　William MacLeod Raine

the streets.

The frankness with which they discussed before Alice Frome things never referred to in good society shocked James.

It appeared that the story of this little factory girl who had been led astray was still urgent in Marchant's mind. At the time of their arrival he had just finished scribbling some verses hot from his heart. Jeff read them aloud, in spite of the poet's modest insistence that they were only a first draft.

"This is a story that two may tell,
I am the one, the other's in hell;
A story of passionate amorous fire,
With the glamor of love to attune the lyre.

She traveled the road at breakneck speed,
I opened the gates and saddled the steed;
"Ride free!" I cried as we dashed along.
Her sweet voice echoed a mocking song."

"'Fraid it doesn't always scan. They seldom do," apologized the author of the verses.

Jeff rapped for order. "The sense of the meeting is that the blushing poet will please not interrupt."

"Nights of the wildest revel and mirth,
Days of sorrow, remorse, and dearth,
A heaven of love and a hell of regret—
But there's always the woman to pay my debt.

'Sin,' says the preacher, 'shall be washed free,
The blood of the Lamb was shed for thee.'
Smugly I pass the sacred wine,
The woman in hell pays toll for mine.

'I am a pillar of Church and State,
She but the broken sport of Fate;
This is a story that two may tell,
I am the one, the other's in hell.'"

There was a moment's silence after Jeff had finished.

"What are you going to call your verses?" the nurse asked.

"I'll call them, 'She Pays.' That's the idea of it."

James was distinctly uneasy. There was positively something indecent about this. He had an aversion to thinking about unpleasant things. Every well-regulated mind ought to have. He would like to make a protest, but he could not very well do that here. He promised himself to let Alice Frome know as soon as they were alone what he thought about her escapades into this world below the dead line.

He moved uncomfortably in his chair, and in doing so his gaze fell full into the eyes of Sam Miller. The fat librarian was staring at him out of a very white face. Before James could break the spell an unvoiced question had been asked and answered.

Marchant was already riding the hobby that was religion to him. "Four dollars a week. That's what she was getting. And her employer is worth two millions. Think of it. All her youth to be sold for four dollars a week. Just enough to keep body and soul together. And when she went to the head of her department to ask for a raise he leered at her and said a good looking girl like her could always find someone to take care of her. Eight months she stuck it out, getting more ragged every day. Then enter the man, offering her some comfort and pleasure and love. Do you blame her?"

"You must give me her address," Alice said softly.

Oscar nodded. "Good enough, comrade. Jeff has looked out for her, but she needs a woman friend." With a sweep of the hand he went back to the impersonal. "Her trouble was economic, just as ours is. Look at it. We've got a perfect self-regulating system that adjusts itself automatically to bring hard times when we're most prosperous. Give us big crops and boom times, and we head straight for a depression. Why?" He interrupted himself with a fit of coughing, but presently began again, talking also with his swift supple hands. "Because then the foreign market will be glutted. Surplus goods won't sell abroad. The manufacturer, unable to dispose of his produce, will cut down his force or close his plant. Labor, out of work, cannot buy. So every branch of industry suffers because we're too well off. It's a vicious absurd circle born of the system under which we live. Under socialism the remedy would be merely to work less for a time until the surplus was used. It would affect nobody injuriously. The whole thing's as simple as A B C."

It had been plain to the first casual glance of James that the little Socialist was far gone. The amazing thing was the eagerness with which his spirit dominated the body in such ill case. He was alive to the fingertips, though he was already in the Valley of the Shadow. To the lawyer there was something eerie about it all. Marchant was done with the business of living. Why didn't he lie down and accept the verdict?

But to Alice it was God-like, a thing to stand uncovered before. His remedies might be all wrong. Probably they were. None the less his vital courage for life took her by the throat.

Jeff nodded at the invalid cheerfully. "We're going to change all that, Oscar. Into this little old world a new soul is being born. Or perhaps the old soul is being born again."

The Socialist caught at this swiftly. "Yes, we're going to change this terrible waste of human lives. I see a new world, where men will live like brothers and not like wolves rending each other. There poverty will be blotted out... and disease and all mean and cruel things that hamper and destroy life. Law and justice will walk hand in hand through a land of peace and plenty. Our cities, the expression of our social life, will be clean and sunny and beautiful because the lives of the common people are so. There strong men and deep-breasted women will work for the joy of working, since all is for the common good. Their children will be free and happy and well fed... yes, and equal to each other. From that highly socialized state, because it is tied together by love, will come that restrained freedom which is the most perfect individualism."

The nurse forced him gently back upon the pillows. "There! You've talked enough to-day."

He lay coughing, a hectic flush above the high cheek bones. Presently, at a look from the nurse, his guests departed.

Outside the building Miller left the rest abruptly. Flanked by the two cousins, Alice crossed Yarnell Way back to that world to which she had always belonged.

James laid down the law to her concerning the folly of such excursions into the unconventional. Alice listened. She discovered that his viewpoint was exactly like that of Ned Merrill. Any deviation from the conventional was a mistake. Any attempt to escape from existing conditions was a form of treason. Trade, property, business, respectability, good form; these were the shibboleth they worshipped. It was just because she did not want to believe this of James Farnum that she had taken him with her to call on Marchant. It was in a sense a test, and he was answering it by showing himself complacently callous and hidebound.

Surely he had not always been like this, a smug and well-clad Pharisee, afraid to look at the truth. In those early days, when they had been friends, with the possibility of being a good deal more, there had been an impetuous touch of ardor she could no longer find. Her cool glance ran down his figure. The man was taking on flesh, the plump well-fed look of one who has escaped moral conduct by giving up the fight. Fat cushioned the square jaw and detracted from its strength. For the first time she observed a hardening of the eye. The visible deterioration of an inner collapse was being writ on him.

Alice sighed. After all she might have spared herself the trouble. He had chosen his path and he must follow it.

At the corner of Powers Avenue and Van Ault Street James left them. It was natural that the talk should revert to Marchant.

"Oscar finds your visits a very great pleasure," Jeff told her.

"The dear madman!" Her eyes were shining softly. "Isn't he brave and optimistic?"

"Yes."

Both of them were thinking how soon the arm of that unseen God of love and law he worshipped would enfold him.

Alice smiled tenderly, and for the moment the street in front of her danced in a mist. "And his perfect state! Shall we ever realize it?"

"We must hope so. Perhaps not in the form he sees it, but in the way we work it out through a species of evolution. Think of the progress we have made in the last five years. How many dark corners in the long disused houses of our minds have been flooded with light!"

"Yes. Why have we made more progress in the past few years?"

Jeff's eyes held a gleam of humor. "This is a big country with enormous resources. There used to be room for all the most active plunderers to grab something. But lately the grabbing hasn't been so good. We have discoveredthat the most powerful robbers are doing their snatching from us. So we've suffered a moral awakening."

"You don't believe that," she said quickly.

"There's a good deal in the bread and butter interpretation of history. The push of life, its pressure, drives us to think. Out of thought grow new hopes and a broader vision."

"And then?"

"Pretty soon the thought will flood the world that we make our own poverty, that God and nature have nothing to do with it. After that we'll proceed to eliminate it."

"By means of Mr. Marchant's perfect state?"

"Not by any revolution of an hour probably. Society cannot change its nature in a day. We'll pass gradually from our present state to a better one, the new growing out of the old by generations of progress. But I think we will pass into a form of socialism. It will be necessary to repress the pre-datory instinct in us that has grown strong under the present system. I don't much care whether you call it democracy or socialism. We must recognize how inter-dependent we are and work together for the common good."

They had come to the car line that would take her home. Up the hill a trolley car was coming.

"May I not see you home?" Jeff dared to ask.

"You may."

They left the car at Lakeview Park and crossed it to The Brakes. Every step of that walk led Jeff deeper into an excursion of endearment. It was amazingly true that he trod beside her an acknowledged friend, a secret lover. The turn of her head, the shadowy smile bubbling into laughter, the gracious undulations of the body, indeed the whole dear delight of her presence, belonged for that hour to him alone.

CHAPTER 21

Many a man has kept his self-respect through a long lifetime of decalog breaking, only to go to smash like a crushed eggshell when he commits the crime of being found out.

—From the Note Book of a Dreamer

THE HERO IS PAINED TO FIND THAT EVEN IN A WELL-REGULATED WORLD THE GODS ARE JUST, AND OF OUR PLEASANT VICES MAKE INSTRUMENTS TO PLAGUE US

Going back across the park Jeff trod the hilltops. He was not thinking about society, except that small unit of it represented by a slender, golden girl who had just bidden him good-bye. And because his heart sang within him his footsteps turned toward the office of his cousin. There had been between them of late an estrangement. Since the lawyer had been appointed general attorney for the Transcontinental and had formed a partnership with Scott, thus bringing to the firm the business of the public utility corporations, James had not found much time for Jeff. He was a member of the most important law firm on the Pacific Coast, judged by the business it was doing, and he had definitely cut loose politically from his former associates. His cousin blamed

William MacLeod Raine

himself for the change in their personal relations, and he meant to bring things back to the old basis if he could.

It was past office hours, but a light in the window of the junior member's private office gave promise that James might be in. Leaving the elevator at the fourth floor, he walked down the corridor toward the suite occupied by the firm.

Before he reached the door Jeff stopped. Something unusual was happening within. There came to him the sounds of shuffling feet, of furniture being smashed, of an angry oath. Almost at once there was a thud, as if something heavy had fallen. The listener judged that a live body was thrashing around actively. The impact of blows, a heavy grunt, a second stifled curse, decided Farnum. Pushing through the outer office, he entered the one usually occupied by James.

Two men were on the floor, one astride of the other. The man on top was driving home heavy jarring blows against his opponent's face and head. Jeff ran forward and dragged him away.

"Good heavens, Sam! What's the matter?" his friend demanded in surprise.

Miller waited panting, his fists still doubled, the lust of battle in his eyes.

"The damned cad! The damned cad!" was all he could get out.

From the floor James Farnum was rising. His forehead, his cheek, and his lips were bleeding from cuts. One of his eyes was closing rapidly. There was a dogged look of fear in the battered face.

"I tripped over a chair, he explained, glaring at his foe.

"Damn you then, stand up and fight!"

Disgust and annoyance were pictured on the damaged countenance of the lawyer. "I don't fight with riff raff from the streets."

With a lurch Miller was free from Jeff and at him again. James lashed straight out and cut open his lip without stopping him. Jeff wrenched the furious man back again. A moment later he made a discovery. The fear of his cousin was not physical.

"Here! Stop it, man! What's the row about?" Jeff hung on with a strangle hold while he fired his questions.

Sam turned a distorted face toward him. "Nellie."

The truth crashed home like a bolt of lightning. James was the man who had betrayed Nellie Anderson. The thing was incredible, but Jeff knew instantly it was so.

Except where the blood streamed down it the face of the lawyer was colorless. His lips twitched.

"Is this true, James?"

The sullen eyes of the detected man fell. "It will ruin me. It will ruin my career. And all because in a moment of fearful temptation I yielded, God help me."

"God help you!" The angry scorn in Miller's voice burned like vitriol. "God help you! you selfish villain and coward! You pursued her! You hounded her. You made your own temptation—and hers. And afterward you left her to bear a lifetime of shame—to kill herself if she couldn't stand it. When I think of you, smug liar and hell hound, I know that killing isn't good enough for you."

"Steady, old man," counseled Jeff.

Miller began to tremble violently. Tears gathered in his eyes and coursed down his fat cheeks. "And I can't stamp him out. I can't expose him without hurting her worse. I've got to stand it without touching him."

Faintly Jeff smiled. James did not look quite untouched. He was a much battered statue of virtue, his large dignity for once torn to shreds.

Miller flung himself down heavily in a chair and buried his face in his hands. James began to talk, and as he talked his fluency came back to him.

"It's the only stain on my life record... the only one. My life has been an open book but for that. I was only a boy—and I made a slip. Ought that to spoil my whole life, a splendid career of usefulness for the city and the state? Ought I to be branded for that one error?"

Miller looked up whitely. "Shut up, you liar! If it had been a slip you would have stood by her, you would have married the girl you had ruined. But you left her—to death or worse. She was loyal to you. She kept your secret, you damned villain. I wrung it out of her to-day when I went home only by pretending that I knew.... And you let Jeff bear the blame of it without saying a word. I know now why her name wasn't unearthed by the reporters. You killed the story because you were afraid the truth would leak out. You haven't a straight hair in your head. You sold out Jeff's bill. You're for yourself first and last, no matter who pays the price."

"That's your interpretation of my career. But what does Verden think of me? No man stands higher among the best people of the community."

"To hell with you and your best people. I say you're nothing but a whited sepulchre," snarled Miller.

Suddenly he reached for his hat and left the office. He was stifling.

He knew that if he stayed he could not keep his hands from his enemy's throat.

James wrung his hands. "My God, Jeff, it's awful! To think that a little fault should come out now to ruin me. After I've gone so far and am on the way to bigger things. It's ghastly luck. Can't you do something? Can't you keep the fellow quiet? I'll pay anything in reason."

Jeff looked at him steadily. "I wouldn't say that to him if I were you."

"Oh, I don't know what I'm saying." He mopped the blood from his face with a handkerchief. "I'm half crazy. Did he mark me up badly?" James examined himself anxiously in the glass. "He's just chopped my face to pieces. I'll have to get out of the city to-night and stay away till the marks are gone. But the main point is to keep him from talking. Can you do it?"

For once Jeff's toleration failed him. "He's right. You are a selfish beggar. Don't you ever think of anyone except yourself?"

"I'm not thinking of myself at all, but of—of someone else. You're wronging me, Jeff. This is not the time to go back on me, now that I'm in trouble. You've got to help me out. You've got to keep Miller quiet. If he talks I'm done for."

His cousin looked at him with contemptuous eyes. "Can't you see—haven't you fineness enough to see that Sam Miller would cut an arm off before he would expose his wife to more talk? Your precious secret's safe."

"It's all very well for you to talk that way," James complained. "I don't suppose you ever were put into temptation by a woman. You're not a lady's man. I'm the kind they take a shine to for some reason. Now this Anderson woman—"

Sharply Jeff cut in. "That's enough. When you speak of her it won't be in that tone of voice. You'll speak respectfully of her. She's the wife of my friend; and before she met you was innocent as a child."

"What do you know of her? I tell you, Jeff, there's a type of woman that's always smiling round the corner at you. I don't say I did right to yield to her. Of course I didn't. But, hang it, I'm not a block of wood. I've got red blood in my veins. The whip of youth drove me on. You've probably never noticed it, but she was a devilish pretty girl."

He was swimming into his phrases so fluently that Jeff knew he would soon persuade himself that he had been the victim of her wiles. So, no doubt, in one sense, he had. She had laid her innocent bait to win his friendship, with never a thought of what was to come of it.

"It happened of course while you were rooming there," the editor shot at him.

James nodded sullenly.

His cousin knew now that more than once he had put away doubts of James. When Sam Miller told him of her disappearance he had thought of the lawyer and had dismissed his suspicions as unworthy. He had always believed James to be a more moral man than himself, and he had turned his own back on the temptation lest it might prove too great for him. It would have been better for Nellie if he had stayed and fought it out to a finish.

James began further explanations. "Look at it the way it is. She put herself in my way."

Two steps carried Jeff to him. Without touching James he stood close to him, arms rigid and eyes blazing. "Don't say that again, you liar. You ruined her life. You let her suffer. She might have died for all of you. She nursed your child and never whispered the name of its father. Sam Miller is charging himself with the keep of your daughter. Do you think she hasn't paid a hundred times for her mistake? Now, by God, keep your mouth shut! Be decent enough not to fling mud at her, you of all men."

James shrugged his shoulders and turned away in petulant disgust. "I see. You've heard her side of it and you've made up your mind. All right. I've nothing more to say."

"I've never heard her side of it. Her own mother doesn't know the truth. Sam didn't know not till to-day. But I know her—and now I know you."

"That's no way to talk, Jeff. I admit I did wrong. Can a man say more than that? Do you want me to crawl on my hands and knees?"

"It's easy for you to forgive yourself."

"Maybe you think I haven't suffered too. I've lain awake nights worrying over this."

"Yes. For fear you might be found out."

"I intended to look out for the girl, but she disappeared without letting me know where she was going. What could I do?" The lawyer was studying his face very carefully in the glass. "My face is a sight. It will be weeks before that eye is fit to be seen."

Jeff turned away and left him. He walked to his rooms and found his uncle waiting for him. Robert Farnum had sold out his interests in Arkansas and returned to Verden with the intention of buying a small mill in the vicinity. Meanwhile he had the apartment next to the one used by his nephew.

"Seen anything of James lately?" he inquired as they started down the street to dinner.

"Yes. I saw him to-day. He's leaving town for a week or so."

"On business, I suppose. He didn't mention it when I saw him Wednesday."

"It's a matter that came up suddenly, I understand."

The father agreed proudly. There were moments when he had doubts of James, but he always stifled them by remembering what a splendid success he was. "Probably something nobody else could attend to but him."

"Exactly."

"It's amazing how that boy gets along. His firm has the cream of the corporation business of Verden. I never saw anything like it."

The younger man assented, rather wearily. Somehow to-night he did not feel like sounding the praises of James.

His uncle's kindly gaze rested on him. "Tired, boy?"

"I think I am a little. I'll be all right after we've had something to eat."

CHAPTER 22

But when your arms are full of girl and fluff
You hide your nerve behind a yard of grin;
You'd spit into a bulldog's face, or bluff
A flock of dragons with a safety pin.
Life's a slow skate, but love's the dopey glim
That puts a brewery horse in racing trim.

—Wallace Irwin

CANARIES SING FOR THE HERO

Part 1

James Farnum had been back in Verden twenty-four hours. A few little scars still decorated his handsome visage, but he explained them away with the story of a motor car accident. Just now he was walking to the bank, and he had spoken his piece five times in a distance of three blocks. From experience he was getting letter perfect as to the details. Even the idiotic joke about the clutch seemed now a necessary part of the recital.

It was just as he was crossing Powers that a motor car whirled around the corner and down upon a man descending from a street car. The chauffeur honked wildly and rammed the brakes home. Simultaneously James leaped, flinging his weight upon the man standing dazed in the path of the automobile. The two went down together, and for a moment Farnum knew only a crash of the senses.

He was helped to his feet. Voices, distant and detached, asked whether he was hurt. Blood trickled into his eyes from a cut in the head. It came to him oddly enough that his story about the motor car accident would now be true.

A slender figure in gray slipped swiftly past him and knelt beside the still shape lying on the asphalt.

"Bring water, Roberts!"

James knew that clear, sweet voice. It could belong only to Alice Frome.

"Are you much hurt, Mr. Farnum?"

"No, I think not—a cut over my eye and a few bruises."

"I'm so glad. But this poor old man—I'm afraid he's badly hurt."

"Was he run over?"

"No. You saved him from that. You don't know him, do you?"

The lawyer looked at the unconscious man and could not repress a start. It was his father. For just an eyebeat he hesitated before he said, "I've seen him before somewhere."

"We must take him to the hospital. Isn't there a doctor here?

Someone run for a doctor." The young woman's glance swept the crowd in appeal.

"I'll take care of him. Better get away before the crowd is too large, Miss Frome."

"No. It was our machine did it. Oh, here's a doctor."

A pair of lean, muscular shoulders pushed through the press after the doctor. "Much hurt, James?" inquired their owner.

"No. For heaven's sake, get Miss Frome away, Jeff," implored his cousin.

"Miss Frome!" Jeff stepped forward with an exclamation.

The young woman looked up. She was kneeling in the street and supporting the head of the wounded man. Her face was almost as bloodless as his.

"We almost ran him down. Your cousin jumped to save him. He isn't dead, doctor, is he?"

Jeff turned swiftly to his cousin and spoke in a low voice. "It's your father."

The lawyer pushed forward with a manner of authority.

"This won't do, doctor. The crowd's growing and we're delaying the traffic. Let us lift him into the machine and take him to the hospital."

"Very good, Mr. Farnum."

"Doctor, will you go with him to the hospital? And Jeff... you, too, if you please."

A minute later the car pushed its way slowly through the crush of people and disappeared. James was left standing on the curb with Alice.

He spoke brusquely. "Someone call a cab, please....I'll send you home, Miss Frome."

"No, to the hospital," she corrected. "I couldn't go home now without knowing how he is."

"Very well. Anything to get away from here."

"And you can have your cut attended to there."

"Oh, that's nothing. A basin of cold water is all I need. Here's the cab, thank heaven."

The girl's gaze followed the automobile up the hill as she waited for the taxicab to stop. "I do hope he isn't hurt badly," she murmured piteously.

"Probably he isn't. Just stunned, the doctor seemed to think. Anyhow it was an unavoidable accident."

The eyes of the young woman kindled. "I'll never forget the way you jumped to save him. It was splendid."

James flushed with pleasure. "Nonsense. I merely pushed him aside."

"You merely risked your life for his. A bagatelle—don't mention it," the girl mocked.

Farnum nodded, the old warmth for her in his eyes. "All right, I'll take all the praise you want to give me. It's been a good while since you have thought I deserved any."

Alice looked out of the window in a silence that appeared to accuse him.

"Yet once"—She felt in his fine voice the vibration of feeling—"once we were friends. We met on the common ground of—of the spirit," he risked.

Her eyes came round to meet his. "Is it my fault that we are not still friends?"

"I don't know. Something has come between us. What is it?"

"If you don't know I can't tell you."

"I think I know." He folded his handkerchief again to find a spot unstained. "You wanted me to fit into some ideal of me you had formed. Am I to blame because I can't do it? Isn't the fault with your austerity? I've got to follow my own convictions—not Jeff's, not even yours. Life's a fight, and it's every man for himself. He has to work out his own salvation in his own way. Nobody can do it for him. The final test is his success or failure. I'm going to succeed."

"Are you?" The compassion of her look he could not understand. "But how shall we define success?"

"It's getting power and wielding it."

"But doesn't it depend on how one wields it?"

"Yes. It must be made to produce big results. Now my idea of a successful man is your uncle, Joe Powers."

"And my idea of one is your cousin, Jefferson Farnum."

The young man sat up. "You're not seriously telling me that

you think Jeff is successful as compared with Joe Powers?"

"Yes. In my opinion he is the most successful man I ever met."

James was annoyed. "I expect you have a monopoly in that opinion, Miss Frome—unless Jeff shares it."

"He doesn't."

The lawyer laughed irritably. "No, I shouldn't think he would." He added a moment later: "I don't suppose Jeff is worth a hundred dollars."

"Probably not."

"And Joe Powers is worth a hundred millions."

"That settles it. I must have been wrong." Alice looked at him with a flash of demure daring. "Valencia said something to me the other day I didn't quite understand. Ought I to congratulate you?"

"What did she say?" he asked eagerly.

"Oh, I'll not tell you what she said. My question was in first."

"You may as well, though it's still a secret. Nobody knows it but you and me."

"And Valencia."

"I didn't know she knew it yet."

Alice stared. "Not know that she is going to marry you? Then it isn't really arranged?"

William MacLeod Raine

"It is and it isn't."

"Oh!"

"I know it and she suspects it."

"Is this a riddle?"

"Riddle is a good word when we speak of your cousin," he admitted judicially.

"Perhaps I asked a question I ought not to have."

"Not at all. I'm trying to answer you as well as I can. Last time I mentioned the subject she laughed at me."

"So you've asked her?"

"No, I told her."

"And she said?"

"Regretted that other plans would not permit her to fall in with mine."

"Then I don't quite see how you are so sure."

"That's just what she says, but I've a notion she is planning the trousseau."

Alice flashed a sidelong look at him. Was he playing with her? Or did he mean it?

"You'll let me know when I may safely congratulate you," she retorted ironically.

"Now is the best time. I may not see you this evening."

"Oh, it's to be this evening, is it?"

"To the best of my belief and hope."

His complacency struck a spark from her. "You needn't be so cock sure. I daresay she won't have you."

His smile took her into his confidence. "That's what I'm afraid of myself, but I daren't let her see it."

"That sounds better."

"I think she wants to eat her cake and have it, too."

"Meaning, please?"

"That she likes me, but would rather hold me off a while."

Alice nodded. "Yes, that would be like Val."

"Meanwhile I don't know whether I'm to be a happy man or not."

Her fine eyes looked in their direct fashion right into his. "I must say you appear greatly worried."

"Yes," he smiled.

"You must be tremendously in love with her."

"Ye-es, thank you."

"Why are you going to marry her then—if she'll let you?"

"Now I'm having Joe Powers' railroads and his steamboats and his mines thrown at me, am I not?" he asked lightly.

"No, I don't think that meanly of you. I know you're a victim of ambition, but I don't suppose it would take you that far."

He gave her an ironical bow. "Thanks for this testimonial of respect. You're right. It wouldn't. I'm going to marry Joe Power's daughter, *Deo volente* because she is the most interesting woman I know and the most beautiful one."

"Oh! That's the reason."

"These, plus a sentimental one which I can't uncover to the cynical eyes of my young cousin that is to be, are my motives; though, mind you, I'm not fool enough to be impervious to the railroads and the ocean liners and the mines you didn't mention. I hope my reasons satisfy you," he added coolly.

"If they satisfy Val they do me, but very likely you'll find they won't."

"The doubt adds a fillip to the situation."

Her eyes had gone from time to time out of the window. Now she gave a sigh of relief. "Here we are at the hospital. Oh, I do hope that poor man is all right!"

"I'm sure he is. He was recovering consciousness when they left.

James helped her out of the cab and they went together up the steps. In the hall they met Jeff. He had just come down stairs.

"Everything's all right. His head must have struck the asphalt, but there seems to be no danger."

Alice noticed that the newspaper man spoke to his cousin and not to her.

Part 2

Though Valencia Van Tyle had not made up her mind to get married, James hit the mark when he guessed that she was interesting herself in the accessories that would go with such an event. The position she took in the matter was characteristic. She had gone the length of taking expert counsel with her New York modiste concerning gowns for the occasion, without having at all decided that she would exchange her present independence for another venture into stormy matrimonial seas.

"Perhaps I shatn't have to make up my mind at all," she found amusement in chuckling to herself. "What a saving of trouble it would be if he would abduct me in his car. I could always blame him then if it did not turn out well."

Something of this she expressed to James the evening of the day of the accident, watching him through half-shuttered eyes to see how he would take her first concession that she was considering him.

He took without external disturbance her gay, embarrassed suggestion, the manner of which might mean either shyness or the highest expression of her art.

"I'd kidnap you fast enough except that I don't want to rob you of the fun of getting ready. How long will it take you? Would my birthday be too soon? It's on the fourth of June."

"Too soon for what?" she asked innocently.

"For my birthday present—Valencia Powers."

She liked it that he used her maiden surname instead of her married one. It seemed to imply that he loved her in the swift, ardent way of youth.

"Are you sure you want it?"

The lawyer appreciated her soft, warm allurement, the appeal of sex with which she was so prodigally endowed. His breath came a little faster.

"He won't be happy till he gets it."

Her faint laughter rippled out. "That's just the point, my friend. Will he be happy then? And, which is more important to her, will she?"

"That's what I'm here to see. I'm going to make you happy."

She laced her fingers behind her tawny head, not quite unaware perhaps that the attitude set off the perfect modeling of her soft, supple body.

"I don't doubt your good intentions, but it takes more than that to make marriage happy when the contracting parties are not Heaven-sent."

"But we are—we are."

Valencia shook her head. "Oh, no! There will be no rapturous song of birds for us, none of that fine wantonness that doesn't stop to count the cost. If we marry no doubt we'll have good reasons, but not the very best one—that we can't help it."

He would not consent to that. "You're not speaking for me. The birds sing, Valencia."

"Canaries in a cage," she mocked.

"You've forgotten two things."

"Yes?"

"That you are the most beautiful woman on earth, and that I'm a man, with red blood in my veins."

Under lowered lids she studied him. This very confident, alert American, modern from head to heel, attracted her more than any other man. There was a dynamic quality in him that stirred her blood. He was efficient, selfish enough to win, and yet considerate in the small things that go to make up the sum of existence. Why not then? She must marry some time and she was as nearly in love as she would ever be.

"What ARE your reasons for wanting me?"

"We smoke the same Egyptians," he mocked.

"That's a good reason, so far as it goes."

"And you're such a charming puzzle that I would like to domesticate it and study the eternal mystery at my leisure."

"Then it's as a diversion that you want me."

"A thing of beauty and a joy forever, the poet puts it. But diversion if you like. What greater test of charming versatility for a woman than that she remain a diversion to her husband, unstaled by custom and undulled by familiarity?"

After all her father would be pleased to have her marry an American business man. The Powers' millions could easily buy for her a fine old dukedom if she wanted one. At present there was more than one available title-holder on her horizon. But Valencia did not care to take up the responsibilities that go with such a position. She was too indolent to adapt her life to the standards of others—and perhaps too proud. Moreover, it happened that she had had enough of the club man type in the late lamented Van Tyle. This man was a worker. He would not annoy her or interfere with her careless pleasures. Again she asked herself, Why not?

"I suppose you really do like me." Her face was tilted in gay little appeal.

"I'm not going to tell you how much. It wouldn't be good for discipline in the house."

Her soft little laugh bubbled over. "We seem to have quite settled it. And I hadn't the slightest notion of agreeing to any-thing so ridiculous when I ventured that indiscreet remark about an abduction." She looked up at him with smiling insolence. "You're only an adventurer, you know. I daresay you haven't even paid for the car in which you were going to kidnap me."

"No," he admitted cheerfully.

"I wonder what Dad will think of it,"

"He'll thank Heaven you didn't present him with a French or Italian count to support."

"I believe he will. His objection to Gus was that he looked like a foreigner and never had done a day's work in his life. Poor Gus! He didn't measure up to Dad's idea of a man. Now I suppose you could earn a living for us."

"I'm not expecting you to take in sewing."

"Are you going to do the independent if Dad cuts up rough?"

she asked saucily.

"Independent is the word." He smiled with a sudden appreciation of the situation. "And I take it he means to cut up rough. I wired him to-day I was going to ask you to marry me."

"You didn't."

"Yes."

"But wasn't that a little premature? Perhaps it wouldn't have been necessary. Or did you take me for granted"

"There was always the car for a kidnapping in case of necessity," he joked.

"Why did you do it?"

"I wanted to be above board about it even if I am an adventurer."

"What did he say? How could you put it in a telegram?"

"Red consoles marooned sweet post delayed."

"Dear me! What gibberish is that?"

"It's from our private code. It means, 'Going to marry your daughter if she is willing. With your consent, I hope.'"

"And he answered? I'll take the English version, please."

"'Consent refused. No fortune hunters need apply.' That is not a direct quotation, but it conveys his meaning accurately enough."

"So I'm to be cut off with a shilling." Her eyes bubbled with delight.

"I reckon so. Of course I had to come back at him."

"How, may I ask?" She was vastly amused at this novel correspondence.

"Oh, I merely said in substance that I was glad to hear it because you couldn't think now I wanted to marry you for your money. I added that if things came my way we would send him cards later. One doesn't like to slang one's wife's father, so I drew it mild."

"I don't believe a word of it. You wouldn't dare."

That she admired and at the same time distrusted was so apparent that he drew a yellow envelope from his pocket and handed it to her.

"This is his latest contribution to the literature of frankness. You see his feelings overflowed so promptly he had to turn loose in good American talk right off the bat. Couldn't wait for the code."

She read aloud. "Your resignation as General Counsel Transcontinental will be accepted immediately. Turn over papers to Walker and go to the devil." It was signed "Powers."

"That's all, is it? No further exchange of compliments," she wanted to know.

"That's all, except that he is reading my resignation by this time. I sent it two hours ago. In it I tried to convey to him my sense of regret at being obliged to sever business relations owing to the fact that I was about to contract family ties with him. I hoped that he would command me in any way he saw fit and was sorry we couldn't come to an agreement in the present instance."

"I don't believe you're a bit sorry. Don't you realize what an expensive luxury you're getting in me and how serious a thing it is to cast off heaven knows how many millions?"

"Oh, I realize it!"

"But you expect him to come round when he has had time to think it over?"

"It's hard for me to conceive of anybody not wanting me for a son-in-law," he admitted cheerfully.

Valencia nodded. "He'll like you all the better for standing up to him. He's fond of Alice because she's impudent to him."

"I didn't mean to be impudent, but I couldn't lie down and let him prove me what he called me."

"If you're that kind of a man I'm almost glad you're going to make me marry you," she confided.

He leaned over her chair, his eyes shining. "I'll make you more than almost glad, Valencia. You're going to learn what it is to—oh, damn it!"

He was impersonally admiring her Whistler when the maid brushed aside the portieres. She had come to bring Mrs. Van Tyle a telegram.

"No answer, Pratt."

After the maid had retired her mistress called James to her side. Over her shoulder he read it.

"Glad he is an American and not living on his father. Didn't think you had so much sense. Tell that young man I want to see him in New York immediately."

The message was signed with the name of her father.

"What do you suppose he wants with you in New York?"

James was radiant. He kissed the perfect lips turned toward him before he answered. "Oh, to make me president of the Transcontinental maybe. How should I know? It's an olive branch. Isn't that enough?"

"When shall you go?"

He looked at his watch. "The limited leaves at nine-thirty. That gives me nearly an hour."

"You're not going to-night?"

"I'm going to-night. I must, dear. Those are the orders and I've got to obey them."

"But suppose I give you different orders. Surely I have some rights, to-night of all nights. Why, we haven't been engaged ten minutes. Business doesn't always come first."

James hesitated. "It's the last thing I want to do, but when Joe Powers says 'Come!' I know enough to jump."

"But when I say stay?" she pleaded.

"Then I stop the prettiest mouth in the world with kisses and run away before I hear the order." Gaily he suited the action to the word.

But, for once swift, she reached the door before him.

"Wait. Don't go, dear."

The last word came faintly, unexpectedly. The enticement of the appeal went to his head. He had shaken her out of the indifference that was her pride. One arm slipped round her waist. His other hand tilted back her head until he could look into the eyes in which a new fire had been kindled.

"What about that almost glad? If I stay will you forget all qualifying words and be just glad?"

She nodded quickly, laughing ever so softly. "Yes, I'll help you listen to the birds sing. Do you know I can almost hear them?"

James drew a deep breath and caught her swiftly to him. "New York will have to wait till to-morrow. The birds will sing to-night and we will not count the cost."

"Yes, my lord," she answered demurely.

For to-night she wanted to forget that their birds were only caged canaries.

CHAPTER 23

"And what are the names of the Fortunate Isles,
Lo! duty and love and a large content;
And these are the Isles of the watery miles
That God let down from the firmament.

Lo! duty and love and a true man's trust,
Your forehead to God and your feet in the dust:
Lo! duty and love and a sweet babe's smiles,
And these, O friends, are the Fortunate Isles."

AND LARKS FOR THE REBEL

Beneath a sky faintly pink with the warning of the coming sunrise Jeff walked an old logging trail that would take him back to camp from his morning dip. Ferns and blackberry bushes, heavy with dew, reached across the road and grappled with each other. At every step, as he pushed through the tangle, a shower of drops went flying.

His was the incomparable buoyant humor of a lover treading a newborn world. A smile was in his eyes, tender, luminous, cheerful. He thought of the woman whom he had not seen for many months, and he was buoyed up by the fine spiritual edge which does not know defeat. Win or lose, it was clear gain to have loved her.

With him he carried a vision of her, young, ardent, all fire and flame. One spoke of things beautiful and her face lit from within. Her words, motions, came from the depths, half revealed and half concealed dear hidden secrets. He recalled the grace of the delicate throat curve, little tricks of expression, the sweetness of her energy.

The forest broke, opening into a clearing. He stood to drink in its beauty, for the sun, peeping over a saddle in the hills, had painted the place a valley of gold and russet. And while he waited there came out of the woods beyond, into that splendid setting, the vision that was in his mind.

He was not surprised that his eyes were playing him tricks. This was after all the proper frame for the picture of his golden sweetheart. Lance-straight and slender, his wood nymph waded knee deep through the ferns. Straight toward him she came, and his temples began to throb. A sylph of the woods should be diaphanous. The one he saw was a creature of color and warmth and definiteness. Life, sweet and mocking, flowed through her radiantly. His heart sang within him, for the woman he loved out of a world of beautiful women was coming to him, light-footed as Daphne, the rhythm of the morning in her step.

She spoke, commonplace words enough. "Last night I heard you were here."

"And I didn't know you were within a thousand miles."

"We came back to Verden Thursday and are up over Sunday," she explained.

He was lost in the witchery of the spell she cast over him.

Not the drooping maidenhair ferns through which she trailed were more delicate or graceful than she. But some instinct in him played surface commonplaces against the insurgent emotion of his heart.

"You like Washington?"

"I like home better."

"But you were popular at the capital. I read a great deal in the papers about your triumphs."

The dye in her cheeks ran a little stronger. There had been much gossip about a certain Italian nobleman who had wooed her openly and madly. "They told a lot of nonsense."

"And some that wasn't nonsense."

"Not much." She changed the subject lightly. "You read all about the wedding, of course."

He quoted. "Miss Alice Frome as maid of honor preceded the bride, appearing in a handsome gown of very delicate old rose satin with an overdress of—"

"Very good. You may go to the head of the class, sir. Valencia was beautiful and your cousin never looked more handsome."

"Which is saying a good deal."

"And we're all hoping they will live happy ever after."

"You know he is being talked of for United States Senator already."

"You will oppose him?" she asked quickly.

"I shall have to."

"Still an irreconcilable." Her smile could be vivid, and just now it was.

"Still a demagogue and a trouble maker," he admitted.

"You've won the recall and the direct primary since I left."

"Yes. We've been busy."

"And our friends—how are they?"

"You should see Jefferson Davis Farnum Miller. He's two months old and as fat as a dumpling."

"I've seen him. He's a credit to his godfather."

"Isn't he? That's one happy family."

"I wonder who's to blame for that," she said, the star flash in her eyes.

"Nellie told you?"

"She told me."

"They exaggerate. Nobody could have done less than I."

"Or more." She did not dwell upon the subject. "Tell me about Mr. Marchant."

He went over for her the story of the little poet's gentle death. She listened till he made an end.

"Then it was not hard for him?"

"No. He had one of his good, eager days, then guietly fell asleep."

"And passed to where, beyond these voices, there is rest and peace," she quoted, ever so softly.

"Yes."

"Perhaps he knows now all about his Perfect State." Her wistful smile was very tender.

"Perhaps."

They walked together slowly across the valley.

"It is nearly six months since I have seen you."

"Five months and twenty-seven days." The words had slipped out almost without her volition. She hurried on, ashamed, the color flying in her cheeks, "I remember because it was the day we ran down your cousin and that old gentleman. It has always been a great comfort to me to know that he was not seriously injured."

"No. It was only the shock of his fall."

"What was his name? I don't think I heard it."

There was just an instant's silence before he pronounced, "Farnum—Mr. Robert Farnum."

"A relative of yours?"

"Yes."

Across her brain there flashed a fugitive memory of three words Jeff had spoken to his cousin the day of the accident. "It's your father."

But how could that be? She had always understood that both the parents of James were dead. The lawyer had denied knowing the man whose life he had saved. And yet she had been sure of the words and of a furtive, frightened look on the face of James. According to the story of the *Herald* the father of Jefferson, a former convict, was named Robert. But once, when she had made some allusion to it Captain Chunn had exploded into vigorous denial. It was a puzzle the meaning of which she could not guess.

"He has several times mentioned his wish to thank you for your kindness," Jeff mentioned.

"I'll be glad to meet him." Swiftly she flashed a question at him. "Is he James Farnum's father?"

"Haven't you read the papers? He is said to be mine."

"But he isn't. He isn't. I see it now. James was ashamed to acknowledge a father who had been in prison. Your enemies made a mistake and you let it go."

"It's all long since past. I wouldn't say anything about it to anybody."

"Of course you wouldn't," she scoffed. Her eyes were very bright. She wanted to laugh and to weep at her discovery.

"You see it didn't matter with my friends. And my reputation was beyond hope anyhow. It was different with James."

She nodded. "Yes. It wouldn't have improved his chances

with Valencia," her cousin admitted.

Jeff permitted himself a smile. "My impression was that he did not have Mrs. Van Tyle in mind at the time."

They had waded through the wet ferns to the edge of the woods. As her eyes swept the russet valley through which they had passed Alice drew a deep breath of pleasure. How good it was to be alive in such a world of beauty! A meadow lark throbbed its three notes at her joyfully to emphasize their kinship. An English pheasant strutted across the path and disappeared into the ferns. Neither the man nor the woman spoke. All the glad day called them to the emotional climax toward which they were racing.

Womanlike, Alice attempted to evade what she most desired. He was to be her mate. She knew it now. But the fear of him was in her heart.

"Were you so fond of him? Is that why you did it for him?" she asked.

"I didn't do it for him."

"For whom then?"

He did not answer. Nor did his eyes meet hers. They were fixed on the moving ferns where the pheasant had disappeared.

Alice guessed. He had done it for the girl because he thought her in love with his cousin. A warm glow suffused her. No man made such a sacrifice for a woman unless he cared for her.

The meadow lark flung out another carefree ecstasy. The

William MacLeod Raine

theme of it was the triumphant certainty that love is the greatest thing in the world. Jeff felt that it was now or never.

"I love you. It's been hidden in my heart more than eight years, but I find I must tell you. All the arguments against it I've rehearsed a thousand times. The world is at your feet. You could never love a man like me. To your friends I'm a bad lot. They never would consider me a moment."

Gently she interrupted. "Is it my friends you want to marry?"

The surprise of it took him by the throat. His astonished eyes questioned for a denial. In that moment a wonderful secret was born into the world. She held out both hands with a divine frankness, a sweetness of surrender beyond words.

"But your father—your people!"

"'Where thou lodgest, I will lodge: thy people shall be my people.'" She murmured it with a broken little laugh that was a sob.

Even then he did not take her in his arms. The habit of reverence for her was of many years' growth and not to be broken in an instant.

"You are sure, dear—quite sure?"

"I've been sure ever since the day of our first talk on the *Bellingham.*"

Still he fought the joy that flooded him. "I must tell you the truth so that you won't idealize me… and the situation. I am enlisted in this fight for life. Where it will lead me I don't know. But I must follow the road I see. You will lose your friends. They will think me a crank, an enemy to society; and they will think you demented. But even for you I can't turn back."

A tender glow was in her deep eyes. "If I did not know that do you think I would marry you?"

"But you've always had the best things. You've never known what it is to be poor."

"No, I've never had the best things, never till I knew you, dear. I've starved for them and did not know how to escape the prison I was in. Then you came... and you showed me. The world is at my feet now. Not the world you meant, of idleness and luxury and ennui... but that better one of the spirit where you and I shall walk together as comrades of all who work and laugh and weep."

"If I could be sure!"

"Of me, Jeff?"

"That I can make you happy. After all it's a chance."

"We all live on a chance. I'll take mine beside the man I love. There is one way under heaven by which men may be saved. I'm going to walk that way with you, dear."

Jeff threw away the reins of a worldly wise prudence.

"For ever and ever, Alice," he cried softly, shaken to his soul.

As their lips met the lark throbbed a betrothal song.

* * * * * * *

William MacLeod Raine

They went slowly through the wet ferns, hand in hand. It was amazingly true that he had won her, but Jeff could scarce believe the miracle. More than once he recurred to it.

"You saw what no other young woman of your set in Verden did, the human in me through my vagabondage. But why? There's nothing in my appearance to attract."

"Valiant in velvet, light in ragged luck," she laughed. "And I won't have you questioning my taste, sir. I've always thought you very good-looking, if you must have it."

"If you're as far gone as that!" His low laughter rang out to meet hers, for no reason except the best of reasons—that they walked alone with love through a world wonderful.

Other books by this author

Man Size

The Big-Town Round-Up

The Sheriff's Son

Angled Trails

William MacLeod Raine

Choose from Thousands of 1stWorldLibrary Classics By

A. M. Barnard
Ada Leverson
Adolphus William Ward
Aesop
Agatha Christie
Alexander Aaronsohn
Alexander Kielland
Alexandre Dumas
Alfred Gatty
Alfred Ollivant
Alice Duer Miller
Alice Turner Curtis
Alice Dunbar
Allen Chapman
Alleyne Ireland
Ambrose Bierce
Amelia E. Barr
Amory H. Bradford
Andrew Lang
Andrew McFarland Davis
Andy Adams
Angela Brazil
Anna Alice Chapin
Anna Sewell
Annie Besant
Annie Hamilton Donnell
Annie Payson Call
Annie Roe Carr
Annonaymous
Anton Chekhov
Archibald Lee Fletcher
Arnold Bennett
Arthur C. Benson
Arthur Conan Doyle
Arthur M. Winfield
Arthur Ransome
Arthur Schnitzler
Arthur Train
Atticus
B.H. Baden-Powell
B. M. Bower
B. C. Chatterjee
Baroness Emmuska Orczy
Baroness Orczy
Basil King
Bayard Taylor
Ben Macomber
Bertha Muzzy Bower
Bjornstjerne Bjornson

Booth Tarkington
Boyd Cable
Bram Stoker
C. Collodi
C. E. Orr
C. M. Ingleby
Carolyn Wells
Catherine Parr Traill
Charles A. Eastman
Charles Amory Beach
Charles Dickens
Charles Dudley Warner
Charles Farrar Browne
Charles Ives
Charles Kingsley
Charles Klein
Charles Hanson Towne
Charles Lathrop Pack
Charles Romyn Dake
Charles Whibley
Charles Willing Beale
Charlotte M. Braeme
Charlotte M. Yonge
Charlotte Perkins Stetson
Clair W. Hayes
Clarence Day Jr.
Clarence E. Mulford
Clemence Housman
Confucius
Coningsby Dawson
Cornelis DeWitt Wilcox
Cyril Burleigh
D. H. Lawrence
Daniel Defoe
David Garnett
Dinah Craik
Don Carlos Janes
Donald Keyhoe
Dorothy Kilner
Dougan Clark
Douglas Fairbanks
E. Nesbit
E. P. Roe
E. Phillips Oppenheim
E. S. Brooks
Earl Barnes
Edgar Rice Burroughs
Edith Van Dyne
Edith Wharton

Edward Everett Hale
Edward J. O'Biren
Edward S. Ellis
Edwin L. Arnold
Eleanor Atkins
Eleanor Hallowell Abbott
Eliot Gregory
Elizabeth Gaskell
Elizabeth McCracken
Elizabeth Von Arnim
Ellem Key
Emerson Hough
Emilie F. Carlen
Emily Bronte
Emily Dickinson
Enid Bagnold
Enilor Macartney Lane
Erasmus W. Jones
Ernie Howard Pie
Ethel May Dell
Ethel Turner
Ethel Watts Mumford
Eugene Sue
Eugenie Foa
Eugene Wood
Eustace Hale Ball
Evelyn Everett-green
Everard Cotes
F. H. Cheley
F. J. Cross
F. Marion Crawford
Fannie E. Newberry
Federick Austin Ogg
Ferdinand Ossendowski
Fergus Hume
Florence A. Kilpatrick
Fremont B. Deering
Francis Bacon
Francis Darwin
Frances Hodgson Burnett
Frances Parkinson Keyes
Frank Gee Patchin
Frank Harris
Frank Jewett Mather
Frank L. Packard
Frank V. Webster
Frederic Stewart Isham
Frederick Trevor Hill
Frederick Winslow Taylor

Friedrich Kerst
Friedrich Nietzsche
Fyodor Dostoyevsky
G.A. Henty
G.K. Chesterton
Gabrielle E. Jackson
Garrett P. Serviss
Gaston Leroux
George A. Warren
George Ade
Geroge Bernard Shaw
George Cary Eggleston
George Durston
George Ebers
George Eliot
George Gissing
George MacDonald
George Meredith
George Orwell
George Sylvester Viereck
George Tucker
George W. Cable
George Wharton James
Gertrude Atherton
Gordon Casserly
Grace E. King
Grace Gallatin
Grace Greenwood
Grant Allen
Guillermo A. Sherwell
Gulielma Zollinger
Gustav Flaubert
H. A. Cody
H. B. Irving
H. C. Bailey
H. G. Wells
H. H. Munro
H. Irving Hancock
H. R. Naylor
H. Rider Haggard
H. W. C. Davis
Haldeman Julius
Hall Caine
Hamilton Wright Mabie
Hans Christian Andersen
Harold Avery
Harold McGrath
Harriet Beecher Stowe
Harry Castlemon
Harry Coghill
Harry Houidini

Hayden Carruth
Helent Hunt Jackson
Helen Nicolay
Hendrik Conscience
Hendy David Thoreau
Henri Barbusse
Henrik Ibsen
Henry Adams
Henry Ford
Henry Frost
Henry James
Henry Jones Ford
Henry Seton Merriman
Henry W Longfellow
Herbert A. Giles
Herbert Carter
Herbert N. Casson
Herman Hesse
Hildegard G. Frey
Homer
Honore De Balzac
Horace B. Day
Horace Walpole
Horatio Alger Jr.
Howard Pyle
Howard R. Garis
Hugh Lofting
Hugh Walpole
Humphry Ward
Ian Maclaren
Inez Haynes Gillmore
Irving Bacheller
Isabel Cecilia Williams
Isabel Hornibrook
Israel Abrahams
Ivan Turgenev
J. G.Austin
J. Henri Fabre
J. M. Barrie
J. M. Walsh
J. Macdonald Oxley
J. R. Miller
J. S. Fletcher
J. S. Knowles
J. Storer Clouston
J. W. Duffield
Jack London
Jacob Abbott
James Allen
James Andrews
James Baldwin

James Branch Cabell
James DeMille
James Joyce
James Lane Allen
James Lane Allen
James Oliver Curwood
James Oppenheim
James Otis
James R. Driscoll
Jane Abbott
Jane Austen
Jane L. Stewart
Janet Aldridge
Jens Peter Jacobsen
Jerome K. Jerome
Jessie Graham Flower
John Buchan
John Burroughs
John Cournos
John F. Kennedy
John Gay
John Glasworthy
John Habberton
John Joy Bell
John Kendrick Bangs
John Milton
John Philip Sousa
John Taintor Foote
Jonas Lauritz Idemil Lie
Jonathan Swift
Joseph A. Altsheler
Joseph Carey
Joseph Conrad
Joseph E. Badger Jr
Joseph Hergesheimer
Joseph Jacobs
Jules Vernes
Julian Hawthrone
Julie A Lippmann
Justin Huntly McCarthy
Kakuzo Okakura
Karle Wilson Baker
Kate Chopin
Kenneth Grahame
Kenneth McGaffey
Kate Langley Bosher
Kate Langley Bosher
Katherine Cecil Thurston
Katherine Stokes
L. A. Abbot
L. T. Meade

L. Frank Baum
Latta Griswold
Laura Dent Crane
Laura Lee Hope
Laurence Housman
Lawrence Beasley
Leo Tolstoy
Leonid Andreyev
Lewis Carroll
Lewis Sperry Chafer
Lilian Bell
Lloyd Osbourne
Louis Hughes
Louis Joseph Vance
Louis Tracy
Louisa May Alcott
Lucy Fitch Perkins
Lucy Maud Montgomery
Luther Benson
Lydia Miller Middleton
Lyndon Orr
M. Corvus
M. H. Adams
Margaret E. Sangster
Margret Howth
Margaret Vandercook
Margaret W. Hungerford
Margret Penrose
Maria Edgeworth
Maria Thompson Daviess
Mariano Azuela
Marion Polk Angellotti
Mark Overton
Mark Twain
Mary Austin
Mary Catherine Crowley
Mary Cole
Mary Hastings Bradley
Mary Roberts Rinehart
Mary Rowlandson
M. Wollstonecraft Shelley
Maud Lindsay
Max Beerbohm
Myra Kelly
Nathaniel Hawthrone
Nicolo Machiavelli
O. F. Walton
Oscar Wilde

Owen Johnson
P.G. Wodehouse
Paul and Mabel Thorne
Paul G. Tomlinson
Paul Severing
Percy Brebner
Percy Keese Fitzhugh
Peter B. Kyne
Plato
Quincy Allen
R. Derby Holmes
R. L. Stevenson
R. S. Ball
Rabindranath Tagore
Rahul Alvares
Ralph Bonehill
Ralph Henry Barbour
Ralph Victor
Ralph Waldo Emmerson
Rene Descartes
Ray Cummings
Rex Beach
Rex E. Beach
Richard Harding Davis
Richard Jefferies
Richard Le Gallienne
Robert Barr
Robert Frost
Robert Gordon Anderson
Robert L. Drake
Robert Lansing
Robert Lynd
Robert Michael Ballantyne
Robert W. Chambers
Rosa Nouchette Carey
Rudyard Kipling
Saint Augustine
Samuel B. Allison
Samuel Hopkins Adams
Sarah Bernhardt
Sarah C. Hallowell
Selma Lagerlof
Sherwood Anderson
Sigmund Freud
Standish O'Grady
Stanley Weyman
Stella Benson
Stella M. Francis

Stephen Crane
Stewart Edward White
Stijn Streuvels
Swami Abhedananda
Swami Parmananda
T. S. Ackland
T. S. Arthur
The Princess Der Ling
Thomas A. Janvier
Thomas A Kempis
Thomas Anderton
Thomas Bailey Aldrich
Thomas Bulfinch
Thomas De Quincey
Thomas Dixon
Thomas H. Huxley
Thomas Hardy
Thomas More
Thornton W. Burgess
U. S. Grant
Upton Sinclair
Valentine Williams
Various Authors
Vaughan Kester
Victor Appleton
Victor G. Durham
Victoria Cross
Virginia Woolf
Wadsworth Camp
Walter Camp
Walter Scott
Washington Irving
Wilbur Lawton
Wilkie Collins
Willa Cather
Willard F. Baker
William Dean Howells
William le Queux
W. Makepeace Thackeray
William W. Walter
William Shakespeare
Winston Churchill
Yei Theodora Ozaki
Yogi Ramacharaka
Young E. Allison
Zane Grey

www.ingramcontent.com/pod-product-compliance
Lightning Source LLC
Chambersburg PA
CBHW021306250626
47155CB00002B/406